Also by the author:

Playing Out the String

PROSPERITY

B. J. Leggett

Livingston Press
The University of West Alabama

first edition
6 5 4 3 2 1

PROSPERITY

A man's dying is more the survivors' affair than his own.

—Thomas Mann, *The Magic Mountain*

I

KELLY'S is always loud after seven when the people at the bar are into their second or third, but especially tonight when the drinks are free, and I have to lean down to hear what Deathridge is saying. "Try to forget you're an ex-cop" is what he's saying as we shake hands under a banner that wishes me well in large red letters. John Deathridge, Chief of Detectives, arrived late, so he is the only completely sober person in the room except for Kelly the owner.

I don't ask him why I should forget I'm about to become an ex-cop, because I think I know. "You're one of the people I'm going to miss seeing. You and Eddie." We stand with our backs to the bar looking out over a room full of policemen, mostly, a few women. Some are in uniform, some in shirts and ties, jackets removed, weapons exposed.

"Hate to lose you," Deathridge says. "You've come to be the one I count on the last couple of years."

"You never mentioned that."

"You don't want your people to get complacent."

I could have told him he was the most honorable policeman I'd run across, which is true, but he's not the kind of man you say things like that to, and I don't want to get sappy at the end. "So have a drink, Chief. On the house," I say instead.

"I believe I will. Who's springing for this?" He's always been suspicious, sometimes with good reason, that we're somehow misusing the section's funds. Crimes Against Persons, that's my section and it contains most of the suspicious characters in the department.

"Well, we all threw in a little. I threw in the most since Eddie reminded me it was my party. Kelly's supposed to be keeping tabs and give me a sign when we have to start buying our own."

Deathridge orders a single-malt scotch, reducing the period of free drinks disproportionately, and Kelly catches my eye and nods. While he's pouring, a paying customer walks in, a much-pierced young man in an obscene tee shirt.

"Bar's closed," Kelly yells at him over the din, gesturing back over his shoulder to a hand-lettered sign on the wall behind him. "Private party."

The kid starts to complain but then notices that a large percentage of the people at the bar are armed. He turns and walks out saying something about why you can never find a policeman when you need one.

"Nice banner." The Chief takes a sip of his drink and steps back to look up over the bar.

"Eddie's work." Eddie Ray Carpenter, nephew of the local blues man James Thomas Carpenter, has been my partner for the last four and a half years. *Good Luck Shake* is what the banner says. "I told him when I came in that he needed to climb up there and put a comma in front of *Shake,* but he said I was through correcting his grammar."

"The literacy level of the department's going to drop noticeably."

Eddie is responsible for the name on the banner, one of several I'm known by in the department. It was after the novel came out that he hung the name *Shakespeare* on me, and it was picked up in the department as a form of derision. But it's easy to predict what happened. Shakespeare is a little long and awkward, and pretty soon Eddie shortened it to Shake, so that's what the people I know best call me, although Deathridge and the other higher-ups have stuck with Robert, and the people who want to mock my literary pretensions still call me Shakespeare. And people I don't know at all use some variation of Lieutenant O'Brian. When I take a phone call I can pretty much judge my relation to the caller by which name is used.

You could say that Eddie is also indirectly responsible for the novel. I stayed on for a masters in English after I graduated from Western Appalachian and always figured I would teach high school like my mother. Then this cop job came along and I found out I was good at it and rose up fairly quickly through the ranks. But I was always a reader, and that didn't change. You can't read Hemingway and Faulkner all the time, and I have a weakness for mystery novels and police procedurals, most of them by women, who seem to have a knack for that sort of thing. I read people like Patricia Cornwell and P. D. James and Sue Grafton. One day Eddie and I were in a vacant apartment across the street from a drug house taking turns at the front window with a camera. While Eddie was at the window, I was reading the new somebody-or-other just to pass the time, and I said almost to myself, "I think I could write one of these things." I mean, I actually knew how a police department worked and I had been shot at, which is something Sue Grafton probably can't claim.

Eddie said it was probably harder than I thought getting published. There was probably some trick these women knew that I didn't know.

"I bet I could do it," I told him.

"Hundred dollars," he said.

"How long do I have?"

"Say a year."

"I got to write the thing and get it published in a *year*?"

"Then don't take the bet."

"What if it gets accepted by a publisher? Is that the same thing?"

"All right," Eddie said. "Clock starts now, June 29. You better get to it—got any paper on you?"

I won the bet, but Eddie got his money back. After the book was accepted but before it came out, I gave him the publisher's proofs to read, and he concluded that one of the characters, the protagonist's partner, shared certain of his speech characteristics. "Man talks just like me."

I had to agree that there were certain similarities, and Eddie recalled that writers had to pay permission fees to use something of somebody else's. Right? I tried to make some distinctions here, but he invented a category, Unique Speech Patterns, for which permission fees were in order. I asked him how much. "Hundred ought to cover it," he said.

I'm telling this story to Deathridge at the bar when Eddie walks over to catch the punch line. "I didn't know how much that sucker was gonna make," he says. "You got off easy."

"I made you famous. Chris Rock was set to play you in the movie."

"Famous don't put the groceries on the table," he says.

The book did make a lot of money. It got up to number eight on the *New York Times* bestseller list, and my agent sold it to a Hollywood producer for the equivalent of several years of a police lieutenant's salary. It got to the casting stage but never got made, which distressed Eddie no end, since he figured he could go to Hollywood as a police consultant and coach Chris Rock on his Unique Speech Patterns.

The most notable of Eddie's speech patterns, not at all unique, is to insert the word *fuck'n,* as he pronounces it, in the midst of two-word names, as in New fuck'n Jersey or North fuck'n Carolina, the most blasphemous usage being the splitting of *Jesus Christ.* The language of policemen is the roughest I've ever heard, but some of the boys were actually shocked at Eddie's variation on taking the Lord's name in vain and a lively theological debate ensued. One side had it that the *Jesus Christ* itself was the offense and you couldn't make it any worse, but the prevailing side argued that if you really had to pay for your sins, then Eddie's creative violation of the third commandment surely cost him double.

But back at the bar, Eddie's talk is obscenity free. Nobody ever uses strong language around Deathridge.

"So what are you going to be doing with yourself?" Deathridge studies his drink, as if asking an idle question, but I figure he's been curious about my decision.

"Man's going back to this little hick town where he grew up," Eddie says. "Can you believe that? Man in the prime of his life quitting his job and leaving all his friends."

"Eddie, it's thirty miles away." And then to Deathridge, "Yeah, I'm going back to Prosperity and see if I can write another novel." That's true as far as it goes, and what it leaves out I've never tried to put into words. Complete this sentence: *You're going back to Prosperity because. . . .*

"You still have family there?"

"They're all gone." *You're going back because you left in disgrace?*

"So you haven't had much occasion to go back."

"Mainly for funerals." *Because you have some vague notion about setting things straight?*

Eddie taps me on the shoulder with the back of his hand. "Here's somebody I got to see." Wanda, our beauty queen dispatcher—Miss Western Appalachian 2005—has just walked in. Eddie meets her at the door and steers her to a table, flashing me a thumbs up sign behind his back.

Deathridge gives me a quizzical look. "A recipe for heartbreak," I say. "My ex-partner never knows when he's in over his head." Actually, one of the things I like about Eddie, twice divorced, is his eternal optimism.

"One of the few benefits of my job is being removed from all the office entanglements," Deathridge says. "How's your. . . .?" He doesn't know quite what to call it, so he just points to my left side.

"Not doing any heavy lifting, but they told me it would be back to normal in a few months." That's the immediate cause of my early retirement. The book and the advance on a second constitute the enabling cause, but the shooting is the immediate cause. Assisting Vice on a drug bust, I took one just below the ribs on the left side. I was lucky, the surgeon told me. There was not a lot under there on the left side. The same spot on the right and I would have been in some difficulty, especially considering the size of the hole, drug dealers tending to favor the larger calibers.

Nothing like being shot to make a man reconsider his career options. Lying in a hospital bed over long boring days, I began to wonder if this was not the time to see if the first novel was a fluke. The agent and the publisher were putting pressure on me, and I figured I had enough to live on for a couple of years. But I didn't make the decision then. It was later, a couple of weeks after the funeral of another gunshot victim who had once been a friend, that I set the retirement date for June 29, the anniversary of the day three years earlier when Eddie and I made the bet.

"That was a nasty business," Deathridge says. "I hope it didn't make your decision for you."

"Maybe speeded it up a little."

Deathridge sets his glass on the bar and looks over the room. "I guess I'll head home. I always feel like the father at these things."

"I'm honored that you came."

"Just wanted to see you off." We shake again. "And you know that if there's ever anything I can do to help in any way . . ."

(Looking back, a small irony here. Deathridge is offering his assistance simply as a conventional farewell, yet quite soon I will be in real need of his help and, to push the irony further, he will be unwilling to extend it. But in recalling events some time after the fact ironies abound, since irony in this sense is no more than ignorance of the meaning of the present.)

I watch him walk across the room toward the door, nodding to men who turn to acknowledge him. There seems to be a kind of energy field around him that makes a wave through the crowd. Even the men who make fun of him for his straight-laced manner must respect him for his absolute integrity in a profession not especially noted for that.

The free drinks having run out, I stand alone at the bar and brace myself for the surge of insincere goodbyes that is about to begin. I'm aware that there are very few people who are truly sorry to see me go. Like Uncle Charley in *Death of a Salesman*, I was liked but I was not well liked. I was good at my job, which gained Deathridge's respect, but that didn't always work to my advantage, since I got to be known as Deathridge's fair-haired boy. But that's not a reason for taking early retirement. The thing is I never quite fit into the community of policemen I worked with. I read poetry and talked about finding a really good olive oil. I had published a novel and I corrected my colleagues' spelling.

Eddie kept me informed on my shifting reputation in the department. "These peckerwoods can't figure you out," he told me once, "and there's some of them think you may be a little—" he made a fluttering motion with his right hand. "I'm the only one understands you. You're the sensitive type, the kind women go for, somewhat like myself. Kevin Costner before he started losing his hair. And sometimes I think you don't exploit that side of yourself enough."

I reminded him that I had just gotten out of what could only be tritely called a bad relationship, and I was trying to give it a rest. "All the same," he said, "these boys are suspicious of a man like you, never married, don't try to jump every presentable woman he meets, eats goat fuck'n cheese for lunch."

Eddie was wrong about Kevin Costner. If life were a movie I

B. J. Leggett

wouldn't be Kevin Costner. Or George Clooney, say. People have a hard time disliking Costner or Clooney, even when they play jerks. People don't have a hard time disliking me. Maybe James Spader. People don't know quite what to make of James Spader. Eddie was right though about my uneasy status in the department, and that was another reason for leaving.

But as some Freudian said, when a man gives you three reasons why he can't come to your party, none of them is the real reason. I have at least three reasons to be standing under a banner that says *Good Luck Shake*, and then there's something else closer to the real reason. In the words of the American poet Jimmy Buffett, some people claim that there's a woman to blame.

II

No one would wish a beautiful woman plainer, but if Jesse McLean possessed average features, my life would be less complicated. When I told her this, she said it sounded sexist. She took her degree at Sarah Lawrence and is always on the alert for signs of sexism. But I said no, I didn't think I was a sexist. I said I was guilty of a bias against ugliness and drawn to beauty in all its forms, including the feminine. This seemed to satisfy her, but she was right. She is uncommonly beautiful and I've made a number of questionable decisions, including quitting my job and returning to a place I thought I was done with.

I think it was the shock of her mature beauty that affected me so much. I had known her only as the kid sister of Bradley McLean of the storied McLean family and my close friend in high school. She was the thin ungainly little girl who was always trying to horn in on whatever it was we were up to. She was something of a pain in the ass and completely devoted to her older brother.

The last couple of years of high school Bradley and I were together almost every day. In the fall he was the quarterback of the McLean County High football team and I was a wide receiver. In the summer he was the pitcher and I was the utility infielder. On weekends he was at my place or I was at his, and always there was this skinny little girl trying to tag along. If there were no girlfriends involved, we tolerated her, so she was around a lot, always trying to find ways to torment me. She called me Bobby, for example, because she knew I hated the childhood name my mother used until the day she died.

After graduation I went on to college at Western Appalachian in Knoxville, severing all ties with my hometown and the McLean family. I never forgot Jesse McLean, but in my mind she was frozen in her pre-pubescent state. When I saw her again after so many years, she had been miraculously transformed in my absence. I couldn't keep my eyes off her, which seemed a sacrilege since the occasion was Bradley McLean's funeral.

Bradley had gone to Princeton, as befits the son and heir of the most prominent family in Prosperity. Had it not been for what happened at the lake the summer before we left for college we probably would have kept in touch, an email now and then, a drink at Kelly's when he was in Knoxville, but that's not the way it worked out.

What happened at the lake, or some similar phrase became the shorthand for what everybody in Prosperity was talking about that summer, although what the phrase conveyed varied markedly. For most people it was just a juicy piece of gossip that involved the two golden boys from the senior class. For the McLean family it was a narrow escape, from which they no doubt quickly and happily moved on. For me and my family it was decisive and we never quite recovered from it, for which, perhaps unjustly, I have always held my father to blame.

My father, who fancied himself an intellectual and read histories and biographies in the evening, never adjusted to Prosperity, where he moved shortly after his marriage when my mother took a job at McLean County High. Because he was a college graduate he saw himself as over-qualified for most career opportunities that came his way, and was infrequently employed. He attributed his fate to the provincial nature of Eastern Tennessee and was certain that a move to the west, California perhaps, was the solution. That was one of his obsessions, moving out west. The other was the McLean family and he concocted various schemes to tap into their wealth. It was this last obsession that I have used to explain to myself his role in what happened.

What happened was that coming back late at night from a drunken graduation party at the lake, Bradley driving, me half asleep, we hit a man named Billy Ratliff, who was walking down the shoulder of the road. Billy Ratliff, known to the young of Prosperity as the Rat Man, had a little shack down by the lake and ran a trotline. He sold catfish in town on Saturdays, but his main source of income was his monthly disability check. He was, in the parlance of that time, slow, in my mother's words, "a simpleton, poor thing." But he was just as dead as if he had been one of Prosperity's solid citizens.

I can talk about this now with a certain degree of detachment. That was not my response at the time. I must have been hysterical, or maybe it was because I had been drinking that I remember only random images from that evening, the way Billy Ratliff's body in the roadside weeds was twisted at odd angles, the way Bradley took charge, flagging down a car and directing the driver to call his father, the way I kept repeating to myself, sobbing, "We killed Billy Ratliff," and then later to Bradley, "He should have been facing the traffic." As if somehow it was Billy Ratliff's fault.

Judge McLean arrived before the sheriff, and I should have guessed that something was up since I saw that my father was with him. The Judge told us not to say anything—he would deal with the sheriff, and he and my father must have walked away to confer, although I don't remember that. What I remember was the Judge talking to the sheriff, silhouetted in the headlights of the cruiser, and my father motioning me into the Judge's car, where we sat together in the back seat. He told me there was a way out of this, but I needed to do what he said. The Judge would take care of it, but it would be hard if his son were the driver. If I were the driver he'd see to it that it would be no more than a one-year suspended sentence, and at the end of the year the conviction would be expunged from my record.

I told him that I was not driving. Bradley was driving. Why couldn't Bradley get the suspended sentence? That was the whole point, my father said. The Judge couldn't arrange it for his own son without the risk of political embarrassment, but he could do it for me, and he kept repeating the arrangement. There would be a hearing, the Judge would recuse himself and bring in a colleague from Chattanooga, I would be given a suspended sentence, and the charge would eventually be expunged. I remember that he savored the word *expunged*, which he must have picked up from the Judge. I said I didn't want to lie about it, and he said it was too late. The Judge had already informed the sheriff that I was driving. Didn't I see that this would be the best for everybody? Including you, I thought later, but not at the time, and it may be that my account of that night is a mix of what I actually remember and what I added later in piecing it together. But one thing is certain. When I climbed out of the back seat of Judge McLean's car,

I was the drunken driver who had killed Billy Ratliff.

Later when I was able to think about it rationally, I understood what had happened. The Judge wanted to avoid a family scandal. Perhaps he thought Bradley's Princeton appointment would be jeopardized. I don't know that for sure, but I do know that certain promises concerning employment with the McLean empire were made to my father.

And the Judge kept his word. After a decent interval my father was offered a job in the McLeans' tobacco warehouse, which he kept at for six months or so before deciding that his talents were being wasted. And I was given the promised suspended sentence, the conviction eventually expunged from my record. But it was not expunged from the minds of the good people of Prosperity, for whom, whatever I had been before, I was now the killer of Billy Ratliff. The remainder of that summer is contained now in two vestiges of memory—the whispers and nudges I encountered whenever I ventured out, which became increasingly rare, and the sounds of bitter argument I heard from my bedroom late at night. In the fall I escaped to Western Appalachian and less than a year after that my father left for parts unknown.

When I ran into Bradley McLean before I left, he was matter-of-fact and unrepentant, said he was sorry it turned out that way but it was not his idea. And it was not that I was angry with him exactly, nor, except for the Judge, with his family. His mother, Audrey, was, I'm sure, not consulted in the matter, and Jesse was too young to know what was going on. For me it was more a matter of being disabused of an illusion, my first lesson in the American class system. The McLean family had treated me well enough until it was in their interest to do otherwise. They were simply acting after their nature. I had not understood the enormous social gulf that lay between Bradley's family and my own, so it was perhaps a kind of resentment rather than anger. My anger was reserved for my father and Judge McLean, who became the villains in my narrative of what happened that night at the lake, my father the chief villain because he sold out his son for the promise of a rich man's favor.

I saw Bradley McLean twice in the years after that summer, first at my father's funeral and then, six years ago, at my mother's. In both cases we shared polite meaningless words, and now, without thinking much about it except that something had come full circle, I had decided to return the favor.

This was toward the end of May, a month or so before the retirement party. I sat across the aisle, a few rows behind Jesse McLean and her mother in the Prosperity Methodist Church, and it was because of Jesse that I caught only fragments of what the minister was saying. He talked a lot about this beloved family that had done so much for Prosperity, very little about Bradley, except for how fortunate he was to have departed so early this vale of tears. I was thankful he didn't launch into a recitation of "To an Athlete Dying Young." But it was Jesse who held me, and even now I can call up exactly the way she looked. She was wearing a black dress with a high collar and a large hat that could have come from a fifties movie starring, say, Ava Gardner. Her profile was old fashioned, classic, and she never wept, never looked away from the pulpit, never moved a muscle during the entire service, as if stillness were the only way to hold in her grief and the slightest motion would send it all pouring out.

After the service, I went down to the reception in the church basement, and saw her standing alone with her mother to receive the mourners, Judge McLean having departed this vale of tears a decade or so earlier. I waited until almost everyone else had filed through then took my turn. I thought she wouldn't recognize me, but I saw by the look on her face that she did. We embraced silently and she began to sob. I tried to say something but nothing came except a muffled, "I'm sorry."

She stepped back finally and wiped the tears with the back of her hand. "Look, Mother. Bobby's come."

Mrs. McLean, who was such a great beauty in my youth, looked drawn and tired. She turned to me with a suspicious look, as if I had come to gloat, but was intercepted by a woman about her age who clasped her hand with both of hers. "I'm so sorry, Audrey. I just hope you can get through all this."

"I hope so too," Jesse whispered beside me, and held on to my arm.

Mrs. McLean turned back to me, weeping openly now after hours of stoic silence. I took her hand and told her how sorry I was.

"You two were so close," she said and then paused. "I've always regretted the way it turned out."

I nodded without coming up with an adequate response. I was not quite prepared to accept so easy an apology, if that's what it was.

"Why don't you go sit down, Mother," Jesse said. "I'll be there in a minute." Mrs. McLean walked over to sit on a folding chair beside a woman I knew quite well, her sister, Jesse's Aunt Helen. Helen Gates gave me a little wave and a sad smile. She had been a good friend of my mother, a friendship that had managed to survive the tension between the two families. Like me she had moved to Knoxville, so we had kept in touch.

Jesse pulled me aside, out of hearing of the two women. "Oh, God, Bobby. This is the worst. The absolute worst."

No worst there is none. The words of a mannered poem on despair echoed somewhere in my head, but this was no poem and Jesse was right—this was the absolute worst. Not only was she confronting the loss of a brother she grew up worshiping but she had to deal with the sensational circumstances of his death. It had made the front page of the Knoxville paper three days earlier, and I had read the account at first in disbelief. Bradley McLean had been found in a plowed field on the family farm outside Prosperity. He had died of a single gunshot wound to the right temple, and a gun lay near his right hand. That first account hinted at suicide, but the follow-up story the next day could not rule out the possibility of homicide, since there was evidence that more than one person had walked across that field to the furrow where the body lay.

I could have told the sheriff's department it wasn't suicide after the first story, and I could have told them that the person who killed him was either a newcomer to the area or not a football fan, because Bradley McLean was well known as the most proficient left-handed quarterback in the history of McLean County High.

"What are we going to do, Bobby? He's gone."

"It doesn't seem real," I said.

"It's real all right." She didn't seem aware that she still had a tight grip on my arm.

"Do they know what happened?"

"I can't think about that right now," she said. "I know that'll come later, but I just can't think about it now. All I know for sure is that he didn't do it. I saw him that morning, and he was happy as a lark, kidding me about my new haircut. Said I looked like something out of a punk rock band. That's why I wore this stupid hat. I didn't want him to be ashamed of me." The tears welled up in her eyes again, and when she looked at me, her face was so naked and so beautiful that all I could do was pull her against me. She clung there, and held on so tightly that I could feel the stabs of pain in my left side. And I felt something else, a kind of hypocrisy, since the sensations I was experiencing were not limited to pity or sorrow. Something stirred in me that I unsuccessfully tried to put down as inappropriate, an odd mixture of sadness and long-held resentment and lust as we stood clinging to each other in the almost empty church basement.

"There was never a question about that with me," I said over her shoulder. "I mean that he could have done it or even provoked it. He was too—" I let it drop but what? Too what? Content? Accepting of life as it came? Maybe *happy* was the right word after all—happy as a lark, as she had said. Bradley McLean, when I was close to him, was maybe the most even-tempered person I knew. But again I was the hypocrite, because when I read that first account of his death I did have a small question about provocation. I had not been around him in a very long time and we had not parted on good terms. Perhaps as the patriarch of the first family of McLean County he had become as ruthless as his father.

But I didn't say that to Jesse. What I said, as if to put an end to things, was, "Your Aunt Helen knows how to get in touch with me if there's anything I can do."

She pulled away, found a tissue in her purse and wiped at her tears. "We do need to talk some more," she said. "Maybe after a little time has passed. Maybe it'll be easier. Will you call me?"

"Yes."

"Promise?"

"Of course."

She tilted her face up to mine and I kissed her on the cheek. "Look at you," she said. "You know all of us little girls were in love with you, except for the ones that were in love with Bradley."

"That's not the way I remember it."

"That's because we didn't tell you. It would have given you the big head." She managed a little smile at last, and at that moment, as she tried to break through her despair, I thought she was the most beautiful woman I had ever seen, but again that must have been because of the charged circumstances, the raw nerves that made everything seem more intense. Like a lot of people who read too much, I have a bad habit of thinking in literary analogies, and later, re-living that scene, I recalled what Poe had said—that the most affecting of all experiences and therefore the most poetical of all subjects is the death of a beautiful woman. Not so, I thought, unable to get her out of my mind, it is the grief of a beautiful woman. And if you had to pick a point where certain nameless things began to take shape, it would have to be that moment in the basement of the Prosperity Methodist Church.

Although I thought of her constantly in the week after the funeral, I didn't call her because, I told myself, she needed time, and I had nothing to say to her that would help her get over Bradley's death. I had my own problems with Bradley's death, and the McLean family, and my complicated response to meeting the adult Jesse McLean. Or maybe it was not that complicated, I decided later. She was simply a part of a world from which I had been exiled, and all the more alluring for that. But I tried not to analyze it too closely. I applied myself to my work, with only partial success. Another week went by, and then I got a call from her Aunt Helen.

Helen Gates, the widow of a still-famous Knoxville trial lawyer who had had connections to the Clinton White House, lives alone. Before I became an ex-cop I would get a call from her every few months inviting me over for dinner. She's a good cook and a charming dinner companion so these were, with one reservation, pleasant occasions. She takes a motherly interest in me, and we talk about the old days in Prosperity, and about my police work, which fascinates her. She wants all the gory details, which I confess to exaggerating in order to keep her entertained.

The one reservation is the result of her vexation at my bachelorhood. She thinks it unnatural somehow that neither her nephew Bradley nor I married, and so she's always trying to fix me up with somebody she's met, and I expect she did the same for Bradley. Sometimes when I arrived I would be greeted with the announcement that she had neglected to tell me that someone else had been invited, drawing out the word to put the blame on her neglect, and then I would be introduced to the unannounced dinner guest, always a woman about my age, always a different one. "Robert, I'd like you to meet Jeanne. She's a loan officer at my bank," or "Robert, I'd like you to meet Jennifer. She's the new junior partner at the law firm." And the next line would always be the same. "I thought you two would have a lot in common." What I had in common with a loan officer or a lawyer, or, once, a dentist, always escaped me, but her matchmaking made her happy and I indulged her. God only knows what she told those women, who were also indulging her. It's hard to say no to Miss Helen, as I have addressed her since childhood.

On a Friday evening about two weeks after the funeral, I was ringing her doorbell, wondering if I was going to be spending the evening talking to a lady accountant or an associate professor at Western Appalachian. The odds were good because I thought I detected more than one voice inside.

She greeted me at the door and waved me in. "So glad you could come. We have a special guest."

And then the voice from the living room. "Bobby?"

"Hello, Jesse," I said, and for no good reason other than the voice and the kind old woman who was guiding me into the living room and the dull ache in my left side I thought how sweet life is, and how gray and overcast my own life had become, so gradually I hadn't even noticed it. I bent down and kissed Miss Helen on the cheek. "How've you been?"

"Very well," she said. "Considering."

"I hope Jesse knew I was coming."

"I believe it was her idea," Miss Helen said.

"It was my idea," Jesse said. She stood up from the sofa. "You weren't going to call me, were you? You promised."

"Jesse must have been a child the last time you saw her before the funeral." Miss Helen interrupted.

"More like a brat. But that was, what, twenty-five years ago."

"And look how well she turned out," Miss Helen said.

"Hard not to," I said.

"You two are embarrassing," Jesse said. "You'd think I wasn't even in the room. But come over here and give me a hug."

We held each other for a moment, this time without tears. "I was going to call you," I said. "I just wanted to give you a little time."

"Liar," she said in a voice I remembered well, the young girl's teasing voice. "But sit down, Bobby. Let's talk about you, now that you're this police detective. What an unlikely thing for you to do."

"That's exactly how the people I work with feel. They call me Shakespeare and think I'm a little—" I did Eddie's fluttering of the right hand. "I'm thinking about taking early retirement."

"But how did you ever choose that line of work?"

"Maybe my lifelong fight against injustice," I said, and Miss Helen gave me a look over her glasses.

"And you've written a novel, of all things. You're just full of surprises. I confess I haven't read it yet."

"Miss Helen's read it. I think she actually liked it."

"Very engrossing," Miss Helen said. "Set right here in Knoxville. You'd recognize a lot of the places, and I believe Robert based the main character on himself. At least I saw a lot of him in the young police detective that solves the—" She couldn't bring herself to say the word. "The crime," she said.

"Do you have any copies? Could you send me one? I'd love to read it."

"Sure. The trouble with writing a novel is that they expect you to write another one. I was thinking about going back to Prosperity to give it a try."

"Really? That would be wonderful. We could see each other. I mean, have lunch at the Rosewood and everything."

"I don't think I'd get much writing done with you around. And I mean that in the best possible way."

"I'll tell you what you ought to do. You ought to rent the lake house. It's just sitting there, and I could give you a good rate." She smiled. "It's real isolated and nobody would bother you, except maybe ever once in a while I would come by and peep in your window."

"You two can work all this out later," Miss Helen said. "Your dinner's going to get cold."

During dinner I half expected some reference to Billy Ratliff and my inglorious exit from Prosperity, but it didn't come up. Perhaps they had agreed before I arrived that it was not to be a topic of conversation. We also avoided the thing that Miss Helen couldn't bring herself to say, but toward the end of the evening I finally broached it. "I haven't seen anything in the paper lately. Have they found out anything?" *They* were the McLean County Sheriff's Department, notorious for its corruption.

Jesse shook her head. "And I don't expect them to. I don't think they even want to."

"We weren't going to talk about it tonight," Miss Helen said. "But since you brought it up I can tell you that Audrey would just as soon let it drop. She says he's gone and knowing the ugly facts is not going to bring him back."

"That's Mother," Jesse said, "but I need to know something, and I need for somebody to have to answer for it."

"Have you talked to anybody at the Sheriff's Department?"

"I talked to Stanton Giles. Has that big house across from the Baptist church."

"What did he say?"

"He said they were doing everything they could, but they had very little to go on. I don't believe him. I don't think they're doing anything, and I think they know more than they're saying. I asked to see the autopsy report, and he said it wasn't complete. Some lab results hadn't come back, he said. But he was that way about everything—always a reason why he couldn't tell me anything. And he was very rude."

"That's a bad bunch," I said. Policemen have a sense of who's on the take and Stanton Giles gives all the signs.

"Just look at that house," Miss Helen said. "How does a man build a house like that on a sheriff's salary?" She paused. "But that's the way it's always been in county politics, and I guess our families are as bad as anybody else in turning a blind eye. I remember your father saying to just consider it a part of their salary that the county doesn't have to pay." She was referring to Judge McLean, who was certainly not above applying the same principle to himself.

18   *B. J. Leggett*

"But couldn't they at least do their job?" Jesse said. "I was hoping—" She looked across the table at me and held my eye. "Well, I was hoping maybe you could look into it. That's what you do, isn't it?"

"It's what I do here. I don't have any authority in McLean County." Or any reason to aid the McLean family, I might have said but didn't, assuming that Jesse was ignorant of past family sins.

"I don't mean officially," she said. "I mean just sort of look into it. Especially if you come over to write your book. I'll make you a deal. You look into it, and while you're there you can have the lake house for free."

Look into it. A couple of weeks later Chief of Detectives Deathridge would tell me to try to forget I was an ex-cop, and I would understand what he meant, that people who know you're a cop or an ex-cop will ask you to look into things, and looking into things without the authority of the state behind you is almost guaranteed to get you into trouble. Not a game you'd choose to play, and I would have politely declined if I could've shaken the feeling that my hand had been dealt some time ago, the night we killed Billy Ratliff—Bradley in fact, I as surrogate—driving home on Lake Road.

III

DRIVING southeast from Knoxville on a curving blacktop, cresting the ridge and looking down on the town of Prosperity, your first thought might be that the person who named it possessed a fine sense of humor. The two rows of brick and wood structures facing each other across a two-lane road appear to announce, if anything, deprivation and neglect. This too would be a deception, for there's considerable wealth in the area, but what signs of prosperity are about—the McLean place, the Giles place, the Cobb place, a few other fine homes, and the vacation houses of businessmen from Knoxville and Chattanooga—are out of town, secreted in little hollows or cloaked by trees on hillsides. Except for the mountains looming to the east and south, a tourist would probably conclude the place wasn't worth stopping for, especially since there isn't a souvenir shop in sight, but then it's not on the way to anywhere else, so not many tourists drive by. To be where I am, on that rise dropping down into the valley, Prosperity has to be your destination.

It started out as McLean's Crossing and was founded—if that's not too grand a word for so modest a locale—by a man named Randolph McLean, an officer in the Revolutionary army who, for his services to his country, was ceded a large tract of land in what became East Tennessee. (This information, by the way, comes from *A History of McLean County* by Audrey McLean, who begins her account: "Some people mispronounce the name of our county. It rhymes with McCain.") Randolph McLean had come across the mountains from North Carolina, and his principal interest was farming, but he built a log house at a place where two roads crossed, and since one of these was the main east-west route for people heading to the western frontier, it became an inn and supply store. It was destroyed by fire in the mid-1800s, and its replacement also burned early in the twentieth century. All that's left is a historical marker that proclaims, among other things, that the inn's most famous guest was Davy Crockett. Nobody knows if this last is fact or fancy.

The name Prosperity dates from the early twentieth century and it was partly an accident. Before the Smoky Mountains National Park was established in 1934 the principal industry in the region was logging, and Randolph McLean's descendants owned thousands of acres of wooded mountain land, the timber rights to which they leased to big logging companies. Although dozens of logging camps were established in Western North Carolina and Eastern Tennessee, the largest and most successful was the camp established near McLean's Crossing, Prosperity Logging and Mining. Its success was mostly the result of the spur line that linked it to the railway in Knoxville, and so large was its operation that the company distributed fliers in Knoxville and the small towns in the region advertising for workers. The flier contained a headline in large capitals—ARE YOU *LOOKING FOR PROSPERITY?*—and the name stuck. (There's another more mundane account of how the name got changed, but I prefer my version, and I've seen one of the original fliers framed under glass in Audrey McLean's guest bathroom.)

All the wooden structures in town date from that time—the late twenties and early thirties, and its downfall as a boom town came with the establishment of the national park, which the McLean family, I am told, fought vigorously, since it meant the end of one large source of revenue. What had been timberland was now National Park land, the boundary of which is seven miles from Prosperity. The logging companies pulled out and moved west, and Prosperity fell on hard times. The town, that is, but not the large landowners like the McLeans, who made millions from the sale of land forming the park. It turned out that, from a strictly financial point of view, the McLeans had been wrong to fight the National Park. They made far more money from the land sale than they would have ever realized from the logging operation, which was hit hard by the depression.

The only hope for Prosperity as a flourishing town was to become a tourist center, a kind of gateway to the Smoky Mountains National

Park. Across the big ridge to the east lay another logging camp named Gatlinburg, and Prosperity's competition with Gatlinburg to become the major tourist center in the area extended well into the forties. But it was Gatlinburg that got the parkway and the title Gateway to the Smokies, some said because the large landowners in Prosperity didn't want to become a tourist center. They wanted it to stay pretty much as it was.

And it has. The town I enter as I come off the ridge pulling a rented trailer filled with my worldly possessions looks almost exactly as it must have looked more than half a century ago. On the right, the first thing you see is the large brick building with the painted windows, Wilson's Grocery and Supply, next to it the small post office, the bank, and then the wooden building with the blue awning that always has a different occupant. Right now it appears to be a beauty shop. Then in succession, Bailey's Hardware, the Rosewood Café, and finally, anchoring the row, Booker's Notions, an establishment people used to frequent from miles around to purchase wallpaper before it went out of style. On the other side of the street there is first the green BP Station where the old guys go for breakfast. It replaced a white frame building with two gas pumps run by a man named Dyer who lost a leg when a tree fell the wrong way. Next to the BP is an office building rented by H & R Block in the spring and a tobacco buyer in the fall, a barber shop with two chairs, a coin laundry, a convenience store that sells mostly beer—Wilson's refuses to carry it—and Edward's Drugs. Edward's Drugs occupies the spot where the original inn had been, or at least that's where they put the historical marker.

You have to go back to a place to see what it really looks like. Growing up here, I never saw it as anything but mundane, and my memory of it during my self-imposed exile did not improve it. But looking at it spread out before me now, I see that with a little work here and there, and the dynamiting of the BP Station, it could even be charming, like a Tuscan hill town.

I pull off at the BP to check the directions Jesse gave me. There was no lake house when I lived in Prosperity, and she said it was a little tricky to find. The lake is Lake Eleanor, formed during the Roosevelt administration when TVA put a dam on the French Broad River that runs through the area out of the North Carolina mountains.

"You'll love it, Bobby," she said when she came by the police station to give me the key. "Bradley stayed there off and on, and there's still a lot of his stuff there. I can't bring myself to go pick it up. But just make yourself at home for as long as you like. No charge, although you will have to get you a box at the post office. There's no mail delivery out there. I don't even think it has an official address."

I told her that I had considered her rent-free offer, but I thought I needed to pay, since the other matter she had brought up that night at Miss Helen's seemed a little dubious to me. "I don't think I could do you much good with that."

"You don't want to look into it?"

"We'll see when I get there. But I wouldn't expect to find out much. Stanton Giles knows who I am, and he's not going to appreciate some ex-cop from Knoxville nosing around in his county."

"You didn't seem so reluctant the other night."

"Your Aunt Helen's wine, I guess."

"Okay, I'll drop it for the time being," she said, and then in a teasing voice, "I hope you weren't too tipsy to remember what else happened that night."

"Just some innocent flirtation," I said.

"Is that what you call it? Those long deep looks across the table, with Aunt Helen chattering away? They didn't seem all that innocent to me."

"I don't remember the evening quite the way you do," I said looking around the station to see if anyone was overhearing our conversation. Eddie had been skulking in the hallway, his curiosity aroused. "But I'll accept your version. I must have been mistaken in my impression of being led on like a lamb to slaughter."

She ignored this assessment. "And don't think Aunt Helen didn't see exactly what was going on."

"I hope we didn't upset her."

"Oh, she loved it. One of her matchmaking dinners finally came off."

I must have reddened at that and she smiled. "I believe I've embarrassed you, Bobby."

"Would you mind not calling me that in here? I've got enough names as it is, and if I was over the line the other night, I apologize."

She gave me one of those looks we had exchanged at dinner. "I've always been attracted to older men, Detective O'Brian or whatever they call you. Maybe it'll make your stay in Prosperity all the more interesting."

A few minutes after she left Eddie was at my desk. "Damn. You been holding out on us."

I gave him a laundered version of my link to Jesse McLean. I've never told him about my troubled relations with her family. I've never told anybody outside of McLean County.

"She come around here much and your reputation as the departmental"—he fluttered his right hand—"is going to be in jeopardy." He thought for a moment. "And she's the one you had dinner with the night before you came in and announced you were leaving us?"

"That's right."

"Things are beginning to come clear. This retirement thing is a good deal fuck'n fishier than you led us to believe."

"Ever the detective," I said, but he was right. The morning after the dinner at Miss Helen's I had walked into Deathridge's office to announce my retirement, effective June 29.

"Can't be done," Charlie Newell had said. "You got to give me at least a month's notice." Charlie is Deathridge's assistant and very much the rules man.

"Why don't you run it by Deathridge before you say for sure."

He did, and Deathridge said that since I'd been out three weeks with the gunshot wound, they would be willing to make an exception in my case, so June 29 it was, and that's why I am at the moment sitting at a fork of a badly-maintained gravel road wondering which branch will take me to the lake house. Jesse's directions failed to mention this particular option, but I figure that Lake Eleanor is somewhere to the left of me, so I take the road to the left and follow it until it dead-ends at a gate in a barbed-wire fence. I retrace the route to the fork and take the other branch to the lake house.

Like everything else the McLean family has anything to do with, the house is tasteful and unpretentious, with one exception. In the living room, on the wall opposite the French doors to the deck, is a large Catherine Wiley oil called, I believe, *Haystacks*. It is the Wiley painting one is liable to come across in coffee table books on American impressionism. Catherine Wiley is Knoxville's most famous painter, an early twentieth-century impressionist who was re-discovered in the seventies. I had read in the local paper that Wiley's best-known painting had been purchased by an anonymous buyer, and here it is, trying not to look like a museum piece in the lake house. On the adjoining wall is a small Picasso drawing I've never seen before. Curious to know if the McLeans would tolerate a print on their walls, I tilt the frame slightly away from the wall to look behind it. The set of wires leading no doubt to a security system gives me the answer.

On the lake side the living room is all glass, and the view is down the lake rather than across it, so that it appears to flow directly into the mountains to the east. Beyond the deck is a covered dock at the bottom of a long set of wooden steps and a fishing boat hoisted up on a lift. I inspect the kitchen and the two bedrooms and baths and discover a study off the larger bedroom. A vase of wildflowers sits on a desk in the study, leaning against it a note addressed to me. I scan down immediately to Jesse's signature along with a telephone number.

> *I guess this is where you'll be composing the Great American Mystery Novel. (You may not know I was also an English major and once did a paper on Hemingway's portrayal of women that got me a B+ from an old guy who was always trying to look down my dress.) I promise not to bother you, but if you get lonely down there remember that I'm only a few miles away, and we could have some deep significant glances and maybe even some innocent flirtation or innocent touching or God knows what, as long as it's innocent. I'm enclosing my cell number, and I'll keep the phone near in case you experience a sudden case of writer's block and require diversion. By the way, there's gin and vermouth and olives and George Dickel in the pantry. I ran into a fellow named Eddie down*

*at the police station who said these were your drinks
of choice. I happen to favor the martini also, which
means we could join up for some innocent drinking as
well. There's also a case of wine. I called Aunt Helen
to find out what we were drinking the other night,
thinking perhaps you might be able to duplicate that
particular state of drunkenness I found so fetching.*

I read it over again, noting that Jesse has a good ear for the rhythms
of prose, which also puts me in mind of the fact that the first sentence
of my own project is as yet unwritten. I consider the possibility of
including such a note in a narrative. What circumstances might I invent
that would cause a woman to compose a note like that?

IV

I WAKE to the sound of unfamiliar birds and a shaft of light on a strange wardrobe. For a long blank moment I am lost before it all comes flooding back, as has happened many times before, once, most notably, in a hotel room in Bangkok after a twenty-hour flight, coming to consciousness to the whistles of the boatmen on the Chao Phraya River. I have thought of these afterwards as moments of innocence before the sins of the past rush in, or the worries of what the coming day will bring. Maybe they're only exaggerated versions of what happens every morning when consciousness precedes memory. The dying man has a blissful moment before it comes to him that his body is riddled with cancer. The murderer stares innocently at the ceiling and wonders, What was it I did last night? Oh, yeah, I shot a man in the right temple in the middle of a plowed field.

I sit up and look out the bedroom window, the mist rising off the water, the mountains bearing an early morning covering of thin clouds, and my past sins announce themselves in quick succession. You are in the house of the enemy, and that constant ache in your side comes from not being careful enough, and outside is a small trailer containing everything you own, and you have quit your job on a whim and left behind your few friends, and today you will try to write the first words of a novel that must be engaging enough to entertain large numbers of people, and you are on the verge of a complicated relationship that every conscious consideration tells you to avoid, and you have half-promised to look into the death of the man whose sin you have borne these many years. How—what? Unlikely.

I have this bad habit of taking stock of things—where am I exactly at this moment? And the only way I've found to fight it is to distract myself, select a task and stick to it. So sitting in bed looking out over Lake Eleanor I make a mental list of Things to Do. *One, unload the trailer. Two, set up the computer in the study. Three, rent a post office box. Four, lay in a week's groceries from Wilson's. Five, call Eddie to give him the cell phone number. Six, under no circumstances call Jesse McLean. Seven, more specifically, resist further entanglement with Jesse McLean. Eight, invent a plot and characters for a novel.* Seven of these seem doable.

Unloading the trailer is the easiest because the most mindless, except at the point when I bring in an armload of clothes, drop them on the bed, and open the closet door. It's half-filled with what must be Bradley's clothes, and I push them to one side. Physical evidence. Victims' and suspects' closets were always regarded as prime hunting grounds in murder investigations, although I've never been big on physical evidence. Contrary to all those police shows with carpet fibers and hair follicles, the way most murders get solved is that you ask everybody in a roundabout way who did it and eventually somebody tells you. Then you deal with the physical evidence. Anyway, I decide that I'm not at the moment conducting an investigation and make another trip out to the trailer.

Setting up the computer is easier than it might have been because Eddie has color-coded all the cables and receptacles, knowing I am not adept at electronics.

"You put the red fuck'n thing in the red hole," he said when we loaded it into the rental trailer. "You put the blue fuck'n thing in the blue hole. You put the yellow fuck'n thing—

"I got it. I understand the principle."

"You sure?"

"Right. I don't know what I'm going to do without you."

"I worry about that. Your lady friend over there never had to set up a computer. She's not gonna take care of you like I do."

"You're not jealous, are you?"

"We did have a nice rapport."

"You'll have to come over to Prosperity."

"That's in the country, right? I never did care much for the country—spiders, cows, rednecks. There's people down in them hollers probably never seen a black man."

"Hey, this is the twenty-first century. They have TV sets. They've seen Tiger Woods, Oprah."

"Ain't neither one of them exactly black but I get your point."

The computer was the last thing to be loaded, and we stood behind the trailer in the parking lot of the police station and made small talk. "Take care," Eddie said. "And try not to rile up that fellow Giles. He's a mean little mother."

"You take care, and let me know who they give you."

"Probably one of them green rookies. Never going to be the same, and I'm holding you accountable."

We shook hands rather formally, and I thought that would be the last I would see of Eddie for a long time. But, as with so many other assumptions over the next few days, I was wrong.

The visit to Wilson's is my formal reintroduction to Prosperity society and the first test of my return from exile. I'm pretty sure to run into somebody from my past since everybody shops at Wilson's, regarded as a regional institution. That's partly because of its longevity and partly because it was one of the last grocery stores to convert to the supermarket format, written up in *Southern Living* or one of those type magazines. Even when I was a kid, it was an anachronism. When I went to Wilson's with my mother's list, I would hand it over to old Mr. Wilson, who sat on a stool by the cash drawer. He would look it up down and give it to young Mr. Wilson, who would methodically remove the items from shelves inaccessible to customers and stack them on the counter. Old Mr. Wilson would tally up the bill and enter the total in a large gray ledger. No money ever changed hands, but at the end of the month my father would come in and settle up or carry it over to the next month if he couldn't pay. We were not one of the more well-to-do families in town.

Two things about Wilson's have stuck in my mind all these years— first, how dark it was inside, the only natural light coming from plate glass windows the fronts of which were always painted over with that week's prices or announcements of new arrivals. The other thing was the metal ladder young Mr. Wilson used to retrieve items from the top shelves. It rolled on little rails attached to the ceiling, and I had never seen anything quite like it, although they must have been common at one time.

After a stop at the post office, I walk back to Wilson's, next door. On the outside it is unchanged, the windows still proclaiming the weekly specials, but when I enter I see the interior is now as bright and sleek as any Kroger, although considerably smaller, and that the checkout lanes are staffed by young girls in khaki shorts and green tee shirts that announce over the left breast *Wilson's. Established 1931.* I also see that young Mr. Wilson has become old Mr. Wilson. He sits in a little cubicle in the front of the store staring into a computer screen, and when I've filled my cart with a lot of stuff I figure I'll never eat I walk over to speak to him. He doesn't recognize me, probably takes me for a salesman.

"Robert O'Brian," I say, shaking his hand. "It's been a while since I've been back."

"Kate's boy," he says.

"That's right."

He frowns, starts to speak, thinks better of it, then says finally, "You here visiting relatives?"

"None left. I'm staying out by the lake. Doing some writing." This last is bravado. I seem to be doing everything I can to keep from doing any writing. "There are some people I'd like to see though. I just saw Miss Edna over at the post office. She said I was the only person she could remember ever asked to rent a post office box. No point in it, she said. She'd save my mail for me, just to come in and pick it up."

I don't tell him what I'm still trying to think through—the exchange that took place when I introduced myself to Miss Edna. "The prodigal son," she said in a tone I couldn't read. "So you finally came back for something besides a funeral." I told her I would be staying at the McLeans' lake house for a while, which produced an arched eyebrow. "Does that mean all is forgiven?" Miss Edna long ago appointed herself our local historian, although my father said that was just her euphemism for town gossip.

"I came in to get a post office box" was my response, for the moment forestalling that particular line of historical inquiry.

"Miss Edna's been there so long she knows everybody around

B. J. Leggett

here," Mr. Wilson says. "Maybe a little unorthodox, but she gets the job done. She's been known to take people's mail home with her so they can pick it up after hours. Of course there's people thinks she steams open some of the more interesting looking pieces."

"I remember hearing that."

"This recent Mexican influx kind of threw her for a loop, so she just throws everything that looks Mexican in a big cardboard box and lets them sort it out."

"Is Byron Holmes still around?" Byron Holmes was my high school English teacher and the man who introduced me to reading and taught me how to write. I dedicated the novel to him.

"He's still living out on that little place in the country. Long retired from teaching. Does some truck farming. If you got any tomatoes in that cart, they came from his place. He'll probably be in with a new batch in a few days."

"I was surprised not to see him at the funeral."

"He and the McLean family have had this running feud about a property line on his place. You may remember that he was one to hold a grudge."

"When he comes in, could you tell him I'm staying out at the McLean house on the lake. Maybe he could drop by some time. There won't be any McLeans around, just me."

"I'll tell him, and I think I've got his number around here somewhere." He searches the top of his desk and locates the card. It says simply *Byron Holmes Produce* with a telephone number. "You can keep that. I've got it written down. Weren't you and Bradley buddies? At one point, I mean. Before the—" He pauses, searching. "Incident" is what he finds. "Down at the lake."

"That's right." I turn to leave.

"I believe y'all were on the only championship football team McLean County ever had," he says, not wanting to let it go.

"We were."

"And you're living in Knoxville."

"Just moved out."

"Did you ever see Miss Helen Gates over there? She and Kate were close, as I recall."

"I had dinner with her and Jesse not too long ago."

"I'm sure that whole family is just numb. Nothing like this has happened around here before that I can remember. It's like one of those TV mysteries."

I remind myself that I'm here to write a novel, not to solve a mystery, then immediately venture my first investigative question. "So what are people around here saying? Anybody know what happened?"

He frowns, then motions me inside the cubicle. "You want to sit down?" He glances over at my cart and gets the attention of the nearest cashier. "Robin, why don't you check out Mr. O'Brian here while we talk."

Robin leaves her post to fetch the cart. "Paper or plastic?"

"Plastic," I say arbitrarily, taking the chair beside the desk. "I haven't seen anything in the newspaper lately. What's the talk here, if you don't mind saying?"

He takes off his reading glasses. "There's some thinks he killed himself because he lost all his daddy's money in the stock market. There's some thinks it has something to do with drugs. There's some thinks it was a jealous husband, and there's some thinks he got in with the wrong crowd."

"In other words, nobody knows anything."

"That's about it."

"Is there any reason to think the family was in financial trouble?"

"It's all speculation. Most of what I hear is from the old guys that take their breakfast at the BP. The market's been taking a beating lately and they've all been losing money from their retirement accounts, so they figure that if poor people are losing a little, rich people are losing a lot."

"Sometimes the rich people are getting what the poor people are losing."

"There's that too," he says. "Like you said, nobody really knows anything. The drug part came up just because drugs have gotten to be big business in this part of the country. It's not like when you were living here. There's people that look like they're from Chicago or Miami been stopped on the highway with rolls of bills and guns in their glove compartments. Half the people that shop here now get their mail

B. J. Leggett

out of Miss Edna's cardboard box."

"And the jealous husband theory is also speculation, I take it."

"Well, now these last two rumors do have some basis. Bradley was going with a woman that was technically married but been separated from her husband for a while. That's no secret. Everybody knows who she is. Shops in here, and I noticed she was not at the funeral. And this bad company angle comes from somebody seeing him at a roadhouse over in Parris County drinking with a pretty rough crowd. One of those old boys in fact used to run cockfights over there and got sent up on a manslaughter charge. But for all I know Bradley was in there on his own and just trying to be sociable. That's the way he was, you remember. You'd never know he was from the richest family in the county that could trace their line all the way back to the Revolutionary War."

Parris County, which adjoins McLean, has always had the reputation of being the place to go to participate in otherwise illegal activities. When I was in high school it was the place to buy bootleg whiskey, which we professed to enjoy. The county seat, Parris City, was reviled from pulpits as a den of iniquity, so it was naturally attractive to the young.

"So what does the sheriff's office say? Do you know if they've followed up on any of this?"

"The sheriff ain't volunteering anything, and there's few brave enough to ask him directly. Anyway, you'll hear all kind of rumors. It's all anybody's talked about the last few weeks."

"It's hard to believe."

"It is," he says, rising. "I miss seeing Audrey McLean. Hasn't been in since it happened. Sends this woman works for her." He looks over at the checkout lane. "I believe Robin's got you all bagged up. We take credit cards now if that's the way you'd like to handle it."

"Wilson's has come a long way," I say. "But I miss the ladder."

Mr. Wilson smiles. "Fellow from the Appalachian Museum came over and bought that off me. I have no idea what he did with it." He sticks out a hand. "I understand how hard it must have been for you to come back." He waits for a response, but I have nothing to say so I nod and shake his hand, then walk over to Robin's register and dig out my Visa.

"Debit or credit?"

"Credit. Did you know Bradley McLean?"

She looks at me without responding, runs the card and hands me the receipt and a pen. "You want me to help you with these?"

"Sure."

"Mr. Wilson says we may be the last ones in the country to take peoples' groceries out."

I follow her to the BMW, which she admires, and ask how one acquires a Wilson's tee shirt.

"The only way I know is to get a job as a bag boy."

"But then I would have to spend the day asking people whether they wanted paper or plastic. How well did you know Bradley McLean?"

"Just from the store," she says. "We voted him the one we'd most like to get trapped in the freezer with."

As we stack the groceries in the back seat I quiz her about what her friends are saying about Bradley's death.

"Love triangle," she says. "You don't want to put that detergent next to the produce."

"Sorry. So what do you mean—that he was shot by some enraged husband?"

"I don't know," she says. "I just know he was too good-looking for anybody to resist and he sort of let you know that he was interested. The way he looked at you. He could have taken me down to the lake any time he wanted to."

I remember that phrase from high school. The most secluded parking places are down by the lake. "But you don't know for a fact that he was involved in some kind of love triangle."

"He was going with a married woman. At least that's what I heard."

"Well, only technically, according to Mr. Wilson. Not as bad as it sounds. Did you know the husband?"

"Never met him," she says. "I don't think he lives around here any more. Where do you want these eggs?"

"Here, I'll take 'em.

She passes me the eggs and shuts the back door of the BMW. "Mr. Wilson's real particular about the eggs. His rule is you ask the person where they want the eggs then they won't complain if they get broken."

"Thanks a lot. Do you accept tips?"

She nods and I fish out a couple of dollars, which she accepts without comment, folds, and sticks in the back pocket of her shorts. "What do *you* think happened?"

I ease behind the wheel, still holding the eggs. "I've just been here long enough to see that it's an honest-to-God mystery." I look up at her as she leans against the edge of the open door. "I wouldn't be surprised if we don't get Geraldo down here with a camera crew."

"Geraldo?" she asks but does not stay for an answer, straightening and pushing my door shut.

I find a place for the eggs in the passenger seat beside the new cell phone and look up into the rear-view mirror just in time to glimpse her pushing the cart back into Wilson's, her khaki shorts so tautly tailored that I can discern the outline of my tip.

V

DRIVING back from Wilson's, I hear the surprisingly effeminate ring of the cell phone in the seat beside me and pull over to the shoulder of the gravel road. "This is Robert O'Brian."

"Don't be alarmed," Jesse says. "I'm not going to bother you. I just wanted to see if everything was okay. And are you always this formal on the phone?"

"A carryover from my former profession. You may be interested to know that you're my first caller on my first cell phone."

"You've never had a cell phone? And by the way, people in the know just call them *cells*."

"I'll try to remember that. The department furnished our phones. I never needed one until now. What I'm wondering is how you got this number. I haven't given it out to anybody. I just took the thing out of the box a few hours ago. Is there something I'm missing here?"

"Okay, you're the detective," she says. "Here's a little test. Tell me where I am and how I got your number."

"Well, since you gave me that small clue, I can tell you that you're at the lake house, probably sitting at the desk in the study, and spread out before you are the instructions for activating the cell phone, including the number."

"Okay, you pass. Now tell me what I'm wearing. Here's a clue— it's very provocative, me thinking of course that you would actually be here."

"I'm on the way back from Wilson's. I'll be there in twenty minutes. Just stay where you are."

"I can't," she says. "I've got an appointment. Maybe tomorrow."

"I liked the note."

B. J. Leggett

"Well, I should hope so. I busted my ass on that. Took me one whole afternoon. It's a big responsibility to write a clever note to a writer."

"The tone was just right."

"I'm glad you liked it."

"The main theme seemed to be innocent relationships, with which I'm totally in agreement."

"It was a little joke," she says. "The old guy who was always trying to look down my dress also taught me about irony."

"But I'm serious." Or half serious. The carnal half of me is already hopelessly smitten, but the serious half says this is big trouble—under no circumstances pursue it.

"I don't understand."

"I don't want to take advantage of the situation."

"And what exactly is the situation in your view?"

"Your brother has just been killed and you're a little manic and maybe a little vulnerable."

"Manic? Is that the way you would characterize me?"

"I don't know. Maybe that wasn't the right word, but I know this conversation has taken a wrong turn, so forget everything I've said and we'll start over again tomorrow."

"Before I get off I have to tell you that you're not the only one who's been analyzing my behavior. I've been in treatment."

"In treatment?"

'I've been seeing this psychiatrist guy in Knoxville."

"I didn't know."

"Anyway, your name came up, and the fact that I felt this attraction, and the good doctor theorized that you and Bradley were so closely associated in my childhood memories that I had transferred my feelings for Bradley to you, but since that made our relationship a kind of incest I told him he was full of shit and he said that the vehemence of my resistance only proved he was right."

"Must be a Freudian."

"And I told him I was attracted to you because you were attractive, which he dismissed as a tautology. So then I thought about it some more and told him that I was attracted to you because of the way I felt when

I was around you, how the gloom disappeared for a while and I had this pleasant burning sensation in a particular portion of my anatomy, which I think embarrassed him a little."

"Jesse, you don't have—"

"And he said that the physical sensation was a sexual fantasy fostered by reading romance novels, which I don't by the way. I told him that the first time I felt it was in the basement of the Methodist Church, and that the proof of my analysis of the situation was that I kept contriving reasons to see you like the dinner at Aunt Helen's and getting you to stay in the lake house and taking the key to the police station, which I could just as easily have mailed."

"You don't have to tell—"

"And he said this was proof of nothing except that I was attracted, but it didn't explain why. And I said why couldn't certain things in life remain a mystery, and perhaps it would be better if he stuck to the part of my life that was in utter despair and stayed away from the part that gave me pleasure."

"I'm not sure—"

"And he said that kind of bi-polar thinking was not healthy, and I said probably not but it was the best I could do at the moment." She stops to wait for my response, which is slow in coming. "You still there?"

"I'm not sure I needed to hear all that, but I can see that I've upset you. I've probably over-analyzed the situation."

"I'm not upset, well, maybe a little, but I will tell you this. You may be a good police detective but as an analyst you suck. You don't need to analyze everything. Just take things as they come, like—I'm running late, got to go."

"Let's start over again at the point where everything fell apart," I say, trying to recover the light tone. "I was supposed to guess what you're wearing."

"All the heart's gone out of it," she says and breaks the connection. I sit for a moment examining the screen of my new phone, then pull off the shoulder and drive back to the lake house, trying to attach a meaning to the conversation so abruptly concluded. *You don't need to analyze everything. Just take things as they come.* Right. She almost said *like Bradley*. But given what, in fact, came to Bradley, this does not seem particularly good advice.

It's only the middle of the afternoon and I have whittled my Things to Do list down to two—Call Eddie and Invent a plot and characters for a novel. I take as much time as I can putting away the groceries, trying to devise some system for storage, but things go much too quickly and I'm now facing the looming confrontation with a blank yellow pad. Only one distraction left, and I place the call to the Knoxville Police Department and ask for Lieutenant Carpenter.

"How's the crime scene in Knoxville?"

"Shake, that you? Well, to tell you the truth, Deathridge is determined to make this the only completely crime-free city in the country. We're all going to be out of a job. They don't need a night watchman down at your place?"

"Who'd they give you?"

"Graber."

"Not as bad as it could've been."

"He's okay, but let's be frank, he's not a very sophisticated man. Mostly tells dirty jokes and talks about his sexual conquests."

"Speaking of which—"

"I know where you're going here. That's another disappointment. The woman is incapable of carrying on a serious conversation."

"Sorry it didn't work out. I saw it coming, but the reason I called was to give you my phone number. This place doesn't have a telephone, so I had to get this cell phone. Or *cell*, as I was just informed people in the know say." I give him the number and ask him to pass it on to Deathridge. I add that it strikes me as a major deficiency of the cell phone that when you buy one you have to spend all your minutes calling everybody you know just to give them your number. Somebody, I suggest, needs to invent an electronic cell phone directory, so that every time one gets sold, the number automatically gets added to the directory.

There is a long silence. "You got way too much time on your hands," Eddie says finally. "I can see already that quitting your job was a bad idea."

"It's just going to take me a little while to get into the new routine.

And by the way, I was thinking, don't you have some time coming?" The idea occurred to me on the way back from Wilson's.

"They owe me a few days."

"You got any plans?"

"Nothing in particular."

"Well, there you are. You should come over for a couple of days. The lake house has two bedrooms, right on the water, ideal vacation spot."

"The lake fuck'n house? What kind of a town is that? All the houses got names?"

"Just this one, as far as I know. Anyway, there's a boat here. We could do some fishing. There's supposed to be big bass in here. This is where they hold one of those television fishing tournaments."

"Fishing?" There's a note of disdain in Eddie's voice. "Fishing? Man, I'm a city boy. From the projects. Fishing's dangerous. You could get one of them little hooks in your eye or fall out of the boat and drown. They always pulling people out of that lake. Fishing." This last under his breath to signal complete dismissal.

"Okay, forget fishing. What about just lying around, relaxing. And Bradley McLean has left a large cache of pornographic videos, including the complete run of *Girls Gone Wild*." I discovered them in the bedroom closet when I was putting my clothes away.

"Well, now you're talking," he says, "but I don't see why a man would want to drive all that way just to see some naked women when you can get that on TV in your own living room. Are you trying to tell me something?"

"Okay, I'll come clean. I halfway promised Jesse McLean I would nose around a little, ask some questions about her brother's death, and I was thinking that might go off better if we temporarily reestablished our partnership. But it was just an idea. Working vacation. Plenty to drink here, nice view, cool breeze, breakfast at the BP, and I haven't even scouted out the local attractions."

"Why didn't you tell me up front you wanted my help?" Eddie says. "Let me get a piece of paper for some directions and I could be over there sometime next week. How about Tuesday?

"Tuesday's good." I give him the directions. "The only tricky part is that fork on the lake road."

"I got it," he says. "The boys are going to be impressed when they find out I'm spending a few days at the lake house."

When I get off, I begin having second thoughts, wondering if it's a good idea involving Eddie, but then I'm always second guessing myself so I let it slide. My problem now is that I have no more chores, so nothing stands between me and that blank sheet of lined yellow paper. I remember the feeling well from the first book—how hard it was to get the writing going every day—until I learned a trick about halfway through. I read somewhere that you should always stop when you've still got something you're burning to put down so you have something to start with the next day, priming the pump. But now I have nothing, no plot, no characters, no crime, and I have devoted very little thought to it, given my current distractions.

In the study I open a package of legal pads and a box of felt tip pens. That's my preferred method of composition—writing it out in long hand and at the end of the day transferring it to the computer. I like the physical sensation of felt tip pen on paper.

Sitting down at the desk, I move Jesse's wildflowers aside, open the legal pad, and print at the top of the first page *IDEAS FOR THE NOVEL*. Something doesn't feel right about the study—too claustrophobic—so I move into the living room and sit on the sofa, facing out over the lake. In the first novel I based the protagonist on myself, or at least an idealized, much wittier version of myself, and his partner on Eddie, as he discovered. There was one main plot and two sub-plots, and the main plot was suggested by an actual murder that had taken place some years before I joined the force but was still much discussed, partly because it involved the kind of investigation that is depicted on TV cop shows and partly because it involved dismemberment, various limbs and organs being unearthed all over town. One side note is that Deathridge, before he became Chief of Detectives, was the lead investigator and was credited with breaking the case.

One of the sub-plots, entirely invented, involved the protagonist's involvement with a beautiful young woman suspected of knowing more than she was letting on. It gave me my title, *A Catch in the Breath*, taken from a William Butler Yeats poem describing a kind of beauty that "made a catch in the breath." Since the female victim had been strangled, I thought this a very fine title, but my editor didn't like it and suggested instead *Body Parts*, which I disliked as obvious and vulgar. He thought my title was a bit artsy for a police procedural, as were the literary epigraphs that opened each chapter, which he also deleted. When I protested, he pointed out that the contract I had signed gave the press the final word on the title and the final text as well as the cover.

So *Body Parts* it was, and the cover, which I disliked even more, featured, as one might have guessed, female body parts, which when put together formed a fairly voluptuous nude figure. These circumstances took some of the joy out of publishing the novel, but the agent said they probably made us an extra hundred thousand or so. I tried to get veto rights to the next title and cover as well as an epigraph clause, but discovered pretty quickly the author's lowly position in the hierarchy of the publishing industry.

In fact, that experience taught me a great deal about the publishing industry, including the impression that it would like to be rid of authors altogether, since they constitute the one element of the process that is unpredictable and not easily reduced to a successful formula. And publishers have almost succeeded in eliminating the author by insisting on a certain type of novel, for example, which always sounds suspiciously like the last blockbuster.

Editors are also frightened to death of a manuscript that does not fit neatly into a type. My agent, a literate man, a writer and therefore probably ill-fitted for his trade, told me from the beginning that, as much as he liked my manuscript, it fell between two stools. It was too literary for a popular novel and too popular for a literary novel, and that was the response of the first editors who looked at it. *Tell me how I can market this and I'll buy it*, one responded.

So the agent, whose name was Christopher, very young, and the lone New York agent who deigned to look at the manuscript, said I was going to have to take it one way or the other, either more literary or more popular. "Are you trying for good reviews or the possibility of large sales?" he asked me. "I'm trying to win a bet," I answered, so popular it was. Out went everything that sounded vaguely like Nick Carraway's ruminations in *The Great Gatsby*. In came more police procedural stuff and more description of scattered body parts. He sold it pretty soon after I had reduced it to the basic murder plot.

But at least I *had* a plot. Now I sit on the sofa looking down at the yellow tablet feeling like a one-trick pony. Okay, what if my protagonist is an ex-cop from a large city police force, say Atlanta, who goes back to his home town and gets involved in a murder investigation? I put that down, look at it for a while, then mark through it. Too autobiographical. That's what I was accused of with the first novel. I need to invent a plot and a protagonist that are not based on my own life. Okay, what if the protagonist is a detective from a large city police department, say Atlanta, who takes a leave of absence to return to his home town because of the death of his father. No, the murder of his father. And he becomes involved in the investigation of his own father's death. I write that down, then mark through it. Too sentimental—all that boring description of the detective's relationship with his father.

I decide the sofa isn't working. Too comfortable and there's no place for the pad except on my knees. I need a table. Maybe the deck would be a good place to write. There's a round umbrella table with chairs that appear to have about the right degree of comfort. I go through the kitchen to the deck, raise the umbrella and create an oval of shade against the late afternoon sun. The chair is comfortable enough without inducing drowsiness, and I start again.

The only thing I like so far is the idea of the protagonist going back to his home town after a long absence. Why would he be going back? How could he get involved in a criminal investigation? I write down these questions, then look at my watch. It's nearing six, the earliest I allow myself a drink. Maybe a martini would help loosen something.

I go back through the kitchen to the pantry. Bombay gin—Eddie was fairly specific in his instructions. There is vermouth, a silver shaker beside the gin, ice in the freezer. I locate a martini glass and a jar of olives.

Back on the deck, I sip the martini and study my notes. *Why would he be going back? How could he get involved in a criminal investigation?* The last one is easy. If he's from a large metropolitan police department, then the small-town cop might need his expertise. I put that down then mark through everything. Too hackneyed. Done to death. Wise-guy city policeman and local hick cop. *One False Move*, *Murder in a Small Town, The Ladies in the Lake.*

I take another sip of the martini, which is excellent, then feel for the cell phone in my shirt pocket, thinking I should call Jesse and try to recover from our last conversation. I look down at the tablet again. The only thing not marked through is the heading, *IDEAS FOR THE NOVEL*. I mark through that, tear out the sheet and squeeze it into a ball. I'm forcing it. Sleep on it tonight. Let it come naturally. I walk back to the study, throw the ball into a little wicker basket by the desk and locate Jesse's note with the telephone number.

"I know why you're calling," she says.

"How did you know it was me?"

"It tells you the number of the person calling."

"I knew that."

"You know, for a police detective you're remarkably out of touch with the twenty-first century."

"It was a source of amusement in the department."

"Maybe I can help you. I'm a whiz at anything electronic. I could show you, for example, how to put my number in your cell, so you don't have to look it up every time you call, which I'm sure you're doing now. Anyway, I know why you're calling. You're calling to say you were wrong and I was right, and you want to find some way to make it up to me."

"I don't know that I would put it that way exactly, but, yeah, basically."

"And I've thought of a way you can make it up. Don't worry—I'm not going to ask you to look into it—"

"Jesse, I need to tell you something." I'm about to tell her that my ex-partner is coming over on Tuesday and that we might indeed spend a couple of days looking into it, but I change my mind in mid-sentence, thinking that our chances of finding out anything substantial are extremely remote and it will only give her false hope. So I say instead, "I was wrong and you were right and we should let this thing take its own natural course."

"This thing?"

"Whatever it is. We should take it as it comes and be happy about it."

B. J. Leggett

"Well, of course," she says. "I've never thought about it in any other way. But we can get back to that later. Right now I'm talking about something else."

"So what do I need to do?"

"Just one thing. All I'm asking you to do is to talk to Stanton Giles. I think the Sheriff's Office is the key to the whole thing, and you know the right questions to ask."

I'm way ahead of her, thinking I ought to talk to Giles before Eddie comes. This is Thursday. I'll call the sheriff's office in the morning, drive over to Adair in the afternoon. But why is the Sheriff's Office the key to the whole thing? "Okay. I'll talk to him."

"Well, that's settled. Now we can talk about this other little issue— whether we should actually be present together in the same room, have physical contact and so on."

"I was just having a martini. I believe your note said that's your drink of choice. How far away are you?"

"Five miles of gravel road."

"Want to come over for a drink?"

"I wouldn't want to interfere with your writing."

"I'm done for the day."

"How did it go?"

"It's always slow at first."

"So how much did you actually write? How many pages?"

"Well, I filled up a page." And then threw it away. Why would a man lie about something like that?

"How long was your first manuscript?"

"About three hundred and fifty pages."

"So you've got only three hundred and forty-nine to go. At that pace you've got only about, what, fifty more weeks and you've got yourself a book. But maybe you don't work on the weekends. Do you work on the week-ends?"

"I don't know. I've never been in this situation before, I mean unemployed. I'll have to figure it out."

"Do you work at night?"

"Never at night."

"So maybe I will come over for one drink—if you promise not to be a Boy Scout. See you in a few minutes."

"I've done my good deed for today," I say. "Agreeing to talk to Stanton Giles." But she's already gone.

B. J. Leggett

VI

ONE difference between my former department and the McLean County Sheriff's Department is that the people I worked for generally knew what they were doing. Sheriff Stanton Giles' greatest area of expertise lies in the art of getting re-elected. He owned a car dealership in Adair before becoming sheriff, and his chief deputy was his head salesman and first campaign manager. Driving to Adair, the McLean county seat, on Friday afternoon, I'm trying unsuccessfully to pull up the deputy's name—Jimmy something. The receptionist said the sheriff would be in all afternoon unless something came up, and not a lot comes up in Adair. As some wag had it, the chief crime in Adair is breaking and entering and falling asleep.

On Thursday night I tried to prepare Jesse for the fact that I probably wouldn't learn much—maybe the results of the autopsy, description of the crime scene, physical evidence recovered, current leads, but not anything definitive or the family would have already been informed.

We had taken our drinks out to the deck, watching the mountains to the east disappear into the dark. "When you talk to him," Jesse said, "I bet you'll come away with the same impression I had. He knows something he's not telling."

"Did you talk to him alone?"

"No, there was this deputy in the room, but he didn't say anything. What did your people think of Giles? They must have had some dealings with him."

"They think he's completely corrupt, that he's had no training in law enforcement, and therefore's not good at it, which makes him defensive and uncooperative. But that doesn't mean he's not a nice person."

She laughed. "That's what I mean about you. I like sitting here with you."

"Nice to have a drinking companion."

"I want you to observe," she said, "how we can sit here and have a drink like normal people. You keep thinking I'm going to rip my clothes off and jump you. But tonight we'll just drink and talk."

"That would be a shame, ripping them off, considering what care you took in their selection."

"Well, it won't happen tonight." I could just make out her smile in the dark. "There'll be time for that later on."

I'm replaying that conversation as I pull into the outskirts of Adair on Highway 411, whose strip malls and fast-food restaurants immediately reactivate my prejudice against ugliness. Only what could loosely be called downtown Adair has escaped the blight of late twentieth-century capitalism. It is the classic small-town square surrounding a brick courthouse with a cupola. The sheriff's office is not located in the courthouse, as I recall, but is out on the other end of Highway 411 that heads off toward Knoxville, or Knoxville Pike as the twenty-five hundred souls who reside in Adair call it.

The receptionist looks up from her computer screen and eyes me with some suspicion when I ask to see Sheriff Giles and I explain that I'm the one who called earlier. She asks me the nature of my business and I tell her it concerns the death of Bradley McLean. She asks my name and writes it down on the pad beside her keyboard.

"That's O'Brian with an *a,*" I say. "Most people misspell it."

She marks through the *e,* prints an *a* above it, tears the sheet from the pad, and disappears through the door behind her desk.

"He can give you ten minutes," she says when she reappears. She gestures over her shoulder. "Through that door, down the hall, second door on the left."

The door is open and Stanton Giles stands up from his desk when I enter. I met him years earlier when I came over to pick up a prisoner for trial, but he would not likely remember, since I was in uniform at that time. He is a small man who helps to confirm my theory that much of the evil in the world is caused by short white males. He is dressed like a lawyer, white shirt, dark suit, dark tie. He wears tiny round glasses and does not resemble the movie caricature of the Southern sheriff.

"Mr. O'Brian with an *a*," he says, giving me his hand across the desk. "Are you any kin to the Prosperity O'Brians? You're not by any chance Kate's son?"

"That's right."

"Then you and I are in the same business."

"Well, not any more. I left the department at the end of June."

"I'm sorry to hear that. I read in the Knoxville paper that you were wounded in a drug raid. I hope it wasn't anything really serious."

I take the metal chair across the desk from him. "It's okay, not life-threatening." I point to my left side. "I still get a little pain, but that's not the reason I retired from the department. I just figured I wasn't cut out for that line of work."

"I see." He sits down, straightening his tie, and his smile suggests that he agrees I wasn't cut out for that line of work.

"And what line of work are you now pursuing?"

"At the moment I'm doing some writing." This is a mistake, I realize almost immediately.

Giles' eyes narrow behind the round glasses. "You're not a journalist?"

"Oh, no. This is just something I'm doing on my own." To say to a man like Stanton Giles that I'm writing a novel would instantly drop me into a category I don't wish to occupy.

"Well, it's nice to have the leisure to pursue your own interests." This is said in such a clipped way as to suggest I am some sort of dilettante. "Where are you living?"

"I'm staying in Prosperity temporarily. And you're still there, I see. Somebody pointed out your house to me." This is not strictly true, but Jesse did say it was across from the Baptist church.

"I like the peace and quiet," he says. "Twenty minute drive." He looks at his watch. "Just what is it I can do for you, Mr. O'Brian?"

"I wanted to ask you about Bradley McLean's death. I jotted down a few questions." I pull a notebook from my shirt pocket and flip it open, a habit left over from my detective days and it is my second mistake.

"Are you conducting an interview?" He pronounces the last word as if it were obscene.

"No, I just wanted to find out how the investigation is going."

"On what authority?"

"I beg your pardon?"

"You're not even a resident of this county and you walk in and want to know how an investigation is going?"

"Actually, a member of the McLean family requested that I talk to you."

"I'm surprised that you and the McLean family are on such good terms. I recall some unpleasantness involving you and that family. Just who was it requested that you speak to me?"

"Jesse actually."

"I see. I had a very long discussion with her and I told her everything I know about the investigation, although she wasn't satisfied with that. And I can see why she would want to send you rather than coming back herself. She was quite rude, made accusations."

"She was upset."

"She addressed me as if I was her field hand. That's always been an arrogant family, but I won't stand for it. Ordered her out of the office."

"She didn't tell me that, but I'm sure you've seen that before. Family members are impatient for results. They don't understand how the process works." The way you and I do, I imply, trying to find some common ground. "I can assure you that these are the most basic kinds of questions, and that the only person I'll share the information with is Jesse McLean." This is also not strictly true, assuming that my ex-partner turns up on Tuesday.

"Does this have anything to do with your writing?" Again there is an odd emphasis on the last word.

"No, nothing to do with that."

"Let me see that." He points to the notebook.

I hand it across the desk. "I don't know if you can make out—"

He raises a hand to interrupt me, then begins reading through the notebook. They are quite basic questions concerning such matters as physical evidence recovered from the crime scene, fingerprints, known associates, friends, lovers, financial records, bank transactions, suspects, motives, autopsy results. He reads through them quickly, flipping over the pages. At one point he mutters "anomalies?" to himself, as if he's never heard the word, then "lifestyle angle?"

He slides the notebook back across the desk. "You ask there about the family's financial situation. I would think they know their own financial situation."

"I just assumed you had checked on it, and I didn't want to embarrass—"

"You know what I think?" He opens a desk drawer and pulls out a folded handkerchief, takes off his glasses and begins polishing them slowly and deliberately. He holds them up to the light, then puts them back on. "I think you're conducting a little investigation of your own. I think maybe Jesse McLean called you up and said this sheriff down here doesn't know what he's doing, so why don't you come down here and see what you can find out. You're the big city detective. You could probably solve this thing in a day or two or maybe in an hour like they do on television."

"I promised her I would talk to you. It's the only thing I promised." This is technically true but evasive. "You're not going to tell me anything?"

"To answer your questions would compromise the investigation." He stands up and leans across toward me with his hands on the desk. "But I will tell you something. If you start nosing around my county, asking questions, stirring things up, I might have to let you spend some time in our local facilities."

"What would be the charge?"

"Interfering with a criminal investigation. And if we don't have a law like that I'll find something else. I don't want you messing around here and I'm not going to have it. No sir. I believe this little interview is over."

We look at each other in silence. "So what should I tell Jesse McLean?"

"You can tell her that she can send you back to Knoxville. You're done here."

I stand, take the notebook from the desk and turn for the door. "Thank you for your time."

"One other thing." He smiles genially. "While you're here I need to know where you're staying, just in case I have to get in touch with you for some reason."

"I'm staying at the McLean's lake house."

"Address and phone number." He takes a tablet from the top drawer of the desk.

"There's no official address. I think people refer to it as the lake road but it doesn't have a name, and the official Lake Road is on the other side of the lake. There's no telephone in the house."

"I assume you have a cell phone."

I give him the number and he writes it down. "I'll tell your one other thing. It's probably not a good idea to get too thick with that family. I have a feeling their best days are behind them."

The receptionist is on the telephone when I walk by her desk. I gesture back to the door behind her. "That's one mean little mother," I say, and she actually smiles, which encourages me to ask if I might consult her telephone directory. Silent, holding the phone to her ear with her shoulder, she fishes it out of her desk and passes it across. I locate the number and write it down in the notebook after *lifestyle angle?*

A large man in uniform walks through the front door. "He back there?"

The receptionist nods, and he strides past me.

"I know him," I say. "Jim something."

"McKinney," she mouths softly with a hand over the phone. Jim McKinney, the sheriff's former campaign manager and chief deputy. It is not strictly true that I know him, but I will in fact come to know him.

Sitting in the car in front of the sheriff's office I start the motor and the air conditioning and then dial the number.

"Sutherland and Anderson," the woman's voice says.

"I wonder if Dr. Sutherland could work me in this afternoon. I'm in town for the afternoon, and it would take ten minutes at the most."

"Have you seen him before?" she asks.

"It's been a while."

"Name and date of birth?"

I tell her and wonder if the O'Brian family's medical history is still on record.

"I have you," she says, "and I'll pencil you in. What time were you thinking?"

"I'm two blocks away. Be right over." Try doing that in Knoxville.

The office is on court square, Anderson having been added in my absence presumably because Roger Sutherland is nearing retirement. He has to be in his seventies by now. Two middle-age women sit in the waiting room. The receptionist, who appears to be the nurse as well, gives me a clipboard with instructions to fill out both sides, takes my insurance card and Xeroxes it. "What's the nature of your complaint, Mr. O'Brian?"

I bend down over the desk, glancing back at the two women behind me. "It's a little embarrassing, I guess. I'd rather describe it to Dr. Sutherland if you don't mind."

She nods, instructs me to take a seat and fill out my recent medical history. When I return it, she points to a door. "Through there, room three. He'll be with you shortly."

I'm sitting on the examination table leafing through an old *Outdoor Life* when he comes in looking not much different from the last time I saw him. "Good to see you, Robert." He offers his hand. "Been a while."

"Six years at least."

"I guess when Kate died. Six years. Doesn't seem that long ago." He looks at his watch. "The nurse said you had an embarrassing medical problem?"

"I lied. I wanted to talk to you privately."

This stops him for a moment. "Climb down off that table and we'll go into my office."

"This might be the best place."

"Okay, what is it I can help you with?"

"You're still the county coroner, I take it."

"Not that it takes up a lot of my time."

"I wanted to ask you about Bradley McLean. Did you conduct the autopsy?"

"I did." He looks at me suspiciously. "And I wrote it up and gave it to Stanton Giles, as instructed. I assume he sent it on to the family."

"He didn't. They don't know anything. Mrs. McLean doesn't want to know anything, but Jesse's getting antsy. She asked me to talk to Giles. I just came from there, but he won't tell me anything. That's why I needed to talk to you and that's why I wanted to talk in here. I don't want to get you into trouble."

"Trouble? Like losing my position as county coroner? I receive the sum of four hundred and fifty dollars for an autopsy, and I'm called on maybe five or six times a year. I could certainly do without the money or the aggravation."

"Are you free to give out the results of the autopsy?"

He considers the question. "I'll be happy to tell you anything I know but only with the consent of the family. Or let me put it a different way. I would feel free to talk to you as a representative of the family."

I pull out the cell phone and hand it over. "Jesse's number is on there. You just punch contacts—"

"I am conversant with the cell phone," he says. "Why don't you get off that table." I take a chair while he places the call.

"Jesse, this is Roger Sutherland. I have a fellow named Robert O'Brian in the examining room who claims to be gathering information on your behalf." He listens for a while then says, "Very good, and will you give my best to Audrey? I'm so sorry." He hands me the phone. "She wants to speak to you."

"What's going on?" she asks.

"Giles wouldn't tell me anything, so I'm talking to Dr. Sutherland about the autopsy. I'll tell you all about it tonight. Maybe you could come over for a drink."

"That was nice last night," she says. "Do you have anything else electronic we could do together?"

"Careful," I say. "I'm not alone."

"I'll see you tonight."

"Right. See you then." I return the phone to my shirt pocket, and Roger Sutherland looks at me with a little smile.

"So," he says. "The plot thickens. What is it I can tell you about Bradley McLean?"

Later, when I relay the information to Jesse, it doesn't sound quite so dramatic, but that's partly because I soften it and omit a couple of details.

The essence of what I tell her is that there were traces of alcohol in the blood but no drugs. He died from a single gunshot to the right temple, and the bullet, which was recovered, almost certainly came from the pistol found at the scene. The downward trajectory of the bullet indicates that the gun was held slightly above his head. An abrasion on the right knee and the dirt on the knees of both pant legs indicate that he was kneeling when he was shot.

He died instantly, I tell her, and I stop at that point. What I don't tell her is that he had two broken ribs and extensive bruising of the torso, indicating that he had been beaten before he was shot, and that the marks on his wrists were consistent with those made by some sort of heavy wire, baling wire perhaps, the kind used in farm work, although no wire was found at the scene.

"The way I see it," Roger Sutherland had said back in the examining room, "he was on his knees with his hands bound behind him with baling wire. He wasn't killed impulsively or in the middle of an argument or because he resisted his attackers. He was savagely beaten and then executed."

"I'm not sure I can tell the family all of that right now," I said. "Maybe after some time has passed."

"Just use your best judgment," he said. "Tell them whatever you think they can handle."

And I do, but it's the wrong call.

VII

THERE'S this to be said for a gravel road—it allows you to spot unannounced guests a good distance away. Standing on the deck on Saturday afternoon, I watch a column of dust approach. Since the road dead-ends at my driveway, I have to assume I am the destination and run through my directory of people who know I'm here. The blur in front of the dust cloud gradually becomes a pickup truck, which eliminates most of the people on my list.

When it gets closer, I see that it is old and somewhat battered, and then it passes in front of the house and I lose sight of it from the deck and walk down the wooden steps and around the side of the house. Byron Holmes has gotten out of the truck and is staring back down the road. He turns and nods. "Ben Wilson told me you were out here. I brought you some produce."

"It's been a few years," I say as we shake hands beside the truck.

"Your mother's funeral," he says. "Let me get this stuff out of the seat." He walks around the front of the truck and retrieves a cardboard box from the passenger side. "Vegetables," he says. "Where do they go?"

"Come on in. We'll find a place."

We walk through the living room, Byron Holmes taking it all in.

"I was always curious about what this place looked like inside. Looks like Audrey McLean. Whatever else you can say about that family, they've got taste." He studies the large painting. "Is that Catherine Wiley?"

"The one in the coffee-table books." I motion him into the kitchen.

"Well, I'll be damned. How did you end up out here, if I may ask?"

"It's a long story," I say. "You got some time?"

"The rest of the day," he says. "I got up early this morning and picked everything that was ripe."

He puts the box on the counter beside the sink. "These heirloom tomatoes are especially good. I don't sell these, just grow 'em for the curiosity of it." Some of them are striped, some jet-black, and some a delicate green. "I could give you the names and histories, but people say I get tiresome when I talk about tomatoes. Anyway, they're good with basil." He brings out a large bouquet. "Just stick the stems in water and it'll keep for a week. Don't put it in the refrigerator or it'll turn black. And some fresh mozzarella and olive oil go good with the tomatoes and basil. I'm sure the McLeans have a forty dollar bottle of olive oil in the pantry, but here's the mozzarella." He holds out a large white mound in wax paper. "Fellow out in California makes this and ships it. The stuff Ben Wilson carries is no good."

"That's very generous of you."

"There's more stuff in the box. Some cucumbers—I can give you a recipe for pickling those—and some new potatoes and some little Japanese eggplants, and I think I put some leaf lettuce in there. The last of the season."

"I'm set for the week."

"It mainly gave me an excuse to come out to see you."

"I'll put these away later. How about a beer after a hot drive."

"I wouldn't say no."

"On the deck. It's got a great view."

"I imagine so," he says. "The McLeans have always occupied the high ground. You might want to put that mozzarella in the refrigerator, and if you've got a big glass I'll stick the basil in some water."

On the deck, Byron Holmes walks over to the railing and peers back down the gravel road.

"You expecting somebody?"

"No, just looking around. You can see a good ways down the road from up here," he says.

"Yeah, I saw your dust when you rounded that bend. Sit down and cool off."

We sip our beers in silence, trying to adjust to our new relationship. I have known Byron Holmes—Mr. Holmes—only as my teacher and mentor. He has known me only as Robert Junior—my father was also Robert O'Brian, and he once saved Byron Holmes' job at McLean County High.

My father was on the school board when Holmes was accused of teaching obscene literature by one of the prominent men in town, Jason Wainwright, president of McLean County Bank and Trust. The offending works were two poems by James Dickey, "Cherrylog Road," in which a couple make love in the back seat of a wreck in a junk yard, and "The Sheep-Child," about the legend held by farm boys that sheep can conceive from humans. The poems were not in the textbook. Holmes, an admirer of Dickey, had mimeographed several of his poems, including these two, and passed them out to the class, which made his action more difficult to defend.

After the accusation became known, the rumors started flying around town, and there was a demand for his resignation. The superintendent called a special meeting of the school board, attracting a larger than usual audience, which included me. I was in the class that got the Dickey poems, and I thought they were great, funny and knowing and in a contemporary idiom unlike the stuff from Tennyson and Matthew Arnold we'd been reading. It was hard for me to see how anybody could be offended by something so absurd. In "The Sheep-Child" the farm boys spread the story that in a museum in Atlanta there's this glass jar that contains the dead offspring of the mating between a human and a sheep, and part of the poem is actually narrated by the dead sheep-child, which I thought hilarious, but apparently some people didn't find it amusing. Anyway, I was curious how it would all come out so I went to the meeting, encouraged by my liberal mother, who thought it would be a good civics lesson.

As I remember it, things didn't start off well for Byron Holmes. The board, including my father, was sitting behind a long table on the stage of the high school auditorium, and old Mr. Wilson, head of the board, asked Jason Wainwright to state his charges.

Wainwright, on the front row in the audience, stood up and repeated what everybody had already heard, that Byron Holmes had distributed certain questionable poems to his eleventh grade English class, that these poems were neither in the board-approved textbook nor on the

B. J. Leggett

course syllabus, that they were obscene, describing acts of fornication and bestiality, and that this was not the first time that word had reached him of Byron Holmes distributing what Wainwright characterized as smut, a word that was new to me at the time. Wainwright concluded that the school board should ask for Byron Holmes' resignation.

"On what grounds exactly?" old Mr. Wilson asked.

"On the grounds of corrupting the morals of our children," Jason Wainwright said and sat down, having scored his points, although some people in the audience must have, like me, wondered about this last remark since Wainwright was in his late sixties and had no children in the public schools.

Old Mr. Wilson then turned to Byron Holmes in the audience and asked him what he had to say. Holmes, who did not rise from his seat, said that he would not say a word in his defense, noting that the issue was censorship pure and simple. He said if the McLean County school board supported Wainwright's charges then he would just as soon teach somewhere else anyway. Wainwright said that would be fine with him and called for a vote from the board.

"A vote has been called for," old Mr. Wilson said, and it was at this point that my father intervened.

"Just a second, Mr. Wilson." My father stood up and leaned across the table, addressing the audience. He wondered, he said, just how many people had actually read the poems in question. He called for a show of hands and only a few went up, including mine, which my mother gently pulled down with a disapproving look.

My father said that he had read the poems, had in fact studied them at some length, even to the extent of going to the library at Western Appalachian to see what others more knowledgeable had said about them. Far from being smut, he said, these were serious poems about— and he paused for a beat—the human condition. I heard a little sigh from my mother at this last phrase, surely the only time the human condition has been invoked at a meeting of the McLean County school board. "Cherrylog Road," my father explained, is a poem about the awful sense of mortality. Why did the lovemaking of these two young people take place in a junkyard full of rusting cars? To juxtapose the sense of love and life and the ravages of time.

Old Mr. Wilson, who knew something about the ravages of time, interrupted. "What was that word?"

"Juxtapose," my father said. "To bring together opposite things."

Old Mr. Wilson nodded, and my father continued. "The Sheep-Child," he said, is about the myths we all live by. He speculated that stories such as the one the poem was based on could be heard on almost any farm in McLean County. Mr. Dickey, he said, has simply given voice to the stories that are our common heritage. He went on like this for a while but then pulled a set of folded sheets from inside his jacket.

"But don't take my word for it. Listen to what scholars have said about James Dickey." He had certainly done his homework and began reading somewhat pompous descriptions of Dickey's work from people nobody in the audience had ever heard of, but each time he read a passage my father would identify the writer as "a professor at Vanderbilt University" or "a well-known authority on American literature" or some other equally impressive title.

Then he turned to the career of Byron Holmes, "educated under the tutelage of the legendary Cleanth Brooks at Yale University." Nobody in the audience had ever heard of the legendary Cleanth Brooks either, but my father had a way of making all these names seem self-evidently important. He recounted Byron Holmes' own publishing record, noted that he was one of the few teachers of literature who was also a published author in some of the leading magazines of the day, and one of the few local faculty who had received a teaching award from the state board of education. He knew for a fact, he said, that Byron Holmes had been offered teaching jobs with higher salaries at the best public schools in Knoxville and at a famous private academy in Chattanooga. But he had turned them down to stay in McLean County. He concluded in a soaring oratorical tone that rather than censoring Byron Holmes for attempting to broaden our children's literary taste with contemporary writers, we should be applauding the presence in our school system of one of the most prominent and one of the most honored educators in the state of Tennessee. He slowly repeated the last point for emphasis. *"We should be applauding Byron Holmes."*

When he sat down there was a moment of complete silence in the audience, then a thin scattering of applause, which slowly began to

B. J. Leggett

grow and then became general across the auditorium. Still applauding, a man on my row stood up and then in little bunches people began to stand until almost the whole audience was standing and clapping. Some people stood no doubt because Byron Holmes had been their teacher or their children's teacher and they knew he was a decent man, others maybe because my father's words had indeed been stirring, and still others perhaps because Jason Wainwright, not one of the most beloved of men, had turned down their application for a loan at McLean County Bank and Trust. But whatever the reason, it was surely my father's finest hour.

After people sat down, old Mr. Wilson looked down at Jason Wainwright and said, "Jason, I was on your side, but who are we two against so many." He banged his knuckles on the table." Meeting adjourned."

Looking at Byron Holmes on the deck finishing his beer, I see he hasn't changed much from that night in the high school auditorium. Even in middle age he affected the style of an old man. I remember once in high school Bradley McLean came across a portrait of Gustav Flaubert, mustachioed and jowly, in a world lit anthology, and when he showed it to me we both started laughing. There was no necessity even to say it. Byron Holmes.

"I was just thinking about the famous school board meeting," I say to break the silence.

"Your father had a gift for that kind of thing," he says. "Should have been a politician."

"Should have been something."

"Maybe he would have found himself eventually," Byron Holmes says. "How old was he?"

"Fifty-two."

"Heart attack, I heard. Somewhere out west."

I nod.

"I knew the two of you were not on good terms after what happened," Byron Holmes says.

"I never forgave him."

"The town was split about fifty-fifty on who was driving that night. I was pretty sure it was Bradley McLean."

"So either I killed Billy Ratliff or I was a perjurer," I say. "Doesn't make much difference. How about another beer?"

He looks at me for a moment, sensing perhaps that it's not a topic I'm comfortable with, even after all these years. "Another beer would be fine," he says. "A man could sit in a place like this all afternoon."

"Nothing to keep us from it."

He has set his empty bottle on the deck beside his chair, and when I stoop down to retrieve it, I see the sheer stockings it rests on. He must have seen them too, since he gives me a quizzical look.

"Jesse McLean," I say. "She stopped by for a drink last night, and it was a little warm out on the deck."

He nods. "She and her mother are the only McLeans I've ever had any use for." He pauses, perhaps to weigh his words. "I'm not prying into your personal affairs, but I'm a little surprised to see you back with that family."

"I'm a little surprised myself. It's mostly Jesse I guess."

"I'm not sure it's a good idea to get too close to the McLeans at the moment."

"That's almost exactly what Stanton Giles told me yesterday. What do you two know that I don't?"

"I don't know what Stanton Giles knows, and I certainly wouldn't want to be associated with that little man, but I'll stick by what I said. I don't know if it'll ever come out—and they've probably got enough money to make sure that it won't—but there's something rotten there, and it led directly to Bradley McLean's death in the middle of that field."

"You want to talk about it?"

"I'm not sure that I do. At least not today."

"Maybe later."

"I don't want to sound too mysterious, but I'm looking into some things that I'm not quite ready to share with anybody else, especially anybody involved with the McLeans. Nothing against you."

"I understand. I'll get us another round."

"If you think these beers are going to loosen my tongue, you're mistaken," he says, smiling.

"No thought of that," I say. "I only picked up a six-pack." When I was young, Byron Holmes had a reputation as a prodigious eater. My father once said that he was the only man he knew who would drop a woman *for* a hot potato. I'm guessing that he is also a lover of good wine and thinking that perhaps Miss Helen's label, which certainly erased my own inhibitions and of which I possess almost an entire case, might be to his taste.

VIII

BYRON Holmes and I agree that Miss Helen's wine is among the best we've ever had. "I don't know that rich people are happier than the rest of us," he says, "but they do get to drink better wine."

We have returned to the deck with the remains of a bottle after a light supper, both of us beginning to lose our reserve. "Speaking of rich people," I say, "I remember hearing stories that the Holmes family was one of the most prosperous in this part of the state."

"Several generations ago," he says. "Second only to the McLeans."

"How'd they lose their money?"

"You may remember the Hemingway novel where somebody asks Bill Campbell that—how'd you lose your money? And he says two ways, gradually and then suddenly. The way I heard it from my daddy, the family had always been profligate, and they maintained their high living by selling off little parcels of land over the years, mostly to the McLeans. But then in the late twenties my grandfather, whose name was Chester Holmes, invested the family fortune in the stock market, and I don't have to tell you what happened then. If there had been a building tall enough in town, he'd probably have jumped out a window. As it was, he put a gun to his head, but he wasn't even successful at that. He lived but he was mentally impaired, had to be taken care of the rest of his life. According to my daddy, he always greeted people by saying, 'I should have seen it coming.' So all we had left is that little piece I'm still living on, and the McLeans even tried to get that."

"Your farm?"

"That's right."

"Why do they want it?"

"Pure symmetry, I guess. They've got the land on both sides, so it's in their way. I say they, but it was Bradley. He was the one that made the proposition. And I guess now that he's gone that's all over."

"You turned him down."

"That was a couple of years ago. He came out, made me an offer that was a lot more than it was worth. But, hell, I wasn't going to sell it to him. Wouldn't give him the satisfaction. And he saw that pretty quickly. That's when he filed the lawsuit over the property line, just out of spite. They own most of the county, and they act like they're entitled to the rest. But I'm talking like he's still alive. I'm sorry that he's dead, but he was not a man I had much respect for."

"That doesn't sound like the Bradley McLean I remember. Sounds more like his father."

"He got to be a lot like the Judge, running a little empire. He did what he had to do, and sometimes the little people like me got in his way. I believe you're familiar with the way the McLean family dealt with people like you and me."

"You think that's what got him killed?" Has Miss Helen's wine worked its spell? Apparently not, since there is silence across the table. "What I mean is, do you think he pushed somebody a little too hard?"

"I said I wasn't going to talk about it." He refills his wine glass. "You're a policeman. Is it your experience that people get murdered over business deals?"

"An ex-policeman," I say. "It's happened, but more often with deals that are not reported to the I.R.S."

"Right," Byron Holmes says, in a tone that makes me think I'm getting closer to whatever it is he does not wish to share.

"I know you don't want to talk about Bradley's death, but I have to confess something. I promised Jesse I would look into it. That's why I was asking. You probably know what goes on in this county as well as anybody, but we'll drop it for tonight. Maybe some time you'll talk to me about it."

"Is that why you came back after all these years? To find out who killed Bradley McLean? You must certainly see the irony in that."

"No, I came back to try to write another novel." At least that's the official reason. The first novel has not been mentioned, and I'm determined not to bring it up, leaving that to the man to whom it was dedicated. I'm not excessively proud of it, but I've always found it curious that Byron Holmes, to whom I sent an inscribed copy on publication, never responded. "I take it you didn't care for the first one." I probably wouldn't have said that without the wine.

"I feel bad that I didn't write you. I appreciated the dedication, and I started to write but I thought you might take what I said the wrong way. I figured we'd have a chance to talk about it sometime."

"It was just a popular novel. I did it on a dare." I don't know why I feel defensive, maybe because I have so much respect for his judgment.

"No need to apologize. It was all right for what it was. Had some nice scenes, but I was a little disappointed it wasn't more ambitious. You could see from reading it that it could have been something."

"The first version would probably have been more to your liking, but people who read it thought it was half literary, half popular. I had to go one way or the other."

"I would have probably gone the other way and taken out some of those body parts," he says. "If you still have that first version, I'd like to read it."

"I'll send it to you. It's called *A Catch in the Breath*."

"Yeats," he says, and we fall silent and watch a nearly full moon ascend above the trees across the lake.

"You working on anything yourself?" When I was in high school, Byron Holmes published some short stories in little magazines, but his specialty was the long essay, in the manner of John McPhee. He did some pieces on Southern culture in quite prestigious magazines.

"I wouldn't want this to get out," he says quietly, leaning toward me as if he is afraid of being overheard, "but I have a contract for a long piece I'm researching at the moment. May take a while."

"What magazine?"

"I'd prefer not to talk about it. It may get me into a little difficulty." He pours the last of the wine. "Maybe already has."

His tight-lipped manner, as with his cryptic allusion to Bradley's death, is uncharacteristic. "Like the James Dickey thing?" I ask, getting up to open another bottle.

"Oh, no, nothing like that. Let's just let it drop."

But I don't want to let it drop. Byron Holmes is one of the least secretive men I have ever known, just the opposite, in fact, loquacious and blunt to a fault. But something has happened or he thinks that something is going to happen, and he's keeping it to himself. While I'm in the kitchen opening the wine I watch him through the glass doors as he walks to the edge of the deck, leans over and looks down toward the lake, then sideways down the gravel road.

When I return, he's back in his chair. "One more glass," he says, "and then I've got to go. This has been very nice."

"Think you're okay to drive?"

"Not a lot of traffic on this road," he says. "I'll be fine."

"So how's your research going? For the essay."

"You need to write Helen Gates and tell her how much we admire her taste in wine," he says.

"I'll do that. So you're not going to tell me anything about what you're working on."

Byron Holmes takes the empty wine bottle and moves it to the edge of the table. "This is Mexico," he says. He places a napkin a few inches from the bottle. "This is Albuquerque, New Mexico." His finger moves across the width of the table and he places the full wine bottle at the far edge. "This is McLean County, Tennessee." He looks at me as if this explains everything. And perhaps it does.

"Are we talking drug trafficking here?"

He nods. "We're talking eighteen-wheelers. We're talking about a distribution point for the east coast. You can see how somebody looking into local involvement might stir up something."

"I'm not sure this article's a good idea," I say, reminded of the occasional ache in my left side. "These people don't fool around."

"That's all I have to say about it at the moment," he says, scraping back his chair. "I've got to go." I follow him as he walks through the house and down the front steps to his truck.

"What would Bradley's death have to do with a drug ring?"

"I don't believe I said that it had anything to do with a drug ring." He climbs into the cab, leaving the door open. "Come by the house next week and I'll supply you with some more produce. I've got some nice lima beans just coming in." He slams the door and backs out onto the gravel road.

Back on the deck, I watch the column of dust drift up, illuminated by the moonlight, and it is surely the circumstances of the evening that lead me to imagine a second column of dust behind the first as he rounds the curve of the lake and disappears from sight.

B. J. Leggett

IX

AFTER Wilson's Grocery and Supply the most storied institution in Prosperity is the Rosewood Café. It does not have Wilson's long history, dating back only to the late eighties, but what it lacks in longevity it makes up for in quirkiness. The Rosewood was opened by a chef from Knoxville named Beals who got tired of competing with the Orangery, the city's most famous restaurant, for the high-end trade. Out in the country, he must have figured, he would have no competition and relatively unsophisticated palates. You have to go all the way to Adair to find even a fast food establishment. So he opened this small, quite ordinary diner, and it worked out for a while, but after a few years he got tired of the long hours, or so he said, closed it down and moved away.

The place sat vacant for a good while, and then five or six years ago a chef from Atlanta who had actually appeared briefly on The Food Channel came up, renovated the space, kept the name, and opened a tiny but exclusive twelve-table restaurant that featured French country cuisine and an extensive wine list. I was long gone from Prosperity by this point, but I got the story from Helen Gates.

His name, she told me, was Sam Rivers, which I thought didn't quite work for a big-time chef—Jean or Jacques Rivers would have been perfect—but you have to work with what you're given. Chef Rivers' show on television had been called *Cooking Without Recipes*, and that was also the name of a cookbook he had published. The concept struck me as somewhat paradoxical since it flies in the face of the very reason that people watch cooking shows and buy cookbooks, and that may have been the reason the show lasted only one season.

The explanation offered by Miss Helen, a real Food Channel

aficionada, was that Sam Rivers lacked the show biz personality of Emeril Lagassee or the affability of Bobby Flay. How he wound up in Prosperity was the real mystery, although as in all things in Prosperity, the rumors pointed toward the McLean family.

The thinking was this. Why would a well-known chef open a small trendy restaurant in the middle of nowhere? Perhaps a few people would drive over from Knoxville or up from Chattanooga, but with so few tables he couldn't hope to turn a profit. And the way Sam Rivers ran the place insured there would be no profit. It was almost as if he tried to find ways of keeping diners out. He didn't take credit cards, for one thing. It was strictly cash or personal check, patrons caught without either being directed to an ATM machine installed by the front entrance. After a while people learned that you didn't just show up and ask for a table. Even if the place was only half full you would be turned away, and pretty soon a sign was installed on the front door announcing that dining was by reservation only. It might just as well have said by appointment only, since you didn't exactly make a reservation. You negotiated a date sometime in the future and left your telephone number with the understanding that the date might be re-negotiated. The only people who didn't seem to have any trouble getting in were the McLeans and their wealthy friends.

Why would a chef operate in this fashion? Clearly, the answer was because his restaurant was being subsidized by the McLeans. They needed a place to take their many visitors and business associates without having to make the long drive to Knoxville. The Rosewood was like an exclusive little country club in which the McLeans were the only members. It was even rumored that Judge McLean, not long before his death, had given Chef Rivers a list of people who were to be admitted without groveling, but this was never verified, and when I once asked Miss Helen about it she just smiled and said she'd like to have a nickel for every wild rumor she'd heard about Audrey's family.

But when I asked Jesse if it was true that her family subsidized the restaurant, she was more forthcoming. "Well, of course," she said. "How do you think the man could stay in business in a little place like Prosperity?"

This was on Sunday morning, when she called with the dinner

invitation. "Mother's not quite up to having people over for dinner, but we could go to the Rosewood."

"The three of us?"

"Just you and me. My treat," she said. "In gratitude for your going to see Stanton Giles for us."

"Not that I learned anything."

"You confirmed my own suspicions."

I told her I had heard some great stories about the restaurant from her Aunt Helen.

"The one about that *New York Times* writer is actually true," she said. "His name was Apple, and I understand he was famous. He wrote up the place for the *Time*'s food section—you know, four-star restaurant in a little hick town—but when Daddy heard about it, he asked them to kill the story, thinking there might be a run on the place."

I mentioned the legendary difficulty of getting a table at the Rosewood on such short notice.

"Sam and I are friends. I don't think it'll be a problem, so what do you say?"

I was sure it would not be a problem. "Sounds great," I said, "except for your treating. Why don't we just go Dutch? I'm sure it's pricey."

"Do you have a problem with people doing things for you?"

"Not really. I just don't like to think of myself as working for your family." In fact I did have a problem.

"Whatever," she said. "You'd better bring some cash. Sam doesn't take credit cards."

"I heard that. How does he get away with it?"

"It's the secret of his success. The more unreasonable he is, the more people think it's the place to be. By the way, where were you last night? I called and nobody answered."

"I must have left the phone in another room. We were out on the deck."

"We? You're already entertaining?"

"Byron Holmes," I said, which produced a moment of silence.

"He's not a friend of my family," Jesse said finally.

"I understand that—some kind of property dispute."

"He and Bradley didn't get along."

"Bradley was suing him," I said. "That's what he told me."

"Then he had a good reason. Bradley got along with almost everybody."

"Byron Holmes is very bitter about it," I said.

"I'm sure he had an opinion about Bradley's death. He has an opinion about everything else."

"My impression was that he did but that he didn't want to talk about it. In fact, I would say his demeanor was on the strange side the whole time he was here. Just between us, he seems to think he's gotten himself into some difficulty with the locals over a magazine piece he's researching."

"Are you saying that Byron Holmes thinks he knows what happened to Bradley but doesn't want to tell you?"

"Something like that. We'll talk about it tonight."

"Around eight," she said. "I'll pick you up if you don't think that's too demeaning."

"Fine," I said.

"I wouldn't want you to feel beholden."

"No problem. Just forget I said anything."

She must have heard the edge in my voice and tried to smooth things over. "Any more work on the novel over the weekend?"

"I haven't picked it up again."

"What's the title, by the way?"

"I don't have a title."

"Then I've got one for you."

"Okay."

"Brief Nudity," she said. "What do you think?"

"We'll talk about it tonight."

And so we do, over drinks at one of the Rosewood's twelve tables in a dimly lit, understated room. It is almost exactly what you might expect in a small expensive New York restaurant that a rich friend has recommended. The wait staff seems to consist of young local women who have undergone intensive training in the French obsession with cutlery.

"So about my title," Jesse says, as we sip our drinks.

B. J. Leggett

"Well, first of all, how do we know it would be appropriate? Maybe there's no brief nudity in the novel."

"If you know it's the title you'll find a way to get it in."

"It does have a certain ring."

"Whenever I watch a movie on a cable channel and the ratings say 'Brief Nudity,' I stay with it," she says. "Or 'Adult Language.' That's another possibility."

I tell her about my battle over the title of the first novel.

"You should have stuck to your guns. *Body Parts* is not a good title. I wouldn't read a book called *Body Parts* unless it was by you, and you still haven't sent me a copy." She smiles and waves at someone behind me. "Here comes Sam."

I'm introduced to the famous Sam Rivers, a handsome middle-aged man appropriately attired in kitchen whites. "Like your dress," he says to Jesse.

"Bobby's a writer," Jesse says. "He's staying out at the lake house."

"Nice place," Chef Rivers says. "I'm especially fond of the view."

"Sam's spent some time at the lake house," Jesse says, and they smile at each other like people who share a secret. "So what should we eat tonight?"

Chef Rivers recommends the celery and celeriac soup with truffles and the goat cheese, beet, and white bean salad. For an appetizer perhaps the warm crab tart, but that also has goat cheese, so if we want the crab tart then perhaps the green salad with pate de campagne and a mustard dressing would be preferable, or if we insist on the beet and goat cheese salad, perhaps we should try the mussels served in rosé rather than the warm crab tart.

In the middle of all this I have to keep reminding myself that I am sitting in the middle of a town so far out of it that the BP station is listed in the yellow pages under restaurants.

For the entree, Chef Rivers is torn between the braised pork shank with primes and juniper and the roasted chicken served on a bed of artichoke pilaf with sautéed onions. For dessert there is no question— the profiteroles stuffed with pear ice cream and drenched with a bittersweet chocolate sauce.

"Why don't we just leave it to you," Jesse says. "You've never disappointed me before. Well, maybe once." They both laugh at that.

Then there is the question of the wine. Sam—as a friend of Jesse I am now instructed to call him Sam, although I resist—Sam is inclined toward a mid-priced California cab that he is particularly fond of, but I have spotted a familiar name and point it out to Jesse. She smiles— Miss Helen's label. "We'll start with this one," she says.

Sam is a little dubious. It might overpower the pork shank. But when Jesse explains that it is a sentimental choice, he acquiesces.

"I can't believe how much money Byron Holmes and I poured down our throats last night," I say after our chef returns to the kitchen. "I had no idea it was so expensive."

"Aunt Helen's one of those people who never ask the price. She first had it here. But I'm not real happy about your giving our special wine to that bitter old man."

"You're kidding, right?"

"Only halfway. He's caused our family a great deal of grief."

"It goes both ways."

"I believe you're taking his side."

"I was sympathetic with him last night. He's been shaken by something. He wouldn't say exactly what, but it gave me an angle on Bradley's death."

"Do you want to tell me about it?"

"You're not going to like it," I say. "But I need to let you in on something. Next week my ex-partner, a man named Eddie Carpenter, is coming over from Knoxville, and we're going to poke around a little bit—if you still want me to."

"I do," she says. "I met your friend briefly at the station."

"This means asking some sensitive questions."

"What kind of questions?"

"Let me try a few on you. You asked me to look into Bradley's murder, but you can't look into something like this without raising some potentially explosive issues. I'm talking about the possibility of Bradley's own involvement in something unknown at present."

"Why would you think that?"

"The way he was killed."

"I'm up to it," she says. "Ask me whatever you like."

74   *B. J. Leggett*

"Alright." I pull the small notebook from my jacket pocket, which produces a giggle from across the table.

"Oh, my god," she says. "This is like a thousand cop shows."

"Cops have to make notes. They have bad memories."

"Fire away, Lieutenant O'Brian," she says, but we pause for the arrival of the warm crab tart with goat cheese and a bowl of mussels in rosé. Between the presentations of wine, appetizers, soups, salads, and entrées I ask Jesse the obvious questions.

How much does she know about the family's finances? Very little. Bradley wasn't inclined to talk business with her, and she wasn't particularly interested. There seems to be plenty of money in the account she draws on. Then she isn't aware of any financial setbacks in recent months? No. Did Bradley seem depressed or preoccupied in the weeks before his death? No. Was there a name of any business associate that came up repeatedly in recent months? No. Any new business associates or new large investments? Not that she knows of. Did he use a cell phone, which would furnish us a list of recent calls? The sheriff's office took it. Then what about home phone bills? She will try to find them. Any noticeable change in his behavior? No. Did he have any enemies that she knew of? Or other people with whom he was feuding like Byron Holmes? Before she can answer we are interrupted by a commotion at the entry.

We are on the celery soup with truffles —and I'm beginning to see why the Rosewood is worth all the trouble—when we hear the angry voices. The hostess is in earnest conversation with a distinguished looking older couple who are both speaking at once. The man, gray haired in a dark suit, is gesturing at the twelve occupied tables and explaining that he made the reservation months ago. Where is his table? I suspect that Jesse and I are occupying it, but neither of us betrays our part in the little drama. Sam emerges from the kitchen at this point, and I wonder how he can possibly pacify a man who looks like somebody who normally gets his way. The room grows quiet and we all hear Sam explain that they have overbooked by mistake—as sometimes happens with long-held reservations, but if the gentleman and lady would like to eat at the bar, which is unoccupied, their dinner and drinks will be courtesy of the Rosewood. This solution seems satisfactory to the couple, who follow Sam to the bar, and the diners return to their plates.

"Two people," Jesse says. "And you've talked to both of them in the last couple of days."

"I'm sorry?"

"You asked about people Bradley was feuding with. There were two. You know about Byron Holmes and the other was Sam, although Byron Holmes was behind that too."

"He was on the outs with your chef?"

"They weren't speaking, but it was all very silly," she says. "I told him he was acting like he was back in grade school."

"Do you know what they were fighting about?"

"Well, first of all, did you know that Byron Holmes grows vegetables and fruit out on his little place?"

"He brought me some yesterday."

"Some of these he grows on land that belongs to us, which he claims is really his."

"He told me about the boundary dispute."

"So when Bradley found out that Sam was buying a lot of his fresh produce from Byron Holmes he was furious, demanded that he stop. Sam said no, it was the best he had found, and the secret of his food was the freshest ingredients."

"That seems like a trivial thing to fight over."

"You would think so, but Bradley was kind of obsessed by that property that he said Byron Holmes was squatting on—and blocking access to our piece beside it. Anyway, he told Sam he hoped he could appreciate the irony. Since he was heavily subsidizing the restaurant, he was paying top dollar for produce being grown illegally on his own property by a man who refused to settle the dispute out of sheer animosity toward our family. But Sam wasn't interested in the irony and said that the kitchen was his domain and he would operate it the way he saw fit. And he kept buying stuff from Byron Holmes and Bradley stopped eating here, even though I know he loved the place."

"Pretty silly on both sides."

"Yes," she says and pauses for a moment. "But there was something brewing there before Byron Holmes' produce came along."

"What was that?"

B. J. Leggett

"Not now," she says. "I'll tell you about it sometime. Next question."

"Well, you don't kill a man over fresh produce," I say.

"Of course not. I'm just trying to answer your questions. But you couldn't say the same thing about land disputes. You've seen all those western movies. A lot of people have been killed over land disputes."

"Byron Holmes is the most civilized man in McLean County. You don't honestly think he had anything to do with your brother's death."

"No, I don't think so. Ask me something else."

I ask her about the married woman that Bradley was rumored to be seeing. Only technically married, she confirms. The husband has moved away and the divorce is pending. But she didn't come to the funeral? She didn't want to fan the rumor fires. "She talked to Mother and me. She was devastated, and still is. Her name is Jill Haynes, and she's moving to Knoxville to work on her masters in social work at Western Appalachian. She can't go anywhere here without being stared at, so she actually has to move away because of this. You're not writing that down in your little book. Believe me, Jill Haynes is a lovely person. I talk to her at least once a week."

I explain that while lovely people may not necessarily kill other people they might unwittingly play a role in their deaths. I want to talk to Jill Haynes if that's possible. Does she have an address or a phone number? Jesse promises to supply me with both. "But you're way off base to think of her as a suspect, and you'll see that when you talk to her."

Suspect. She has used a term picked up from reading mysteries. I tell her that when I was a real policeman in Crimes Against Persons we very seldom dealt with a neat list of suspects, one of whom had to be guilty, as in English crime novels. When we investigated a violent crime it was usually pretty clear who did it and why. But there were usually two other problems. The first one was trying to find enough evidence for a conviction, and the second was simply trying to find him. Almost always him, rarely her. "And that's almost certainly the case here," I say. "I'm sure Jill Haynes had nothing to do with it, but I'd still like to talk to her. And maybe that's enough for tonight. Here comes the waitress with our entrées."

Sam, apparently unable to decide between his two recommendations, has sent one of each. "Braised pork or roasted chicken?" I ask. "You choose and I'll take the other one."

She chooses the chicken, and after the waitress has made an elaborate display of reorganizing our table, we allow Sam Rivers' cuisine to distract us from Bradley's murder. When Sam comes out to solicit our responses, we of course rave appropriately, and he seems pleased. My theory is that chefs, like comedians, are people who desperately need the attention and approval of the people around them and will go to great lengths to secure it, like profiteroles filled with pear ice cream and covered with bittersweet chocolate.

"God, I'm stuffed," Jesse says after the profiteroles. "Wasn't it wonderful?"

"It was indeed. But let me ask you one more question while I'm thinking about it. Knowing everything you know about Bradley's social life and work and whatever else—temperament, friends, habits—is there anybody that comes to mind that could have had anything to do with it?"

She shakes her head. "Nobody. That's why it's so hard to accept. That somebody would have done that to Bradley."

Why don't I believe her? "Maybe he got himself into something a little shady."

"You're thinking drugs."

"Maybe. I'm guessing that's what Byron Holmes thinks."

"Then you're both wrong," she says. "Bradley would have no reason to get involved with the drug business for the money. We're already filthy rich. And he wasn't on drugs. I would have seen that. He drank too much, but there were no drugs."

"Okay, let's let it go for tonight." I signal for the check. "Are you ready to take me home?"

"I hope I can fit behind the wheel," she says. "By the way, I didn't bring any cash. I thought if going Dutch made you happy then paying the whole thing would make you ecstatic."

"My pleasure." It's my punishment for refusing the largess of the McLean family.

The check is as hefty as I anticipated, and I count out the cash. "I couldn't afford to do this a lot. That was my whole month's budget. Doesn't your family get a courtesy discount?"

"We've always paid our way," she says. "I'll get the next one."

As we leave, a number of people acknowledge her with smiles and waves. "The man in the blue jacket owns a string of McDonald's in Knox County," she says in a soft voice, leaning against me. "The old guy by the window with the mousy wife is a lawyer from Knoxville, and the goofy-looking guy in the bow tie is an allergist with a local TV show."

"Is it always full?"

"Almost always," she says. "Sam learned the trick in Atlanta. If you try to keep people out, they'll break down your door. He's a genius in his own way."

The genius appears again from the kitchen and approaches us. "I wonder if I could borrow Jesse for just a moment for some business?"

"Of course."

They walk ahead out into the parking lot, and I follow at a discreet distance. He is explaining something in detail, and Jesse mostly nods. At one point he takes her hand. Whatever the issue, they seem to be in agreement and I can't help observing that they seem very close.

The conference over, he walks back to me. "I hope you'll come again."

"I'll try to save my pennies."

We're both quiet on the way back to the lake house. Whatever Sam Rivers has told her has darkened her mood. She stops in the driveway and gives me a smile. "It was fun," she says with no conviction.

I open the car door but can't quite bring myself to leave her like this. "So you're going to give me Jill Haynes' phone number and address and your recent home phone bills."

"Come by tomorrow and I'll see if I can find them. Did you have fun?"

"Fun. I'm not sure that's quite the right word. Kids have fun. I believe Sam Rivers upset you."

"Just business."

"It was hard to miss the intimacy between you two."

"We dated for a while."

"Dated? How quaint."

"Well, we had a torrid little affair, if you must know."

"The man's a little old for you."

"I thought I explained my weakness for older men."

"You did. Goodnight, Jesse."

"Wait a minute," she says. "Shut your door. I wasn't going to get into this tonight, but I see that this person who wanted to keep our relationship innocent is showing a little jealousy."

"Maybe just a little surprised to have a glimpse into the private life of Jesse McLean." I pull the door shut and lean back in the seat.

"Sam and I went out several times not so very long ago. One night we were at the lake house and Bradley found us together and got very angry."

"He was always protective of you."

"He knew we had been seeing each other. I think it was just the physical shock of seeing his baby sister going at it like a little rabbit."

"Spare me the details."

"Well, he caught us, and he yelled and screamed a while, and one of the things he said was that you don't fuck the help, which Sam never quite forgave him for, so there was always this little tension between them, and then the Byron Holmes thing stirred it all up again."

"I understand."

"You probably don't understand," she says, "but thanks for saying it. Anyway, we're not seeing each other at the moment, but I don't know that it's quite over."

"I could see that."

"You don't miss a trick," she says and smiles. "So there you have it, and good night." She leans over and kisses me on the cheek.

"Good night, Jesse." Walking up to the front door—the McLeans' front door—I'm thinking that I've missed several tricks. As an ex-policeman I should have known that things are almost never as they first appear—most especially, that this thirty-something woman is not quite the provocative little college girl she affects. Unlocking the door, I think of a variation on the old Chinese curse. My curse doesn't have quite the same ring but is surely as perilous—may you meet an interesting woman.

B. J. Leggett

X

THE McLean farm is a half-mile off the blacktop that leads to the national park, and you reach it on a gravel lane that hasn't changed in my absence. The main house—there is also a smaller guest house— is imposing, a two story white brick with a large front porch, but architecturally nondescript from having been added onto over several generations. Since the McLean family hates ostentation above all else, it has suited them perfectly. Pulling up into the circular driveway, I don't know quite how to feel, seeing the place again after so many years. I settle arbitrarily on nostalgic.

Bradley and I spent a large portion of our summers at the two ponds on this farm. The larger pond—called the old pond—was for swimming, and the new pond, dug by Judge McLean and stocked with bass and bluegill, was for fishing. As a kid, Jesse loved swimming and only tolerated fishing, so I remember her mostly at the old pond, horsing around on the floating dock Bradley and I built.

I expect her to answer my knock, but it is Audrey McLean who opens the door. It's almost eleven, and she's still in her robe. Her eyes have the vacant look I observed in the basement of the Prosperity Methodist Church.

"Jesse told me you were coming by," she says. "She's down at the old pond working on her tan. Said to send you down there. I expect you remember the way. And how to unlock the gate. The key's still in the same place."

"Of course. Bradley and I . . . ." I start to tell her that Bradley and I devised the security system, including the hiding place for the key, but then think better of it.

"It's all right to talk about him," she says, still holding the door open. "You boys spent a lot of time down there—and Jesse too, always pestering you."

"Be good to see it again after all this time," I say because I can't think of anything else to say, and turn to leave. "And good to see you, Mrs. McLean."

"Robert." I turn back to face her. "I want to say again how sorry I am about what happened all those years ago. I hope you don't still hold it against us."

"I'm not sure how I feel about it anymore."

"It was a terrible thing."

"It was that."

"I appreciate your coming to the funeral."

"It seemed like the right thing to do."

"And I appreciate what you're doing with Jesse," she says. What I'm doing? What am I doing? "Giving her so much attention. She's going through a hard time, and she needs a little distraction."

So that's what I'm doing—distracting Jesse. Does Audrey McLean honestly believe I'm being attentive to her daughter as an act of charity? "It just sort of worked out this way. I needed a place to write, and she offered the lake house."

"It's nice to have you in there. I don't like it to sit vacant. It's so isolated, and the local kids make free use of the deck. Or so Bradley said. He spent a lot of time there. And I'm sure Jesse'll be there a lot. I hope she doesn't get in the way of your work." She pauses. There's something she's trying to say to me. "Jesse can be very impetuous. You may have to stand your ground. You have more experience of the world."

I nod. She can't quite say it. *Please be responsible* is what she wants to say. *She's very vulnerable. Don't take advantage of her.* Or at least that's what I read in her face.

"I wouldn't want to take advantage of the situation. You have my word on that." I actually mean it, but it's a foolish thing to say, and I immediately regret it, especially since Audrey McLean takes it a step further.

"I wouldn't want Jesse to think we've been conspiring behind her back."

"She won't hear it from me," I say, sensing for the first time that I've been out-maneuvered. But it isn't something you can take back. *No, wait. I can't promise not to hit on you daughter or to keep secret this little pact we've just made.* What I say instead is, "Do I need to move the car? I'm blocking your drive."

"It's fine where it is. We don't get many guests these days." She gives me a little wave. "Thank you for understanding, Robert." Standing at the open door, she watches me as I walk across the lawn and down to the fenced lot that leads to the main barn.

You have to walk past the barn and down a little hill to get to the gate to the pond. I remember that it was kept locked, and the key kept under the cattle tank, as everybody in Prosperity knew. The pond is in a little swale in the pasture behind the barn, surrounded by a grove of trees. It has been there so long and fits so perfectly into the landscape, with a little dogleg to the left, that it appears a natural thing. The story Bradley told me, however, was that in the early nineteenth century some ancient McLean in a funny hat dammed up one end of the swale when he located a spring at the bottom of the hill. Since it's spring fed, it's so clear you can see the bottom in all but the deepest places, and that's why it's the swimming pond. Or such was the case when I spent the better part of my summers here.

It's maybe a football field wide but very long, covering six or eight acres in all. Anybody but the McLeans would have called it a lake. The summer after our junior year Bradley and I concocted a plan to have our own private beach by trucking in commercial sand, but we abandoned the project after a couple of loads when we saw how much work it was going to be.

The path down to the pond is beside a fence row, and the reason is that you might have to make a quick escape through the fence depending on which field the bull is in. Today I can't locate a bull, just a herd of cows who look up intently when I pass then lose interest.

As I make my way down the hill to the pond I can see Jesse through the trees lying on a towel by the diving board. She is, as I should have guessed but didn't, appropriately naked.

"Hey, put something on. I'm coming down."

"Hey, Bobby." Through the foliage I have a glimpse of her pulling up a pair of white shorts, and when I break through the trees I see that she's draped a towel around the back of her neck, the two ends almost succeeding in covering her breasts.

"What is it with you and nudity?"

"I don't want to get suntan lotion on my blouse."

"I see. I just talked to your mother, who believes you're somewhat impetuous." I don't tell her that I have just made a foolish promise to her mother and then compounded it.

"In what way?"

"Like lying down here naked as a jaybird."

"Americans are such prudes about the body," she says as if she has just popped in from the South of France.

"All the same, would you mind covering yourself?"

"They're just breasts. Everybody's got 'em."

I suppress a desire to say something inappropriate and direct my gaze out over the old pond. "Were you able to locate the phone bills and Jill Haynes' address?"

"They're in the beach bag."

"Thanks. I think I'll head off."

"Please don't go," she says. "Try to relax. It's just us and the cows. I brought you a towel, and I've got some beer in the cooler. Why don't you take off your shirt and whatever else you'd like and we can lie here side by side and look up at the clouds. Then you won't have to look at me."

"I don't particularly enjoy lying in the sun. I tend to turn red."

"Then we'll find you some shade. It's so peaceful here."

And indeed it is. She locates a sunny spot with shade beside it, and I spread the towel in the grass, hang my shirt on a bush and lie down.

"Isn't this nice?" she asks after a while.

"It's okay."

"Bring back memories?"

"Unfortunately, yes."

"But we won't talk about the old days. That's one of the things I've learned from my sessions with the good doctor. We'll talk about the present. So ask me some more questions."

And so it is that I lie beside a half-naked young woman, the most

B. J. Leggett

beautiful I have ever known personally, and talk about death. Someone observing us from a distance—and for all I know, someone is observing us from a distance—would have seen two topless sunbathers lying on their backs and conversing while looking straight up into the heavens.

"Ben Wilson told me that Bradley was seen in some bad company not too long before his death."

"I wouldn't doubt that. He liked red-neck bars."

"Did he have a favorite?"

"There's a place over in Parris County he went to a lot. It's called Pearl's, I think. Big Confederate flag painted on the side of the building."

"Were you ever there?"

"That's not my idea of a fun evening."

"Do you know any names? People he might have met there or drank with?"

"I could give you some names, but I don't see where you're going."

"By a lot you mean several nights a week?"

"He went out a lot. I didn't always ask him where he went. Bradley loved drinking in bars. I don't."

"Do you think he had a drinking problem?"

"He drank a lot. Mother worried about it, but I wouldn't say he had a problem. He just liked to drink. But I'm not even sure what the point of the question is."

"Let it go. I'm really shooting in the dark."

"It might be easier if we could look at each other."

"Probably not. What do you know about the criminal element of McLean County?"

"I'm not sure we have one, except for the Sheriff's Department."

"The Sheriff's Department aside, surely this place hasn't changed so much since I was here. I'm talking about the kind of people that in my time used to get into fights in bars and steal hubcaps, which I never quite understood, by the way, but let that go. Is there somebody people think of as the chief troublemaker around here? Somebody you wouldn't be surprised to hear had gotten himself arrested in Knoxville trying to hold up a convenience store."

"Oh, that's easy. Cotton May. Or at least he's the most interesting troublemaker."

"Cotton May. Doesn't ring a bell."

"The family moved in after you left. His father owns May Transport in Adair. Has a fleet of big trucks."

"Ah." This I utter somewhat more emphatically than I intended.

"Ah? Was that some kind of policeman ah? Does this mean that you've solved the crime?"

"It doesn't mean anything." In fact, I was remembering Byron Holmes' reference to eighteen-wheelers presumably full of drugs. "Why is Cotton May such an obvious candidate for chief troublemaker?"

"Anybody around here you asked that question to would have given you the same name. From high school on, he was always in some kind of trouble. As a matter of fact, I think he did rob a convenience store. In Adair, but his father got him out of it someway. His father's got a little money, which probably explains it." A little money for Jesse probably means a lot of money for anybody else.

"What does he do, Cotton May?"

"You mean besides hanging out at Pearl's?"

"That's his place?"

"No, but he's apparently a regular, along with his sidekicks."

"What does he do for a living?"

"I think he worked for his father for a while. I don't know that he does anything now. Lives out on a little farm on the Sevierville Highway, but they don't farm it."

"Ah."

"There you go again. Is it significant that he lives on a farm? Half the people in Prosperity live on farms. I live on a farm."

"Farms have big barns and sheds. Places to store things."

"Yes, farms tend to have barns," she says. "Is there somewhere you're heading with this?"

I borrow Byron Holmes' ploy. "This is Mexico." I draw a small circle in the sky above us, then another above it. "And this is Albuquerque." I trace a line from Mexico to Albuquerque then across the sky to the right and draw another circle. "And this is McLean County."

There is a long silence beside me, and then I see her hand above us, the middle finger extended. "And this is the international sign for smart asses who talk in riddles."

"Drug trafficking," I say. "Byron Holmes thinks there's a route from Mexico up through Albuquerque and across the country to somewhere around here. Like a hub for the east coast."

"And what would Cotton May's part in this be?"

"Well, they would need transportation and a place to store the merchandise. He's got both."

"Cotton May is too dumb to figure out something like that."

"Then maybe somebody else figured it out, and he supplies the trucks and the storage space."

"This is a small town. People would talk."

"Well, apparently people have talked. Byron Holmes must have picked up on something. Isn't his place also off the Sevierville Highway?"

"It's closer in to town, but not all that far from the May place."

"Maybe he saw something suspicious. I don't know what, but I do know that Byron Holmes is not a crank. If he thinks there's something going on, I'd be inclined to believe him."

"Did he mention Cotton May by name? Or what about that deputy Jim McKinney?"

"He didn't mention any names."

"You'd have to know Cotton May to understand why you're wrong about him being a professional criminal. He's annoying, but he's strictly small time. Except for the convenience store, the sort of thing he does is usually not blatantly criminal, unless you wanted to push it. You know, getting drunk and knocking down mailboxes, stuff like that. Then his daddy comes around and pays for the damage."

"Did he ever get involved with your family?"

"Well, Bradley caught him and his friends having a party on the deck at the lake house one time—everybody drunk, beer cans all over the place. He ran them off, and don't say ah, because the next time he saw him Cotton May apologized."

"Do you know him?"

"I speak to him when I run into him."

"What's he like?"

"About my age. Blond. Good-looking, which is probably responsible for a lot of his trouble. Actually kind of charming when he's not drunk. Dresses like a cowboy, boots and all. Reminds me a little bit of James Dean in *Giant*. Do you know that? Anyway, can we leave Cotton May? Next question."

"Why did you bring up Jim McKinney?"

"You wanted troublemakers. He's a troublemaker. Next question."

"I'm all out. I need to talk to Byron Holmes again. Find out what he knows, if he'll tell me."

"Let's say Byron Holmes is right, and there's a big drug ring operating right here in McLean County and Cotton May is smack in the middle of it. What would that have to do with Bradley?"

"That's what I haven't been able to figure out."

"Are you back to him being a drug dealer?"

"I'm sure he was not a drug dealer. I never suggested he was a drug dealer."

She is silent so long I think maybe she has dozed off, but then I hear her stirring beside me. "Is that where you got shot?"

"That's it."

"Can I touch it?" I feel her fingers move along the scar. "Seems to be healing okay."

"A permanent reminder of a careless moment. Never should have happened."

"Is this why you quit?"

"I've never been able to figure out all the reasons I quit, but that was one of them."

She's quiet again for a long time. "Funny isn't it," she says finally, "that McLean County High's two football heroes should both end up being shot."

I can't judge the tone of her voice. "I was luckier. A few inches to the right and I would have been up there with Bradley."

"Up there," she repeats. We're looking up into a cloudless sky that seems endless.

"Just a figure of speech," I say.

"Then you don't share the belief of the Prosperity Methodist Church?"

"You mean is Bradley up there somewhere looking down on us? If he is, then maybe you ought to put some clothes on."

"Don't joke. I'm serious. What do you think happens when you die?"

"Nothing."

"What do you mean nothing?"

"Eternal oblivion."

"You mean nothing for ever and ever? Other people eating at the Rosewood and drinking martinis, and you're nothing?"

"I've thought about it a lot. I can't see any way around it."

"God, that's hard, especially right now. Can't you give me just a tiny speck of hope?"

"That's what the Prosperity Methodist Church is for."

"But you don't know for a fact that there's not an afterlife."

"If it's any comfort," I say, "think of all the time that existed before you were born and all the time that'll exist after you die. Your entire lifetime is like a billionth of a second in the broad scheme of things, so if you live to be ninety years old, the difference between the time of your death and Bradley's is just the blink of an eye."

Another long silence, and then I hear the rustle of fabric against skin. "Since our lives are so insignificant in the broad scheme of things," she says, "I'm just going to slip these off."

XI

AFTER becoming acclimated to my new residence I find myself spending most of my time on the deck overlooking Lake Eleanor. On Tuesday morning I pour a cup of coffee and sit down at my customary station, watching the sun burn the mist off the water. When I judge myself sufficiently awake, I flip open the legal pad and begin my daily list of Things to Do. One, compose the first sentence of the novel. This is the new strategy. Rather than trying to map out the whole thing I'll simply start writing with the hope that once something is on paper the words will begin to flow. It could work.

Two, organize the notes on Bradley McLean's murder. That's in preparation for my ex-partner's arrival today, assuming he hasn't changed his mind. Three, check the McLeans' phone records. Not much hope there, since Jesse said Bradley normally used his cell phone, now in the custody of the McLean County Sheriff's Department. Four, interview Jill Haynes. Not much hope there either, but if I were a working policeman, she would be the first person I would talk to. I wonder if Giles has talked to her. Five, visit a bar called Pearl's near Parris City. This is strictly a lark, but why not?

But first the novel. A simple sentence shouldn't be all that tough. I sip the coffee, flip the page, and look down at the bare lined yellow surface. I decide some dry toast would be good, and perhaps one of Byron Holmes' heirloom tomatoes, sliced with mozzarella and basil and olive oil. After I've eaten I wash the dishes and return to the yellow pad. I write *Chapter One* at the top of the page, look at it for a while then write, *If he had known more about her, he would never have gotten involved, or at least that's what he told himself afterwards.* So what if you picked up a book that began like that? You would put it back down. I wince at the hard-boiled banality of the prose and mark through it. I try again: *Something strange had happened to _____ in his absence. She had become a beautiful young woman.* I read it over. It's not strange for someone to become a beautiful young woman. I mark through *strange* and substitute *wonderful*, then mark through *wonderful* as trite, then mark through the whole sentence and try again. *If he had not gone to _____'s funeral none of it would have happened.* It appears I'm unable to get away from the McLeans. I write, *Bradley McLean was once middleweight boxing champion of Princeton*, mark through it and write *It was a dark and stormy night*, tear out the sheet and go to the kitchen for another cup of coffee. Back on the deck, I look at what I have written and rejected. Why not write about the situation in which you find yourself? It's a good story and a genuine mystery. It has wealth and a beautiful woman and an evil sheriff and God knows what else around the bend. Why not write about it? For one thing, you don't know how it's going to turn out, or given the inaction of the local sheriff's department, if in fact it will turn out. There's probably a better than fifty-fifty chance that Bradley McLean's killer will never be apprehended.

I look out over the lake then close the legal pad. Clearly this isn't working, but I've fulfilled the letter of the law. I've composed several bad first sentences for a bad novel. Now on to number two on my list. By noon I have a dozen pages of notes on Bradley McLean's murder. I hear the cell phone ringing somewhere in the house, and finally locate it in the bedroom.

"You should keep your phone close by," Jesse says.

"What's up?"

"Remember when we were lying together at the old pond?"

"It was yesterday."

"I mean do you remember what we were talking about with your eyes so gentlemanly averted?"

"We talked about a lot of things."

"Do you remember a name that came up—Cotton May?"

"He's in some notes I just made."

"Well, expect a visit from him sometime soon."

"And what would be the reason for his visit?"

"I ran into him this morning at the bank and I told him there was a writer staying at the lake house and that you were working on something set in this particular locale and that you would like to talk to people who knew the area and he ought to drop by and chat. You know, local color, stories about Prosperity."

"I'm not writing anything set in this locale." I'm not writing anything set anywhere.

"Then you see how quick I was. I knew you wanted to talk to him so I made up this little story. Right on the spot."

"Very clever."

"So I'm just calling so you can get your story straight before he gets there."

"He's coming today?"

"I imagine so. He was very curious about you, so he'll probably be there just to check you out."

"Does he know I'm an ex-cop?" I walk back through the house and out on to the deck.

"It didn't come up. What difference would it make?"

"I wouldn't want him to think I'm talking to him as somebody possibly involved in criminal activity." Standing at the railing, I see a swirl of dust heading my way. "I think I see him. Or it could be Eddie. He's coming down today."

"Today should be interesting," she says. "You can tell me all about it tonight." And she's gone.

As the dust cloud gets closer, I see that it is produced by a white pickup truck, and I surmise I am about to meet the man Jesse has nominated as Prosperity's chief troublemaker, a view, she added, that was almost universally held. Just why he is the obvious candidate is what interests me. What is it about Cotton May that says guilty to the people who cross his path?

I WAS once involved in a late-night conversation at Kelly's on the subject of the intuitive detection of criminality. Eddie and I had somewhat drunkenly challenged an old cop named Bernie Dukes, whose position was that policemen, he in particular, possessed a sixth sense about guilt. His claim was that if you put, say, five people, including the perpetrator, in a room with him, after thirty minutes he could tell you who did it. Eddie told him that he was full of shit, recalling how many times he himself had been wrong, and Bernie's conclusion was that Eddie clearly didn't have it, but he did. Eddie, who loves a fight, came back with the argument that everybody was guilty of something, so how did Bernie know whether the guilt he was picking up was for that particular offense? Undeterred, Bernie responded that that particular offense would be what they would be talking about.

"So you never been wrong?" Eddie winked at me.

"Never," Bernie said.

"And if you were wrong just one time, then you'd have to admit that you don't have it. Cause if it's a sixth sense it's always there. It don't go on and off."

"Okay, but I never been wrong." Careful, Bernie, I thought.

"I believe you told us that guy Maples was guilty as hell." Eddie gave me a little smile of triumph. "Remember that one, a couple of years ago? Well, he's a free man today, declared innocent by a jury of his peers."

"That don't mean he's not guilty."

"Hell, Bernie, if that's the way you going to argue, I don't know what I could say to change your mind. So if everybody else thinks somebody's innocent, and you the only one thinks he's guilty, then you win?"

"That's right."

"And the DNA says he's innocent and you say he's guilty?"

"That too," Bernie said.

"What do you think, Shake? You got it too? You can tell when a man's guilty?"

After I've had a lot to drink I tend to pontificate. "If I've learned anything in my brief tenure here it's that nobody knows anything. Nobody's got it. If criminals weren't a whole lot dumber than we are we'd never catch anybody." I was in my Nietzschean phase at the time, and I had adopted Nietzsche's dictum that there are no facts, only interpretations. Questions of relative guilt or innocence fell under the category of interpretation. "Bernie, I have to agree with what my partner says."

"Which part? He says a lot."

"That you're full of shit."

Prosperity's chief troublemaker, obviously familiar with the layout of the lake house, comes up the deck stairs with a six-pack of beer, and I see immediately why Jesse has invoked the image of James Dean. He's very slight, wearing faded jeans, a white dress shirt, and western boots, and he has short blond hair and the kind of shy half smile Deans' character Jett Rink affected in *Giant*. Probably Cotton May is too young ever to have heard of *Giant* or even James Dean, but the resemblance is uncanny.

"You the writer?" He sets the beer on the umbrella table and walks over to the rail, his hand extended.

"That's right." We shake and I motion for him to take a seat.

"Jesse said you needed a little local color."

"That was more her idea than mine." I'm a little uncomfortable with the pretense. I follow him to the table, sit down, and close the legal pad that contains my notes on the murder.

Cotton May points to the pad. "What you working on there?"

"Just some preliminary notes. Nothing serious. Jesse said she ran into you at the bank."

"That's right. How do you two know each other?"

"I used to live here."

He squints at me across the table. "So you've known her a long time."

"When I knew her before, she was maybe ten or eleven."

"She's filled out some since then and I know some people that'd like to get a little piece of that, yours truly not excluded." He pauses and gives me a knowing look. "Maybe you already have, you living out here in the lake house and all. You don't have to answer that. You want a beer?"

"It's a little early for me. You go ahead." I'm quickly forming a dislike for Cotton May and thinking maybe Bernie Dukes was on to something.

He twists the cap off a bottle of something I don't recognize and takes a swallow. "Me and old Bradley had many a beer on this deck. Real shame what happened."

"I wasn't aware that you and old Bradley were close." I can't keep the sarcasm out of my voice. "What I heard was that he had to run you and your friends off."

He stares at me for a moment, then grins and looks down at his boots. "Well, that was a little misunderstanding. There was a rowdy crowd out here one night, and I tried to keep 'em quiet, but they sort of got out of hand. I apologized to him later—you can ask Jesse—and told him it wouldn't happen again and it didn't."

"So you're saying you two were friends?"

Cotton May ignores the question and points to the legal pad again. "So what kind of writing you doing? I figure you for one of those travel writers that likes to come in and write up the local customs."

"Something like that."

"I took an anthropology course over at Pellissippi State, and we had to write up some of the local customs. I may have embarrassed this little girl that taught the class, because I wrote about capping gnats."

"I don't think I'm familiar with that."

"You never heard about capping gnats? Well, you know most of these boys around here never been circumcised—that's a necessary part of it—and they have this game where they sit out in the yard on a summer evening with their peckers out, and—you may have seen this with dogs—pretty soon the gnats start swarming, and the object of the game is to trap the gnats in the foreskin. When one lands you got to jerk it up real quick and trap him before he flies off." He demonstrates the motion of jerking up the foreskin. "The one with the most gnats at the end of the night wins."

"What does he win?"

Cotton May grins. "Well, I've never actually seen this, you understand, so I couldn't tell you if money changes hands. I've just heard stories about it."

"You don't have to make things up just to entertain me."

"I swear to you this is a true story. You're free to write it up, maybe get it published in one of those travel magazines. I might even be able to find one of the boys to demonstrate for you. Maybe we could get Jesse McLean out here as a referee and have a contest. You circumcised?"

"I'd appreciate it if you left Jesse out of this."

"Well, of course," he says. "I didn't realize you were close. You seem a little old for her."

"She's a friend."

"I understand." His expression is the equivalent of a wink. "No more about Jesse. Do you want some more local customs?" He picks at a loose corner of the label on his bottle. "You sure you wouldn't like to join me?"

"Maybe later," I say. "You want me to put your beer in the refrigerator?"

He shakes his head. "I'll just put it here in the shade." He sets it on the deck and slides it under the table with the toe of his boot. "You know the English drink their beer room temperature. Funny about different customs in different places."

"Since you're the local customs man around here, you must have heard some of the rumors about Bradley's murder."

"Well, first of all, it ain't established that it was a murder. They found a gun next to the body, was what I heard, and the shot that killed him came from that gun."

"It's hard to shoot yourself when your hands are tied behind your back with baling wire." This is almost certainly a mistake, but it's out before I see that.

Cotton May looks at me with his half smile. "You seem to know more about this than I do. I hope you didn't get me out here under false pretenses."

"Bradley was my friend at one time."

"I know who you are." He is suddenly matter-of-fact. "You're an ex-cop from Knoxville that got himself shot. Now you're coming in here thinking you're going to find out who killed Bradley McLean."

"I guess both of us are here under false pretenses."

"I was just messing with you. But I can tell you that not much happens around here I don't know about, including the way you left here a long time ago. Killed a retard."

"You know everything that happens around here, then you must know about the drugs."

"What drugs?"

"Illegal drugs—a lot of illegal drugs."

"In McLean County? You got to be kidding. You must be confusing us with Chicago or New York City."

"But if there was drug traffic in McLean County, you would know about it?"

Cotton May doesn't like the implication of the question and reverts to his Jett Rink manner. "Some of the boys may smoke a little grass now and then—no different from any other place." He leans across the table and lowers his voice. "I may have smoked a little bit myself. I hope that don't shock you. But, hey, we got off on the wrong track with the drug business. I guess you don't want to hear any more local color."

"Not particularly."

"There was one I was going to tell you. It has to do with the way the locals deal with people that try to stir things up."

"Like me?"

"Nothing personal, you understand. But you know the mountains is like a big garbage disposal. There's people gone in there that never came out. Some get lost, but mostly it's bears. And if you wanted somebody not to come out all you'd have to do is tie him to a tree and pour a little molasses over him. Of course you have to take off his clothes so they don't find a belt buckle in the bear shit. It's happened, and sometimes he'd get a little note before it happens and it just says *bear meat*."

"These are the kind of stories you need to save for the tourists in Gatlinburg."

"But you can see the possibilities. Say you got some woman that's bugging you. I'm not talking about Jesse McLean, but say like Jesse McLean. What the boys would do is take her up in the mountains, maybe have a little fun with her, then sit her down naked in front of a tree and spread her legs like this." He makes a V with two fingers. "Then you tie her down, and right here—" he points to the notch in the V—"you'd pour your molasses or your honey and then find some place to watch the fun. Of course you'd have to make sure you were way back in the woods because there'd be considerable screaming."

"Is this a threat?"

"These are just local stories like Jesse told me you wanted to hear. Sorry, there's that name again."

"You really are a disgusting little prick."

"Whoa." Cotton May holds up his hands in a defensive manner. "You don't want to take this personal."

"You're trying to scare me off. That tells me something right there."

"I don't know what you're talking about." He reaches under the table for the six-pack and stands up, pushing his chair back. "Before he died—well, naturally it would have been before he died—old Bradley said I should use the deck out here any time I wanted to. I'm assuming that offer still stands." He's walking toward the steps.

I follow him to the edge of the deck. "The only thing I took away from the Knoxville Police Department was my service revolver. It's in the bedroom, and if you or one of the boys ever sets foot on this deck while I'm here, I'll fucking shoot you."

Cotton May looks up from the bottom of the stairs. "You're not a policeman any more. If you're going to threaten people, then you better keep your eyes open." He looks down toward the lake. "Maybe you didn't notice, but you're pretty much all by yourself out here. There's all kind of things could happen to a man out here miles from another living soul."

"If anything happens I'll know who to look for."

He runs a hand through his hair and shrugs, then walks out of sight around the corner of the house. I hear the truck engine, then watch the trail of dust until he turns the bend.

XII

"SOME fool just tried to run me off the road." Eddie drops his bag on the sofa and scans the room. "Nice place."

"White pickup?"

He nods. "Do you know who this is?" He has bent down to read the signature on the Catherine Wiley oil.

"That would be Cotton May in the white pickup and Catherine Wiley on the wall."

"This the real thing?"

"The McLeans, as a rule, disdain copies. Same for the Picasso over there on the next wall."

Eddie walks over to examine it. "Pablo fuck'n Picasso. Looks like something that took him about five minutes. Now here's a man had a real racket. Dash off something like this while he's waiting to get a haircut and sell it for a hefty sum."

"Right. Except I don't think he needed haircuts."

"Well, you get my meaning," Eddie says. "How do you know this is not a print?"

"Look behind it. It's hooked up to some kind of security system."

"A lot of good that would do out here in the boonies."

"Think about it. Five miles of gravel road to get back to town. By the time you got back with your Picasso somebody'd be waiting for you."

Eddie thinks about it. "A man's pretty much isolated out here, that's true. But that goes for you too."

"Cotton May reminded me of that. He may be somebody we'd be interested in getting to know. Right now he's in a rotten mood because I threatened to shoot him."

"That ain't like you, Shake."

"The little prick got under my skin."

"Well, he was clearly pissed," Eddie says. "After he nearly hit me he turned around in a field and followed me down here. For all I know he's still out there."

"He seems to take a proprietary interest in what goes on around here. He also threatened me, if I'm not mistaken. As did the sheriff, by the way—wants me out of here. I may be in a little difficulty, nothing serious."

"What you got yourself into?" Eddie gestures toward the paintings. "People this rich ain't like you and me, and they didn't get this way by being nice to their neighbors. Now you working for them? You don't want to get yourself on the wrong side. I believe that's what you may have done here."

"It's even more screwed up than you think. Remind me to tell you about it some time."

"Couldn't be much more screwed up."

"This rich family and me go back a long way, and I've been on the wrong side before."

"You know what I think? If your lady friend wasn't drop-dead fuck'n gorgeous you wouldn't be in this little difficulty. Am I right?"

"Eddie, you're always right."

He points to his left side. "How you feeling?"

"I haven't thought about it all day, so I guess that's a good sign. We'll check that off the list."

"You been on your own, what, a week? And look what's happened— you got a little redneck on your ass, and the local sheriff trying to run you out of the county."

"But now you're back to watch out for me. Why don't you sit down and relax. How about a beer? We can go out on the deck and admire the view."

"Do these rich people have regular beer or is it some fancy shit?"

"I've got your brand right here. Relax. Things are not that bad."

"I'm going to get you out of this fix one last time, and then you're on your own." He walks out to the deck and leans over the rail on the right, looking to see if the white pickup has departed.

"Is he still there?" I bring out a couple of beers, sit down and open the legal pad.

"Don't see him. What's with the tablet? You finish your novel?"

"Very funny. I made some notes. You want to hear this?"

"Sure. Let's see what kind of mess you got yourself into."

I tell him everything I know about Bradley McLean's death, concluding with Byron Holmes' suspicion of a county drug ring and my recent conversation with Cotton May. Then I lean back to wait for a response.

He's frowning, looking out over Lake Eleanor. "You forgot everything I taught you? You remember when you did this for a living? Even when you had the guy cold you still had to make an airtight case before the people on the third floor would touch it. And what've you got? You got rumors and what somebody suspects is going on. You got a small town punk and a retired schoolteacher."

"Got to start somewhere. I'm not saying I've got anything. I'm just saying this is where we start."

"Why do we have to start?"

"Because if we don't this is headed for the OU files." That's what we called them in the department—Open Unsolved. When people stop working them they go to the bottom of the case loads. They might get picked up later, but the odds are against it. People who watch crimes being solved weekly on TV probably make the assumption that if you commit a murder, say, the chances are good that you're going to get caught. In fact, the majority of crimes go unsolved.

"So?" Eddie spreads his arms. "It goes into the OU files. It won't be the first."

"Indulge me. If this was all you had, where would you go with it?"

"First of all, this sounds too much like work. I thought I was taking a vacation. But you know exactly where you would go if we were working this case back in the department. We'd talk to this Jill Haynes woman. You got to go there first. Then you got to figure what the hell's going on with the little prick in the pickup truck and your old schoolteacher, since that's all you got."

"Exactly."

"But we're not gonna find jack shit."

"You got to start somewhere."

"You said that." He sighs audibly. "This is going to be nothing but trouble. I can see that right now. In addition to having nothing to go on, we got no jurisdiction down here. We're two private citizens poking around in people's business."

"It's a free country. You can talk to anybody you want to."

"In theory. It don't always work out that way."

"We can probably talk to the woman this afternoon. I'll see if I can get Jesse to set it up. And tonight I thought we might go over to this bar in Parris City where Cotton May and his crowd hang out. At the very least we can take in some local color."

"Drinking with a bunch of rednecks," Eddie says. "That ought to be a whole lot of fun."

"I've missed your sarcasm. How about another beer?"

"You know what we're doing here." It's not a question. He's looking out over the lake again, frowning.

"No, Eddie. What is it that we're doing?"

"We're playing. We're going through the motions. Just to please that young woman—playing detective."

"Maybe you're right, but what could it hurt?"

"What could it hurt? I believe you've already had a clue. You can stir things up. Make people want to do things to you. Like shooting you in the fuck'n head."

"Maybe that's the only way we're going to find out anything—stir things up, make somebody do something stupid."

"Just as long as you understand what we're doing. We're going to play like cops for a few days, then I'm going back to Knoxville and we ain't gonna know any more about who killed the man than we do now."

AFTER our conversation with Jill Haynes, I figure Eddie is probably right. When you talk to a lot of people associated with crimes over the years, they tend to fall into certain categories, and I categorize Jill Haynes as somebody trying to distance herself as far as possible from the murder of Bradley McLean. If she knows anything, it's clear very early in the conversation that we aren't going to get it out of her. Eddie and I talk to her in a condo in Adair—well-furnished, tasteful, reminding me a bit of the lake house decor. Maybe McLean money is in evidence here also.

"I wish I could be more helpful," she keeps saying. But she does everything she can to be as little help as possible. She sits on the sofa, Eddie and I in uncomfortable wingback chairs. She offered us coffee, which we decline. She sips from a mug as she professes her ignorance about the affairs of a man she's been seeing fairly regularly for a good while.

I ask her about his business dealings. Does she know what sort of enterprises he had been engaged in shortly before his death? No. He never talked about business. Did he talk about other people he was involved with? No. What about his family? Just Jesse. They talked about Jesse a lot. She's very fond of Jesse. Does she have any reason to think the family is in financial difficulty? No. How long had they been seeing each other? Maybe a year and a half. How often did they go out? Once or twice a week. Were there prospects of marriage, an engagement? No, they just enjoyed each other's company. Technically, she's married. Did her estranged husband object to the relationship? No. He's living in St. Louis. They are not in touch. When was the last time she saw Bradley? Maybe four or five days before he died. Did he seem different in any way? No. Can she think of anybody who wished him harm?

"I wish I could help you," she says again, "but I can't. I've thought about it a lot and there's nothing I know about Bradley or his family or his business that would help you."

"Nothing?" Eddie says. "That covers a lot of ground. It could be something that don't seem important, a passing reference. For instance." He gets up and walks over to the window, which looks out on downtown Adair. "A woman once told me something she heard her husband say over the phone a few days before he was killed. Meant nothing to her, just a name. But it turned out to be crucial to the case."

He turns back from the window, catching my puzzled look. "This was before Mr. O'Brian here joined the department. But let me ask you this—did your friend ever get calls on his cell phone when you all were out together?"

"Sometimes," she says.

"And you heard his end?"

"Well, yes."

"And that didn't tell you anything about the nature of the call?"

"It was mostly just yes and no and I'll call you next week."

"So," Eddie says, "did you think he didn't want you to know the nature of the call?"

"I'm not sure what you're implying," Jill Haynes says, "but what I thought was that he didn't like to mix business and pleasure. I'm so sorry I can't be more helpful, and as I said, I've thought about it, and if there were anything, believe me I would tell you. So I don't think there's any point in dragging this out any further."

I get up to leave. "I guess Stanton Giles has talked to you."

"Actually, Jim McKinney."

"His deputy."

"That's right," she says.

"And you told him the same thing—you'd like to help but can't."

A slight pause before she answers. "That's right."

"So I guess we'll be going. Thanks so much for talking to us."

"I did it for Jesse," she says, steering us toward the door.

"And if you think of anything later on, you can get in touch with me through Jesse."

"I've already thought about it. There's not anything more." She shuts the door, and Eddie gives me a raised eyebrow look in the hall.

"Beautiful young woman," he says. "I guess the pleasure of her company was worth the ride."

"What was that story about the woman hearing her husband on the telephone? I never heard that."

"Sometimes you have to be a little creative," Eddie says. "I was just trying to give her an example of the kind of thing she might have missed."

"I don't think she missed a thing. I think she just wants to get out of the whole mess, and the last thing she wants to do is become a witness."

"Is that the way you read it? I think you may be a little off there." We've stopped in the hallway at the door leading out to the street.

"So how do you read it?"

"Two possibilities," Eddie says. "One, she's protecting somebody, maybe Bradley McLean. Two, somebody got to her. Maybe scared her a little."

"She didn't look scared to me."

"Very polished young woman, doing her best to act natural. If she'd really wanted to help us she could have given us something, but she'd made up her mind not to let anything slip out. And she knew she didn't have to. We got no authority down here."

"So that was more interesting than I thought." We walk out of King's Plaza Condominiums and cross the street to my car, parked at a meter in front of the offices of Sutherland and Anderson, General Practice.

"About to get more interesting," Eddie says. "Man in a uniform leaning on your car."

"That's Jim McKinney, the deputy sheriff."

"Why would he be leaning on your car?"

"I have no idea."

"Mean looking," Eddie says under his breath as we approach the car.

"Officer McKinney, I believe." I offer my hand. "Is there a problem?"

He ignores my hand. "A problem? Yeah, I'd say there's a problem. The sheriff is real disappointed in you." He pushes himself away from the car. "He thought he'd made himself clear when you had that little talk. You do remember that?"

"You're probably referring to the McLean investigation. I can assure you—"

"I don't want to hear it," McKinney says. "I'm telling you that if I see you and your buddy nosing around here again, I'm going to haul your ass in. I don't know how to make that any clearer."

"Actually, if you don't mind my joining in the conversation," Eddie says in his most soothing tone, "I can't speak for Mr. O'Brian here, but it's not exactly clear to me. I mean, nosing around. What exactly does that mean? We can't be in your little town here? We were talking to a friend of a friend of Mr. O'Brian's. Is that a crime in this town?"

"I know who you were talking to," McKinney says. "And I know why you were talking to her. So let's don't be cute here. We all know exactly what I'm talking about and it's not going to happen again. Now is that clear?"

"Well, I hate to keep disagreeing with you," Eddie says. "But what is it that we can do around here without getting ourselves in trouble with the law? I was thinking about going over to that little café down the street and having a beer and maybe a cheeseburger. Would you consider that criminal activity?"

Officer McKinney doesn't respond, but his look darkens. "I believe Eddie is asking for a little clarification," I say. "This is not the old west. You can't just tell people to be on the next stage. We're not doing anything wrong, and I'd hate to have to get a lawyer involved in this, but I know a little about the law, as does my friend here, and you can't go around threatening people."

"I know who you are and I know who your friend is, and I know I can make your fucking life miserable. Call that a threat or whatever you want to. I'd say it's a fact."

"You know, that's what impresses me," Eddie says. He has returned to his soothing tone. "You know who we are. You know who we were talking to. You know what we were talking about. You know whose car this is. You must know everything that goes on in this town. That's very impressive."

McKinney does not have a response. "That's all I have to say. I can make your fucking life miserable, and I'm not just talking about the law. I'd say a reasonable person might think seriously about getting the fuck out of here and leaving the police work to the people elected to do it."

"I didn't realize you were elected, but I understand where you're going with this," I say, thinking there isn't much point in escalating the argument. "You can tell Sheriff Giles we got the message."

"Yeah, well I guess the proof of that will be what we're talking about the next time I run into you." McKinney turns and walks across the street in the general direction of the King's Plaza Condominiums.

"Do I detect a recurring theme here?" Eddie says.

"What's that?"

"There's some people want you out of McLean County."

"The deputy was fairly clear about that, wasn't he?"

"Nice man," Eddie says. "Real fuck'n professional. But he told us a lot."

"Like what?"

"Like why Jill Haynes was afraid to talk to us. How did the man know we were going to talk to her? She told him. He'd warned her about talking to you, and she calls him up and says he's coming over and there's nothing I can do about it because I promised the McLean woman, and he says keep your mouth shut. That's the only way I can figure it."

"It's not the only way, but I can't give you another one at the moment. That would mean that Jill Haynes might actually know something. It might also mean that McKinney and maybe Giles know something too."

"Would that be surprising to you?"

"I can't say that it would."

"You know, Shake, this is a lot more interesting than I figured. I don't mean to say we're going to find out anything, but it's an interesting situation you got yourself in. Maybe you could use it for the novel. What you got so far?"

"I got nothing. I don't have a plot. I don't have characters. I don't even have a crime."

"So what's wrong with this one?"

"Several things, but the main thing is that one of the rules of the mystery novel is you solve the mystery. Like you said, we're not likely to do that, and it doesn't look like local law enforcement wants it done either."

"Well, hell," Eddie says, "you the writer. Make it up."

"If you were writing it and knowing what you know, who would your killer be?"

"I think maybe you should go with the deputy. Man's mean enough to shoot somebody in the head."

"Another rule of the mystery novel is that the most likely suspect can't turn out to be the killer."

"Is that right?" Eddie thinks about this for a moment. "Well then you'd fool 'em all, wouldn't you?"

XIII

DRIVING back, we run into a thunderstorm just outside Prosperity, and when the road begins to disappear in the sheets of rain, I pull over into the lot of the New Hope Baptist Church to wait it out. Eddie has been quiet since we left Adair. I've seen this mood before and figure our encounter with Deputy McKinney has thrown him into a funk. To fill up the silence I begin talking, rambling really, about my history with the McLean family. I tell him everything, including my feeling of betrayal by my own father and my vague sense of coming back to Prosperity to set things straight. When I finish—with my father's death somewhere out west—we sit in silence staring at the water lashing the windshield.

"I'm surprised you never told me that before," Eddie says finally. "That's a lot to carry around with you."

"I never told anybody, but you see how this thing with Jesse McLean is real complicated."

"I can see how you didn't learn anything from the first time," he says.

"This is mostly about Jesse, and she wasn't involved the first time."

"She's a McLean. It's a family that uses people like you and me."

"You don't have to tell me about the McLeans. And there's another complication." I tell him about my impulsive pledge to Audrey McLean. "That bothers me, making a promise I'm not sure I'm going to keep."

"That ain't the part that bothers me," Eddie says. "Don't mean nothing what you told her mother."

"What part is it that bothers you?"

"The part where they find you in a field with a bullet in your head. That part."

B. J. Leggett

"Now why would anybody want to do that?"

"For the same reason they did it to her brother."

"We don't know the reason they did it to her brother."

"But we can guess, and my guess is that he knew something or he was a part of something that somebody didn't want to get out. Now you're in the same place he was, right? At least if you do what his sister wants you to do. You'll know what he knew."

"I don't think it'll ever come to that. You said so yourself."

"Well, it ain't from your lack of trying."

"You may be a little too melodramatic about it." But I see his point.

"It's not like you ain't already had a few hints that there's people here would just as soon you moved on or disappeared."

"And why would you blame Jesse for it?"

"She's put you in the middle of it. You'd think if she cared all that much about you she'd try to keep you out of it. Same thing all over again. That family's still using you."

"I'm a grown man. It was my choice." I'm aware that Eddie is getting the better of the argument.

"You think about it, Shake. If anything happens, it ain't gonna happen to the McLeans. You don't seem to get what's at stake here."

"What would you have me do?"

"Call Deathridge. Get your old job back. Get out of this hick county."

"I can't do it, Eddie. Not at the moment anyway. I sort of gave my word that I'd look into it, and I'll be damned if I'm gonna be run out of town by some redneck deputy."

"Your word," Eddie says. "You gave your word to Jesse McLean. You gave your word to Jesse McLean's mother. Your fuck'n word. I'll remember that when I pick up the paper some morning and see where a former Knoxville police detective was found dead in somebody's barn."

"Okay, I'll grant you that the situation is a little more complicated than I reckoned on, and there may be a certain amount of danger involved, especially in the unlikely event that I find out something, but the one thing I know you're wrong about is Jesse McLean. She's not the villain in this. How about a change of plans for tonight? I thought we might go over to this bar in Parris City, but we can put that off. Why don't I fix us some dinner and call Jesse to see if she can come over? You two need to get to know each other."

"I got nothing against the woman personally you understand. It's what she and her family have gotten you into. Twice, I'm talking about. Ain't no dinner going to change that."

"Even so. You need to talk to her. Have a drink together. A hundred says that when the evening's over you'll be on my side, admitting how wrong you were."

"I won't take your money," Eddie says. "I think the rain's eased up a little. You want to give it a try."

"Hundred dollars." I pull out onto the highway.

"I won't take your money."

Whether he would have taken my money would have been hard to figure. The evening starts out badly, goes downhill from there, then takes a curious turn at the end. Jesse isn't halfway through her first martini before she begins to sense Eddie's disapproval—disapproval, I see, not just for putting me in harm's way, but for her easy display of privilege and wealth, for owning a lake house decorated with expensive paintings, for having a psychiatrist, for the way she dresses and laughs and talks, for being exactly what she is.

Her response is to create a caricature of herself, as if to meet his expectations. She adopts a kind of rich white woman voice and begins pronouncing her words slowly and distinctly. She becomes over-solicitous and artificial, as if speaking to a not especially bright dinner companion. She insists on calling him Edward. "Edward, in what part of Knoxville do you live? Are you out west, which is, I'm told, the desirable area?"

He retaliates by addressing her as Ms. McLean or simply ma'am. "No, ma'am, I live in East Knoxville, over by the projects. My neighbors are mostly drug dealers and pimps, maybe a few welfare mothers."

She responds as if he has replied that he lives in a gated community. "Bobby says you're currently unattached. We'll have to introduce you to some of the local girls. They would probably find you somewhat exotic. I mean being a policeman and all. Maybe we could have a little dinner party here and show you off."

"Bobby?" He gives me a quizzical look.

"It's a long story," I say.

"I don't think I'll be around here that long, Ms. McLean. Be heading back to the projects." He has also adopted a new voice, his southern plantation voice.

"Well, you're welcome to stay just as long as you like. We should all go to the Rosewood one night. We have this marvelous restaurant here. Bobby, did you tell him about the Rosewood?"

"Not yet." I recognize after a while that she's playing her Aunt Helen, and it's quite a performance. "Eddie's only here for a couple of days. I'm not sure country life suits him."

"Speaking of the local girls," she says, "one of the checkout girls you may remember from Wilson's said to tell you hello. What was her name? Lolita? The little blonde in the tight shorts? I believe you made a real impression on her."

"Robin, I believe." I profess not to remember Robin's shorts and attempt to shift the direction of the conversation. "We were over in Adair today talking to Jill Haynes, but we didn't find out anything of significance." That's not exactly true, but I've decided not to bring up our encounter with Deputy McKinney.

"I believe I told you that when her name first came up," Jesse says. "She doesn't know anything. So what did you think of Adair, Edward?"

"Quaint," he says. "And it's Eddie if you don't mind."

"Sorry. You told me that, didn't you? You just seem like an Edward to me. The name Eddie seems so, what? Northern, like somebody you'd meet in a poolroom in Cleveland. And you should call me Jesse, as I reminded *you*. Bobby—do you object if I call you Bobby? People are so picky about their names—could I have another one of these?"

I've never seen this act before, and it doesn't appeal to me. I suspect that she had a martini or two before she showed up. But I can't blame it all on her. Eddie isn't exactly a prince himself, although I understand his attitude. He's being condescended to, and he's annoyed at being put in the situation. At one point he interrupts one of Jesse's idle reflections on policemen—how *fascinating* their lives must be, and what interesting *people* they must encounter—by saying simply and abruptly, "So your family pretty much owns everything around here."

I take it as a deliberately provocative remark—over the line, but I'm wrong, as is so often the case with Eddie. He's always a couple of moves ahead of me, sometimes more. We are eating out on the deck by this point. I concocted a pasta and a salad, and Jesse brought some bread from the Rosewood and a couple of bottles of wine.

"Not everything," Jesse says without looking up, "but a good part of it. Why do you ask?"

"I think the salad came out pretty well," I say. "Those are heirloom tomatoes and the basil is local, and the mozzarella came from some boutique cheese maker in California."

"It's special," she says and looks across the table at Eddie in the soft light. We are surrounded by the dark now, but Jesse has brought out a couple of floor lamps from the living room. "My father used to say that it was bad form to talk money at the dinner table. Why did you ask me that?"

"I was wondering about the bank," Eddie says. "Your family own the bank?"

Jesse starts to answer, but I interrupt her. "As I recall, it's owned by the Wainwright family, or at least it was when I—"

"We bought it," Jesse says. "We have controlling interest in the bank. My brother Bradley was president of the bank. My family's wealthy. I'm not going to apologize to you about that."

"Did he spend time there?"

"He was not a dilettante. He was a very responsible person. But he wasn't a *teller*. He didn't *work* there. I'm not sure what you're getting at."

But I think I see what he's getting at. "I believe what Eddie's interested in is the access Bradley might have had to local financial records, large deposits, unusual transactions, things like that. But I'm not sure this is the time to go into it."

"Not exactly what I'm interested in," Eddie says, "but close. And when is the time to go into it? I thought that's what Ms. McLean wanted—for somebody to look into her brother's death."

"It is what I want." I note that Jesse has dropped her Aunt Helen voice. "And I'm still not sure what you two are talking about."

"We may not be talking about the same thing exactly," Eddie says. "What Shake's talking about is your brother's knowledge of local financial transactions, like whether somebody suddenly came into a great deal of money. What I'm talking about is more specific. Money laundering is what it's called. Maybe you've heard of it."

"Shake?" She gives me a look and a little smile, and it's the first time I've liked her all evening.

"That was the name I had in the department. You know, short for Shakespeare. After the novel came out."

"So Eddie calls you Shake. I can't wait to hear what you call him." She's back, and I'm elated. I couldn't have taken much more of her little rich girl performance.

"Eddie," I say. "I call him Eddie. Do you understand what he's talking about? Money laundering?"

"I know what it is but I'm so lucky to have you two professionals here to explain it to me professionally while I enjoy this wonderful meal you've prepared."

"I'm sure Eddie would be happy to explain it if you promise not to talk like your Aunt Helen anymore."

She shoots me a look. "Whatever are you talking about?"

"I was trying to show you off, and you came on like somebody from the Junior League."

"Sorry," she says. "That's the way I get when I'm uncomfortable. It keeps people at a distance, but you saw right through it, didn't you?" She looks across at Eddie. "Sorry, Eddie. It's okay if you don't like me. I have this thing about people liking me, but my shrink says I've got to move past it. Not everybody's going to like you, he says. I don't think he likes me very much. But anyway, I'm just rambling on here. I think I've had way too much to drink, and it's all your fault, Bobby, for making those wonderful martinis. So now you two have to put up with the drunken rich lady confessing all her sins. I drink too much and I talk too much and I want everybody to like me. Later on, I'll probably break into uncontrollable weeping. What a drag I am tonight." She pauses. "No need to respond to any of this. Just tell me what money laundering has to do with my brother, and we'll all pretend I'm not acting like an idiot. Could I have just half a glass more of that nice wine? I might as well go all the way."

"It may have nothing to do with your brother," I say, pouring the wine, "and I'm not sure about Eddie's take on this. We haven't talked about it." I give him a puzzled look. "You want more wine?"

He shakes his head. "Trying to keep my wits about me. I'm sorry, Ms. McLean if I've made you—"

"Oh, God." She interrupts him. "I thought we had moved past the formal names. Will you please call me Jesse."

He nods.

"So, Eddie, tell me about money laundering."

"Before you do," I say. "I'm curious about when you came up with the idea."

"After the rainstorm," he says. "When we were driving back through town, I saw this tiny little bank over there by the grocery store, like a little toy bank. And I remembered what your old teacher said— what's his name?"

"Byron Holmes."

"Byron Holmes tells you he thinks there's some kind of big drug operation going on around here. So what if he's right and somebody's got all this drug money on his hands? That's the hardest problem for drug dealers—harder than getting it or selling it—figuring out what do with all the money. So what does he have to do? He's got to hide its real source, make it look like it came from some kind of legitimate operation."

"Got that," Jesse says. "Except that maybe Bobby didn't tell you that Byron Holmes is also a writer with a vivid imagination. He's full of conspiracy theories, most of which involve my family."

"Well, put that aside for the moment"—a pause—"Jesse." Looking from one to the other I see her smile and Eddie's little grin. Now they're both becoming charmers.

"Let's say, just for the sake of the argument, that in this case he's right," Eddie says. "You see the problem. All that money that's got to be cleaned up. There's a lot of ways of doing it, but the easiest way would be to own a bank or know somebody who does. And the best kind of bank to own would be one with the fewest number of employees, like that little bank in town. What's it called?"

"Prosperity Banking and Trust," Jesse says, frowning now.

"A man with bags full of drug money who had unlimited access to that bank would think he'd died and gone to heaven. Not many people looking over your shoulder there. Banks are supposed to be on the lookout for certain signs of money laundering, but let's say somebody's turning a blind eye, not reporting suspicious transactions. You see what I'm getting at. And once the money's transferred to a legitimate bank, you're in the clear. It's that first bank that has to be working with the bad guys."

"So you're saying that my brother was laundering money through his bank, setting up dummy accounts, taking in cash without reporting it. No way. No way he could get away with that. There's too much regulation there."

"Not necessarily what he's saying." I'm thinking that Jesse knows a little too much about money laundering. "Even if the bank were involved, it could be somebody else, the manager, another employee."

"The thing to remember," Eddie says, "is that this is all talk, just talk among the three of us. It don't mean nothing. But you can't have it both ways. You want somebody to look into it, you got to go with it wherever it goes. Here's a plausible explanation. Your brother got involved with some criminal types. Then he tried to get out or he threatened their operation in some way."

"What if he just found out that somebody else was laundering drug money?"

"It's possible," Eddie says, "but not as likely as the first possibility."

"But you didn't know Bradley," she says. "What would make you even suspect that he was involved with professional criminals?"

"The way he was killed," Eddie says, and I shake my head, trying to catch his eye. *No, she doesn't know all of it.* But he's looking at Jesse. "On his knees with his hands tied behind his back with baling wire? Tortured and then executed? That's not your amateur killing or the heat of the moment. That's a professional. Maybe not the first time he's done it."

I can't look at her but I hear the little noise she makes. "You didn't tell me that," she says softly. "Why didn't you tell me how my brother died?"

I can't conceive of a proper response to the question, and we sit in silence, the only sound the wind in the trees below the deck.

"I'm sorry," Eddie says finally. "I thought you knew."

"I should have told you."

"What else do you boys know? I might as well have it all."

"There's nothing else."

"Maybe one thing," Eddie says. "The chances of Shake finding out who killed your brother are about zero. Everything's against it, mostly local law enforcement. You probably ought to know that too."

"Is that what you think, Bobby?"

"I'm not as pessimistic as Eddie, but, yeah, I'm not real crazy about the position I'm in."

"Okay, we'll stop it right here. Thanks, Eddie, for being honest with me. I guess I can't say the same for him." She doesn't look at me.

"He was trying to do the right thing," Eddie says. "Maybe he gave his word to somebody. The man's always been a romantic."

"Is that what you call it?"

"He has this kind of Southern attitude about protecting the womenfolk. I hope you won't hold it against him."

"Hey. I'm here. This is me you're talking about. How come I'm suddenly the villain?" In the face of two more likely candidates, I might have added.

They both ignore me. "What an evening," Jesse says, addressing herself to Eddie. "At least I didn't break down in uncontrollable weeping. You seem relatively sober. Maybe you could drive me home."

"I'd be happy to."

"I'll drive you home," I say.

"I'll go with Eddie," she says.

XIV

You'd think you would see from the start that it's a dream, so faded and badly lit, with people you know changing into one another, but it fools you every time, so that when you wake you will thank God that you don't have an exam in a course you've neglected to attend for the entire term, Health and Physical Education, and can't find the room and walk through empty hallways, opening doors onto deserted classrooms and read on a blackboard *Bobby O'Brian killed the Rat Man*. And then when you find the room people are finishing up, turning in their papers to an attractive young woman, who nods and smiles at them then turns to you and frowns, Mrs. McDonald, the science teacher who hates you, and she gives you the exam and the first question contains the word *zygote* and you can't remember what that means, and it's hard to concentrate because workmen are hammering in the next room and is the figure in the hallway Bradley McLean?

I wake to a room flooded with light and the sound of Eddie knocking on my open bedroom door.

"What time is it?"

"After nine," he says. He's dressed and his bag is on the floor beside him.

"You leaving? I thought you were going to stay for a couple of days."

"I thought I might as well get on back. You remember last night? Your lady friend called it off."

"Well, just for the fellowship," I say, and the memory of last night comes back. "But I could be joining you. She may kick me out."

"She'll be all right," Eddie says. "It was mostly the shock of hearing the details. You remember with the relatives. They know he's dead but they can't take the details. But that was my fault. I thought she knew."

"Not your fault. I was wrong, should've told her everything."

"All the same I probably went too far, but the woman was getting on my nerves."

"Mine too. But then you two seemed to hit it off pretty well there at the end. If we'd made the bet, I would've won."

"I think I'd have to call it a draw," Eddie says. "Three hours of being a bitch and forty-five minutes of being civil. I'll call it a wash since the civil part came at the end. Anyway, I might as well take off and let you two make up. Now you can have all the time you need for your writing."

I wish he hadn't mentioned the writing. That's the kind of thing I worry about when I'm still in bed at nine in the morning, and the idea that now I'll have to start on the novel is depressing. "At least let me fix us some breakfast."

"Fine."

"I'm going to take a quick shower. Why don't you put some coffee on? By the way, do you know what a zygote is?"

"Not exactly, but I think it's something you learn about in sex education."

At breakfast I play my trump card. "I never thought I'd see the day when you and the McLean County Sheriff's Department are on the same side."

He looks at me calmly over his coffee mug. "Coffee's good," he says. "What do you think?"

"I mean, I got threatened by Giles and McKinney and Cotton May to no result, and you're here less than twenty-four hours and you accomplish exactly what they wanted. You couldn't have done it any better if you'd been working for them."

"So you don't like the coffee?"

"Forget the coffee for a minute. We're talking about something important here."

"I'm doing it for your own good," Eddie says evenly. "I'm pretty sure that's not McKinney's motive. Can't speak for the other two. I wonder if I could have a little more of the eggs. What's that green stuff in there?"

B. J. Leggett

"Basil. I'm trying to use it up before it goes bad."

"Eggs with basil," Eddie says. "I don't guess you got any goat cheese in there."

"You're trying to get us off the subject again. It doesn't matter what the motive is. The results are the same. I don't mind calling it off, but I'd like it to be my idea."

"What is it you can possibly do without getting yourself in trouble?"

"There are a couple of things I'd like to check out, just for myself—not for Jesse McLean or the McLean family, but for me. I'd like to know what Byron Holmes knows. I think it's considerable, and I don't think the deputy could object to me talking to my old English teacher. And I'd like to go out to that dive where Cotton May and his bunch hang out. It's a public place, and it's not in the county, so I don't think the sheriff's office has jurisdiction over there."

"Maybe you ought to take Bernie Dukes instead of me. Solve the whole thing. You remember he can finger a guilty man after a ten minute conversation." Eddie gets up and takes his dishes to the sink. "I don't know about you, Shake. You're starting to act like some kind of movie detective."

"I'm serious about this. I think if you put a little pressure on this kid he might do something stupid."

"Yeah, like taking a shot at you."

"Anyway, you asked me what I could do and I told you."

"And you want me to do it with you."

"I thought it might be more interesting that way. We could go over to Byron Holmes' place this morning, and go to the bar in Parris City tonight. Tomorrow you're back in Knoxville with some fresh vegetables. So what do you say?"

"I'm not sure how much help I can be."

"I've been thinking about that. Let's say you tell Byron Holmes in an off-hand way that you've heard from somebody in the department that there was big time drug activity in McLean County. Has he heard anything?"

"That would be a lie, wouldn't it? You want me to lie to your friend?"

"It's not exactly a lie. You heard it from me, and I get my last check from the department at the end of the month."

"You always was one for splitting hairs," Eddie says.

I remember the house, off the Sevierville Highway five or six miles out of town. A forties farmhouse with a deep front porch, it looks as if it belonged exactly where it sits, behind it a lot and a weathered barn that leans slightly to one side, and visible behind that the cultivated fields, small fenced-off patches. Byron Holmes' farm sits in a small valley, a choice location and one of the few level plots of land around. The thing I remember most clearly about it is the creek that marks the back boundary, too small to have a name, but he called it Frenchman's Creek in honor of William Faulkner, one of his literary heroes.

"This is what's called a farm," I inform Eddie as we make our way up the gravel drive. "Probably your first time on a farm."

"I got on my good shoes," he says. "We gonna have to walk through any cow shit?"

"I don't believe Byron Holmes owns any livestock. He's a truck farmer, a trade I'd be happy to explain."

"You could pretty much figure it out," Eddie says. "I mean, hell, I'm not from the country but I'm not stupid." He gets out and looks around. "Don't seem to be nothing stirring, but there's a truck down in the field. Let's get this done."

We find him at the far end of the field sitting at a picnic table in a packing shed. He is culling tomatoes, separating them into buckets on the table. A young boy, maybe fifteen, is assisting him, emptying the buckets into hampers and carrying the full hampers to the truck and stacking them in the bed. Byron Holmes looks up at our approach. "You have to separate the number ones from the number twos," he says. "Places like Wilson's and the Rosewood Café buy the number ones, and the locals buy the number twos at half the price. Taste exactly the same. The ones with the bad spots you throw away or feed to the hogs. You all in the market for tomatoes?"

"I wanted you to meet my ex-partner Eddie Carpenter down from Knoxville."

They exchange pleasantries, and Byron Holmes nods toward the boy walking back from the truck. "And this is my partner Jesús, up from Mexico. The two of us take care of the place."

Jesús hoists another bushel of tomatoes, and we watch him walk back to the truck, lift the bushel into the bed, then climb up after it. "Good worker," Byron Holmes says. "I couldn't do it without him. Be happy when he's old enough to drive—turn it over to him and sit on my front porch and watch the traffic go by." He gestures toward a stack of wooden shipping crates. "Drag a couple of those over here in the shade. They make pretty good seats."

And so we do and sit in the shade of the packing shed and talk about farming. Byron Holmes points out the contents of each patch and explains the order of their harvest. The strawberries come in the earliest, he says. In the spring. That's the money crop, but they're labor intensive. "Have to call on my friends from south of the border," he says. "That's how I got to know Jesús." We are informed of the peculiarities of various vegetables, as only a scholar of his trade can recite them, and I glimpse a hint of a smile on Eddie's face. Perhaps Byron Holmes glimpses it also, for he stops in the middle of his monologue on the differences between his tomatoes and the inferior Granger County tomatoes that are so highly touted by people who really don't know tomatoes. "But I guess you boys didn't come out here to get a lecture on farm produce."

"So you like farming better than teaching?" Eddie isn't quite ready to divulge the purpose of our visit.

"I'd have to say that I do."

"Keeping you busy in your retirement," Eddie says.

"I manage to stay busy. The truck farming takes up the spring and summer, and I still have my writing." He adds after a pause, "And lately a bit of photography." This last said as if to himself.

"It's not easy, I imagine. The farming." Eddie keeps up the small talk as if he's got all day.

"It's not easy, I'd have to admit. You know what some biologist said—Nature abhors a garden. You can imagine what she thinks about a truck farm. But then school teaching is a lot harder than people think, not physically but it grinds you down after a while, standing up there day after day in front of a bunch of young people who spend most of their waking hours thinking how they can make your life miserable. And the capacity for ignorance in your average teenager—they not only embrace it but they resent any effort on your part to combat it. So I'd have to say that I've enjoyed my little farm a good deal better than my profession. I don't have to answer to anybody but Jesús there."

As we watch the boy arranging the tomato hampers in the truck bed, Byron Holmes shakes his head and frowns. "Folks blame his people for everything that's gone wrong around here lately, but they're mistaken. I mean Mexican immigrants in general." We wait for clarification, but it is not forthcoming. Instead he straightens his leg, reaches into his pocket and produces a penknife. He takes a tomato from the pile in front of him and cuts it into quarters, popping one in his mouth. "This field's planted with a variety called Big Boys, always been my personal favorite except for the heirlooms. You want a taste?"

"We just had breakfast," I say. "Got a late start this morning."

"In what way are they mistaken?" Eddie asks quietly.

Byron Holmes looks at him for a moment. "It's the homegrown variety that's causing all the trouble," he says. "The pure products of America. These Mexicans like Jesús and his family just want to work, make a little money, maybe send some of it back to their people. It's the local white trash that's getting out of hand."

"How do you mean?" Eddie asks innocently. "You mean there's a criminal element around here?"

Byron Holmes pauses. "I just mean they got no respect for other people or for the law or for anything else."

"You know it's interesting that you should say that." Eddie leans back on his wooden crate and crosses his ankles in front of him. "I heard something from a colleague about a local drug ring in this part of the country. You heard any talk about it?"

Byron Holmes looks from one of us to the other before his gaze settles on Eddie. "Robert Junior must think I fell off a turnip truck. I told him the other night I had said all I meant to say about that, and now I'm thinking that's why he brought you out here, to see if he could get something more. Maybe I'm wrong about that, but I don't intend to talk about it. No offense to you."

"None taken." Eddie shakes his head. "But Robert Junior? How many names has he got?"

"Named after his father," Byron Holmes says. "Sometime you

B. J. Leggett

need to get him to tell you how Robert Senior kept me from being fired for teaching dirty poems. It's a good story, and maybe a local drug ring would be too, but I'm afraid you're not going to be able to get it from me." He folds the penknife, straightens his leg, and returns the knife to his pocket. "Did Jesse McLean put you up to this?"

"No, she's out of it," I say. "I'm still poking around. Can't seem to let it go, and you're my only source of information. I thought you might be willing to talk to a policeman, but I see you got your mind made up."

"That's right," he says. "And you're still trying to be a policeman yourself. That's not a real good idea."

"I told him the same thing," Eddie says. "A man could get his self killed out here in the sticks. Already been threatened by a deputy sheriff and some local character."

"Cotton May," I say, watching Byron Holmes' face for a reaction.

"I'm not surprised," he says, betraying nothing. "One of the worst students I ever had. Couldn't keep himself out of trouble then and I'm sure probably not now. That's his place across the creek there, so we're kind of neighbors."

"I figured maybe Cotton May was the leader of the local criminal element," I say. "He didn't want an ex-policeman from Knoxville asking questions. Told me about a local custom, tying people to trees up in the park and applying honey to attract the bears. You ever heard of that?"

"Bear meat," Byron Holmes says.

"That's right. Before they do it, Cotton May says, they send you a note that says bear meat."

"So far as I know, nobody in this county ever fed anybody to a bear," Byron Holmes says. "There are scary things going on, but I'm not going to talk about Cotton May or the local criminal element. I've got my reasons. I'm not just being a cranky old man. But I'll not be short-tempered about it. I don't get many guests out here, and I wouldn't want to be inhospitable. Let's walk up to the house. How long you going to be with us, Mr. Carpenter?"

"Eddie," he says. "Got one more assignment. Robert Junior here's taking me out to a place called Pearl's tonight, then I'm off tomorrow."

"Well, we'll have to fix you up with some tomatoes and maybe some greens and some freestone peaches to take back with you. The peaches made this year after a two-year hiatus. You married, Eddie?"

"No, Eddie says, "but I do cook. I'd be happy to have some McLean County produce."

"We'll get Jesús to gather you up some stuff. I wouldn't want your trip out here to be entirely fruitless." He stands up from the bench but stops halfway and frowns, as if searching his memory. "I believe Milton uses that play on words in *Paradise Lost.* " He straightens up, with a hand on his back. "Only attempt at humor in the entire poem, so far as I can tell."

XV

"NEVER seen a parking lot that was solid pickup trucks," Eddie says. "You think this fruity little car's gonna be all right?"

We're sitting in the BMW looking at a two-story high confederate flag painted on the side of a brick building.

"Well, now that you bring it up. You got any suggestions?"

"It was my car, I think I'd take it across the road to that feed store. No use tempting these boys."

"Make them walk across the road at least."

"Right."

I park in front of the Parris County Co-Op, and we walk back across the road to Pearl's.

Whoever decorated it apparently got a good deal on unfinished barn wood and used farm implements. There are old tin cola and cigarette signs nailed to the barn wood walls, along with various planters and cultivators scattered around. The faux-rustic decor is curiously artificial given the fact that we actually are in the country. Pearl's is divided into two floors, with the bar on the first and, from the sound of it, pool tables and video games on the second. The barroom is large, maybe fifteen tables, about two-thirds of which are occupied. I gesture toward an empty table in a corner, and we walk over and sit down under a rusty tin sign advertising something called Garrett's Snuff.

"Poor man's Cracker Barrel," Eddie says.

"Yeah, except the Cracker Barrel was already the poor man's something or other."

"See any of the criminal element?"

As a matter of fact, I do. "That guy in the hat in the far corner with the two older men. That's the one tried to run you off the road."

Cotton May looked up but feigned indifference when we walked in. Now he's leaning across the table in conversation with his cohorts, a man in a Cardinals baseball cap and a bearded man actually wearing overalls, although they seem more costume than clothing. Cotton May tilts his head in our direction, and the three look over.

"You want to talk to the cowboy?" Eddie says.

"I think they'll be over here soon enough."

A man two tables away catches my eye and points a thumb toward the bar. "You got to get your own drinks," he says. "No waitress, except on the week-ends."

"I guess we sort of stick out like your little sissy car." Eddie stands up. "I'll get us a couple. What are you drinking?"

"They've pretty much figured out we're not regulars. I'll have a beer, I guess. Your brand. This doesn't look like a martini place."

"Probably serve it in a fruit jar," Eddie says.

Pearl's is oddly subdued, at least at the moment, not at all like Kelly's where you can hardly hear the person across the table. There is music playing, but not blasting, and I can discern the click of the billiard balls above along with the sounds of electronic games. I turn around to watch Eddie conversing casually with the handsome older woman tending bar. He pays for the beers and drops a couple of bills in the tip jar. Eddie fancies himself a generous tipper. He walks back to the table with a little swagger, as if he is in his element, and I guess he is.

"I see they had your brand."

"Bartender said she don't do martinis," Eddie says. "Nice lady. See if you can guess her name."

"The eponymous Pearl," I say. "Just a shot in the dark."

"That's why you were once a big-time detective, and what was that word again?"

"Eponymous, referring to the person something is named for—like the eponymous McLean family that furnished the name for the county or the eponymous Hamlet that furnished the name for the play. But how did you get her name?"

"We had a friendly little conversation. She allowed as how I was one of the few black men she had ever had the pleasure to serve. And she hoped I would feel right at home."

"And I'm sure you do."

"Maybe more than you, and you actually come from around here. Because I don't use words like *eponymous*, especially with people like your friend over there in the cowboy hat."

"Cotton May attended Pellissippi State. Told me so himself. Regards himself as an intellectual, keeper of local history and customs. I believe he's coming over."

We too feign indifference, aware that Cotton May is approaching, followed somewhat reluctantly by his two cohorts.

"Uncanny," Cotton May says. They have brought their beers over, so I figure they're here for a while and motion to the two vacant chairs. The man in the overalls drags a chair over from the next table and they sit. "Uncanny." Cotton May shakes his head.

"My friend Eddie Carpenter. Cotton May."

"This is David Earl." Cotton May motions to the man in the baseball cap. "And the farmer there is Terry." They nod, somewhat amused at the occasion.

"What's really uncanny," Cotton May says, "is this is the table more or less reserved for Bradley McLean when he was alive, and you came straight to it. He always sat there where you are with his back to the bar, and regulars would get up when they saw him come in. People who didn't know would find out pretty quick it was Bradley's table."

"The privileges of the eponymous McLean family," Eddie says and we all look at him.

"So Bradley was a regular," I say to break the silence.

"That's a fact," Cotton May says. "Several nights a week."

"I wonder if he was in here the night he was killed."

"That I couldn't tell you," Cotton May says. "You doing an investigation?" He turns to his companions. "You see him in here that night?"

"I don't believe I was in here that night," David Earl says.

Terry shakes his head. "I never heard anybody say they saw him in here that night. A Monday, I believe it was."

"But he was here three or four nights a week," Cotton May says. "How about yourself?"

"Yeah, maybe more," he says. "You like to drink with people you know."

"What's with the flag out there? I don't see the connection with Pearl."

"Well, you see this used to be called The Rebel before Pearl took it over. She thought about having it sandblasted off, but some of us convinced her it was a local landmark. There was a picture of it in one of those southern magazines a few years ago. Pearl's is the place to be."

"So I've heard."

"So what do you think, Eddie?" Cotton May smiles and takes a sip of his beer. "I hope the flag didn't get you all riled up. And, by the way, Eddie, that's an unusual name for an Africo-American. You all are usually named something like JaJuan or Abdul or Racheed, or some shit like that."

I glance over to see how Eddie is taking Cotton May's inventive nomenclature, and he's smiling, gearing up for it.

"That's a fact," Eddie says in a tone that might be taken as mockery. "People around here seem to have a thing about my name. Young lady last night said it sounded like somebody from Cleveland."

"Right," Cotton May says.

"Of course she had some right to say that, herself having the eponymous McLean name." Eddie pauses. "But in your case it's like the kettle calling the pot black, so to speak."

"How's that?" Cotton May frowns.

"Man named Cotton talking about people's names. I was trying to figure what your middle name might be. Swab, maybe."

Cotton May does not find this amusing, although the other two are grinning now.

"Patch," Terry says and laughs.

"And, of course," Eddie says, "no doubt one of your friends has pointed out that yours is the only name here makes a complete sentence."

They all look puzzled at that.

"It's the answer to the question, Does anybody at the table give blow jobs."

They don't get it, but then Terry snorts and says, "Like *might*. Cotton might."

"You know," Cotton May says, "there used to be a word for people like you."

"What was that?" Eddie is still smiling.

"Uppity," Cotton May says. "And uppity was not what your older Africo-American wanted to be known as. Get you in big trouble."

"I guess that's why there's so few of us Africo-Americans around here," Eddie says. "But then there was a name for people like you."

"And what was that?"

"Hey." I believe it's time for an intervention. "You guys take it easy. I wouldn't want us to get into it our first time at Pearl's."

"No, the man said he had a name for people like me. I'd like to hear what it is."

Eddie is looking at the bar behind me, frowning now. "Southern gentleman," he says at last. "You're clearly one of them southern gentlemen that used to own plantations and such."

"I don't believe that was the word," Cotton May says.

"Well, you know, I'm here as a guest of the McLean family," Eddie says. "I wouldn't want to get anybody riled up." I'm pleased he's backing off but a little surprised. "Come on up to my neighborhood sometime and maybe we can finish this conversation."

"I don't think so. Like to keep my hubcaps," Cotton May says. "You gonna be around here a few more days? Maybe we can finish it down here."

"Leaving tomorrow," Eddie says.

"Taking your friend with you?"

"He's here for a while, I believe."

Cotton May stands, and his companions take the cue. "I'm going to cut you a little slack tonight, Eddie," he says, "being as how you're a guest of the McLean family and you're leaving tomorrow. Maybe we'll run into each other again some time."

"Mighty white of you," Eddie says.

Colton May frowns. "There's something you don't seem to understand. You're in my place now, and the people in this room are my people—if you get my meaning."

Eddie's smile broadens and he looks over at me. "Should we be scared?"

"I'm going to make a point of running into you again," Cotton May says.

"Looking forward to it," Eddie says as they saunter back to their table.

"Thanks for not pushing it. We were seriously out-manned."

"Yeah, wouldn't do to get into it in a place like this," Eddie says. "But I might've played it different if I hadn't seen who just came in."

I turn to see a familiar figure in uniform at the bar. "Deputy McKinney. You think he sleeps with that thing on? What is that anyway? That's a very distinctive grip."

Eddie squints at the bar. "You're looking at a Colt Python with a six-inch barrel. You don't see many of those any more. Used to carry one myself with a four-inch. Easy to tuck under your jacket."

"Why'd you stop?"

"Deathridge outlawed the Python because of the penetration. They fire a .357 Magnum cartridge. Go right through a person, hit innocent bystanders. Anyway, I figured a little skirmish would make him too happy. Outsiders down here disturbing the peace."

"He's out of his jurisdiction."

"They don't seem to pay much attention to little niceties like that around here," Eddie says. "You want another beer?"

"Why not? I'll get this round. Give me a chance to speak to the deputy."

The bar is crowded, but the other drinkers have given McKinney his space, and I lean in beside him.

"Deputy."

He looks up, gives me a cold stare, then returns his gaze to his drink.

"You're off duty, I take it."

He does not respond.

"Buy you a drink? What is that, bourbon?"

He finishes off his drink and looks up. "O'Brian, I've said everything to you I need to say. Now go back and join your black friend."

"Certainly. I just need to get a couple of beers."

"I don't think so."

"I beg your pardon?"

"You look a little unsteady on your feet. I think you've had too much to drink already."

"You're saying I can't have another beer?"

"That's what I'm saying."

"On what authority? We're not in McLean County. You've got no authority here."

"You got to cross the county line to get back home. Then you're in my territory."

"I see."

"Hate to have to run you two boys in."

"I don't doubt for a minute you'd do it. You wouldn't object if we had a couple of soft drinks, would you?"

He holds up his glass. "Pearl, another one of these."

"We'll limit ourselves to Diet Cokes so as not to raise our blood sugar to a dangerous level."

"You're beginning to get on my nerves," he says. "Bar's closed to you."

"Even for a Coke?"

"Bar's closed."

Pearl comes over with his drink. "Don't sell this man anything else," McKinney says.

"Can he do that?"

She shrugs and gives me a little smile. "He's the one got the gun," she says.

XVI

I'VE been aware of the headlights behind us since shortly after we left Parris County. Probably nothing, I think, but then when I turn onto the lake road, they follow and I change my mind. It's not a road that takes you anywhere else.

"We may have a little problem here," I say to Eddie. He's dozing beside me.

"How's that?"

"Somebody's been back there for a good while."

"Not much reason to be on this road," Eddie says. "Not many houses."

"One," I say, "and we're in it."

"Wouldn't do no good to try to outrun him."

"The road dead ends where we're gonna be sleeping tonight."

"If we're lucky." Eddie turns around. "Looks like a white truck, far as I can make out."

"What I figured."

"Guess you got what you wanted."

"You're the one pissed him off."

"I did it all for you, but I seriously underestimated the man. Figured he was all talk."

"Maybe he just wants to talk some more. Can you see if he's got his buddies in there?"

He turns back around. "Can't see inside, but he struck me as the kind of person likes to have a little backup. You got a weapon?"

"I didn't figure I'd need it. The only thing I'm carrying is a cell phone."

"I don't know who the hell you'd call," Eddie says. "I don't believe

Deputy fuck'n McKinney would be much assistance."

The lights behind are closer now. I remember a turnaround on the lakeside just beyond the curve ahead. "I don't like the idea that they're going to follow us all the way to the lake house. I think I'll pull over and see if they go on by."

Wrong move. They don't go by. We watch the headlights stop then ease back slowly around the curve and out of sight, so that the only sign that they're still there is the illumination of the fence posts across the road.

"So much for that idea," Eddie says. "I think they'll just sit there until we take off again. Not as if these characters got anything else to do out here in the wilds."

"I can't figure if this is serious or just a little boyish fun," I say, but then we hear the shot and feel the car tilt a fraction to the right.

"I believe they just shot out one of your rear tires," Eddie says, as we hear a second shot and feel the car level itself again. "And there goes the other one. We got to get the hell out of here. The sons of bitches are trying to kill us."

"Get to the front," I say. The shots came from the rear. What happens next would no doubt have appeared comical to a witness of the scene, who would have seen the two car doors open simultaneously, two men roll out, hit the ground and slither to the front of the BMW.

"Take off," I say. "This way, and then down to those trees." We run, keeping the car between us and the direction of the gunshots, then cut down the bank toward the lake. The bank slopes down toward a grove of trees by the edge of the water, and as we reach the trees we hear two shots in rapid succession. The matter-of-fact thud of the rounds against the tree trunks is sobering. An innocuous *tuk* is the closest I can come to approximating that sound, but you can't help thinking what one of those *tuks* would do to a skull.

"Do you think they're hollow points?" I ask, for no good reason. I have thrown myself down behind a trunk that now doesn't seem quite adequate. Eddie is leaning back against a tree, his hands on his knees, breathing hard.

"Un fuck'n believable."

Another shot and a *tuk* above my head. "Shooting high," I say.

"Just trying to scare us."

"Assholes."

"How many different guns you hear?"

"Fuck'n cretins."

"I think there's just one gun up there." *Tuk.*

"Redneck sons of bitches." *Tuk. Tuk.*

"You'd think they'd be doing some whooping and hollering, maybe a few rebel yells." It's eerily quiet except for the gunshots and the *tuks* and a quick hissing sound in the leaves when a round misses a tree trunk.

"Ignorant shits. I should never have come out to this dumb-ass place," Eddie says. "People down here are fuck'n crazy."

"They're not trying to kill us. They're just trying to scare us off."

"Well, it's sure as hell working," Eddie says.

My cell phone rings. I dig it out of a pocket, flip it open and hear Jesse's voice.

"I'm over it," she says. "When can I see you?"

"I'm kind of in the middle of something right now." Another shot and a *tuk* in the tree beside me.

"I don't mean tonight. Is your friend still there?"

"He's leaving tomorrow—if things work out."

"What things?"

"We'll talk tomorrow." *Tuk.* "I really do have to go."

"You're trying to get rid of me."

"I'll explain it all tomorrow."

"What needs explaining?"

"Please, Jesse."

"Call me," she says.

"I couldn't help noticing you didn't tell your friend you were being shot at," Eddie says.

"I didn't want to get her shot at. What's she going to do, drive down here in her little convertible and rescue us?"

"Must be something she could do. I would say just the presence of other people on the scene might be helpful."

"I'm telling you they're going to get bored with this and take off. They've made their point." Another shot.

B. J. Leggett

"Maybe not quite," Eddie says. "I believe I heard glass with that one."

"Oh, shit."

Another shot and a tinkle of glass. "I hope you got a low deductible," Eddie says. "I believe that was the windshield."

"I'll sue the fuckers."

"We never actually saw anybody, you know. I don't think you got a case."

"You saw the white truck."

"How many white pickup trucks you think they got in this county? And we keep saying them, but I'm not sure there's more than one up there."

"I'm going to nail him."

We hear the roar of an engine. "Looks like the fun's over for tonight," Eddie says. "How far we got to hike?"

"A mile or so. I'm going to nail the son of a bitch."

"Be sure and let me know what happens," Eddie says, "cause I'm gonna be a good ways from here."

XVII

In later years I have come to see that my mother, Katherine Marie O'Brian, Kate to her friends, Miss Katherine to her students, and six years dead, held an increasingly darkened view of life, which she attempted to cover over with various tricks and devices. Some of these she passed on to me. After the Billy Ratliff thing, when I had become moody and angry, she sat me down at the kitchen table, handed me a school tablet, and had me draw a line down the middle of the page. At the top of the left column I was instructed to print *NEGATIVE* and at the top of the other *POSITIVE*. Then she left the room and I dutifully filled in the columns, making sure the positives outweighed the negatives. I wasn't exactly fooled by this exercise, but it was curiously therapeutic, and I have returned to it over the years, if not always on paper.

Lying in bed, watching the pattern of the sun on the wardrobe across the room, I picture the negative column. *One, last night you and your friend were repeatedly fired upon by a person or persons unknown. Two, your friend wants to put as much distance between the two of you as possible. Three, your relationship with the woman who got you into this has become problematic. Four, there is no reason to believe you can assist in identifying her brother's killer. Five, in fact, your continued presence in McLean County is tenuous at best.* What else? *Six, your car is sitting on the side of a gravel road shot all to hell, and your insurance papers are packed away somewhere, including, most essentially, the phone number of your agent, whose name and company you do not recall.*

I'm pretty sure there's more, but I want to turn to the positive column, picturing it on the lined tablet. *One.* Nothing comes. *One.* There must be something. *One, you and your friend survived last night's shooting.* No, that's hardly a positive. I mentally erase it. *One, if this is the bottom, then things have to look up from here on out.*

Wrong. The cell phone on the bedside table rings. Jesse, I guess, and what will I tell her about last night?

Wrong again, although it's another familiar voice. "What the hell's going on over there?"

It's the closest to profanity I've ever heard from Chief-of-Detectives Deathridge.

"There's a lot going on, Chief. Which part are you referring to?"

"I've been informed that you and Lieutenant Carpenter were involved in a shooting last night."

"If getting shot at constitutes being involved in a shooting, then, yes, sir, we were."

"You didn't exchange fire?"

"We were both unarmed. We were returning home from a local bar."

"That's not the report I got."

"Then you were misinformed." I give him a fairly accurate account of the incident, omitting only the verbal skirmish between Eddie and Cotton May. I conclude with the observation that, as far as I can determine, there was only one shooter, and that in all probability his motive was simply to put a scare into us.

"And why would he want to do that?"

"I've been inquiring into the particulars of a local investigation." I stop, aware of how my language had reverted to the jargon of the police report. "A man named Bradley McLean was killed. Maybe you remember it."

"I do."

"There are people here who seem to resent my, ah, intervention into the situation."

"And just what is your interest in the case?"

"His sister, who's living here, asked me to, well, make some inquiries. She felt the local authorities weren't pursuing it with any urgency."

"I see. And Lieutenant Carpenter has been assisting you?"

"Well, not exactly. He just happened to be down here during his time off." I can see where he's going.

"But he accompanied you during some of these inquiries?"

"Well, he was there, yes. But he was not actively involved. In fact, he tried to discourage me from pursuing it."

"As I would," Deathridge says. "Robert, I'm no longer your supervisor, and I can't tell you what to do, but I can tell you that what you're doing is almost certain to get you into trouble, as you saw last night, and I can't have one of my own men involved. Is Carpenter there?"

"Yes, sir."

"Would you mind putting him on?"

"Certainly. It may take a minute. I'll have to locate him."

I rap at the open door of Eddie's bedroom. He's sitting on the side of the bed in his underwear, staring at the carpet, his hand extended toward me.

"This is—"

"Give me the phone," he says. "I heard."

I turn toward the door, but he points me to a chair and I sit, not uninterested in what is to follow.

"Yes, sir," he says and falls silent. "That's essentially what happened. I would have to say in addition that I exchanged words with a local character at a bar in Parris County, and he's the likely perp." He pauses. "No, sir. There was no return fire. My service revolver's locked in my glove compartment and we were in Shake's car." Pause. "I'm coming back today. Be back at work tomorrow morning." Pause. "In your office?" He turns his gaze to me and rolls his eyes. "Nine o'clock. I'll be there." He gestures toward me with the phone. "Wants to speak to you."

"Yes, sir?"

"A couple of things, Robert." His voice has lost its edge. "Officially, I'm strongly opposed to private citizens trying to conduct police business, as you probably know, and I suggest that you inform Stanton Giles that your inquiry has been concluded. Just a suggestion, but am I clear about where I stand officially?"

"Yes, sir."

"Unofficially, I would have to say that the McLean County Sheriff's Office does not always operate by the book. These are not men you want to push too hard."

"That's my impression also."

"One other thing. Your job here is still open if you have a change of heart about early retirement. I haven't put the paperwork through."

"I don't think I've had a change of heart, but could I ask you a question?"

"Fine."

"How did you hear about the incident last night?"

"McLean County Sheriff's Office."

"Giles?"

"That's right. He called me this morning and I told him I would speak to you."

"Now, that's very interesting. How would he know? This happened in a rural area miles from any living soul. The only person who could have reported it would have been the shooter. Why would he report his own crime?"

"I have no idea, but it sounds to me as if you're still making inquiries."

"You couldn't help me on this?"

"I could not."

"There's something really rotten over here."

"You have no authority. I have no authority. You're dealing with lawfully elected county officials."

"You're saying there's absolutely nothing that can be done?"

He's silent for a moment. "I'll give it some thought," he says finally. "One condition. Give me your word that you'll stop whatever it is that's stirring people up over there."

"All right, you've got my word on it."

"Your best decision would be to accompany Lieutenant Carpenter back to Knoxville today."

"No, sir, I've still got a few personal things to tie up here."

"We'll talk again," Deathridge says and breaks the connection.

I look over at Eddie, who hasn't moved from his position on the side of the bed. "Sorry if I got you into trouble."

"Not serious trouble," he says, still staring at the carpet. "Just a little lecture in his office tomorrow on the general topic of off-duty behavior. I can handle it."

"Interesting that Giles finally got what he wanted through

Deathridge. That business last night. How would Giles know about it? Even if somebody heard the shots, how would they know who was involved?"

"Couldn't tell you," Eddie says, "but I've lost interest in it."

"This is important. We need to think it through."

"What I need is some coffee," he says. "We got things to do before I leave. Got to take care of your car, get hold of your insurance agent."

"I got a slight problem on that. When I moved down here, I packed away a bunch of papers, and I can't remember about the insurance."

Eddie shakes his head. "Give me your phone. I'll take care of it."

"How do you know who to call?"

"You got the same as me." He retrieves his wallet from the table by the bed. "Make the coffee. I'm going to take care of it, but this is the last time. Me and Deathridge can't be around all the time. You got to learn to be responsible." He has located the card in the wallet. "Give me the phone."

"You want breakfast?"

"Coffee," he says. "The sooner we get this done the sooner I can get out of McLean fuck'n County." And then more softly, to himself, "Never been in a place they shoot you just for the sport of it."

B. J. Leggett

XVIII

I POUR the coffee into a thermal pot I found in the pantry, locate two of Bradley's Princeton mugs, and take everything out to the table on the deck, then, curious, walk to the back railing and look down the lake to the right. The grove of trees where we took shelter a few hours earlier is visible just at the point where the shoreline curves sharply to the east, and there is the BMW on the side of the road, tiny and, from this distance, unmarred.

When Eddie comes out, I point wordlessly to the now bucolic scene and when he gives me a puzzled look I say, "You can see it from here."

He sits down and pours his coffee. "Here's the deal," he says. "We're meeting the tow truck at ten. You got a camera?"

I nod.

"You need to make pictures of the damage for the insurance. They're taking it to someplace called East Tennessee Collision in Adair. Two to three weeks. You all right with that?"

"I don't know that I've got much choice."

"We could have pushed it in the lake, but it's too late now. Your insurance gives you two weeks of car rental, and there's a place in Adair. I'll drop you off on my way back to Knoxville. I'd try to talk you into going back with me but I know it wouldn't do any good."

"Thanks for taking care of it."

"No problem."

"If you need me to talk to Deathridge, I will. I'll tell him it was all me."

"I'll make that clear." He looks at his watch. "We got about an hour."

"Would you do me a favor? I'd like to get out there a little earlier, look around the car. We might pick up something."

"I'm going to indulge you this one last time."

It could have been worse. The side windows and the windshield are still largely intact, but they now bear sizable holes with spider webs of cracks running to the edges of the glass. There are tiny shards in the seats and on the ground outside, but there are no bullet holes I can see in the metal.

"There's honor even among assholes," I say. Eddie is searching the ground for casings. "He didn't fire into the metal."

"I don't see anything on the ground," he says, "but the windshield slug ought to be inside the car somewhere."

The windshield hole is on the passenger side, and I locate the hole in the front passenger seat, follow the trajectory into the back seat, locate a second hole, and dig the round out of the upholstery. "Pretty good shape. I'd say fairly large caliber revolver."

"Not my field," he says, "but I'll take it back with me if it'll make you feel better."

"I'd appreciate it. It's the only piece of physical evidence I've managed to gather since I've been here."

"Here's another piece." Eddie is kneeling beside the car on the passenger side. "I believe this is going to complicate things a little bit."

He points to the ground beside the door. "This is where he was shooting from. You see this?"

The grid of a boot sole is plainly visible in the dust. Then I see that there are several more, all identical.

"What strikes you about this?" He draws a circle in the dust around the most prominent.

"Not the right size."

"Right," he says. "Not what you would expect. Cotton May was wearing cowboy boots. This is more like a work shoe, and larger. Your man's got tiny little feet."

"Could've been one of his buddies."

"Could've been."

"We may have to rethink the whole business."

"You probably need to get some pictures of these," he says.

"I was pretty sure it was Cotton May. You said it was a white pickup."

"And I said there's a lot of white pickups around here. Be interesting to know what the deputy drives."

"Actually, we know somebody who could probably tell us. I fish out my wallet, find the card that says *Byron Holmes Produce* and punch in the number. "Just out of curiosity," I say when he picks up, "what kind of car does Jim McKinney drive?"

"You talking about the deputy sheriff?"

"That's right."

"Only thing I've ever seen him in was a police car. Why do you need to know?"

"There was a little incident out here last night. I thought maybe he might be involved."

"He's the one man around here you don't want to get crossways of," Byron Holmes says. "I could tell you some stories."

"I believe you. Anyway, thanks. You going to be around tomorrow? I was thinking about dropping by."

"Probably better if I come over to your place," Byron Holmes says.

"Why's that?"

"I don't think you want to be seen around here. Somebody might get the wrong idea."

"The wrong idea about what? Has something happened?"

"We've had a little vandalism. Somebody tried to burn down my barn."

"We've had a little vandalism here too," I say. "We need to talk."

"Call me tomorrow," he says.

LATER, in the parking lot of the car rental in Adair, I inform Eddie that I now have a workable theory of what's going on. He holds up both hands in surrender. "I'm out of this," he says, "and if I'm not mistaken you told Deathridge you were out of it too."

"This is just between us."

"Go write your novel." We walk back to his car and he slides behind the wheel.

I lean in the open door. "I can't just quit cold turkey. I got to ease off."

He turns the ignition and shuts the door, sliding down the window. "I've said all I'm going to say."

"I'll call you about the slug."

"No, I'll call you. With Deathridge on my ass and all, I probably won't see you for a while."

"We'll always have Parris."

He shakes his head sadly, pulls out of the parking lot, and heads north on 411 toward Knoxville.

B. J. Leggett

XIX

WITH Eddie gone I find my solitude at the lake house for the first time oppressive. After an hour or so of staring at a black sheet of paper and thinking of reasons not to call Jesse, I decide to drive into Prosperity with the excuse that I need to replenish my grocery supplies and check my mail.

No mail, Miss Edna informs me, and she hopes I haven't driven all this way for nothing. Why not give her my phone number and she will call me if anything comes in, except of course for junk mail. Something that looks personal, she says. I give her my cell number.

At the grocery it is of some comfort to see Mr. Wilson at his computer and Robin at her post in her regulation khaki shorts. She gives me a conspiratorial smile when I push my cart up to her register.

"Find out anything about Bradley McLean's death?"

"How did you know I was looking?"

"Word gets around. They said you were a policeman from Knoxville and you came down here to find out who killed him."

"I haven't found anything, and I've been told to stop looking. You still hold to the love triangle, I take it."

She nods. "But I don't think they're ever going to find out."

"Is that the consensus? What do your friends say?"

"Different things," she says, passing a plastic jug of milk across the scanner.

"Anybody ever bring up somebody named Cotton May?"

"How do you know him?"

"I've run into him a couple of times."

She rings up my total and takes my credit card. "You want me to take these out to your car?"

"Sure. You don't want to talk about Cotton May?"

"I don't really have anything to say about him." She walks ahead, pushing the cart.

Outside, I see Jesse's car parked in front of the bank. "You do know who he is?"

"Everybody knows Cotton May."

"Like that's where you go to get drugs?"

"I don't see your car."

"It's that little one over there."

"What happened to the other one?"

"In the shop. Cotton May's probably responsible for putting it there. You ever hear anything like that? He and his friends shooting up somebody's car?"

She shakes her head.

"What about robbing a convenience store?"

We are at the car now, and she leans across the cart and looks past me in the general direction of the Rosewood Cafe. "One of the things my friends say is that it's probably not a good idea to be seen talking to you."

"So next time I come in I should go to another cashier?"

She shrugs, and we put the groceries in the back seat. When I offer her a tip she stuffs it into her back pocket and, without looking at me, turns the cart around, and walks briskly back into Wilson's.

I wait for a sighting of Jesse, leaning against the car and observing Prosperity's social scene. Miss Edna comes out of the post office, locks the door, and heads home for lunch. A black Mercedes pulls up in front of the Rosewood, and Sam Rivers in his kitchen whites gets out, carrying a large burlap bag. When he sees me he sets the bag down beside the car and walks over.

"I haven't seen you since the night you and Jesse came in. I hope we didn't disappoint you." We shake hands formally.

"Not at all. I've just been tied up with one thing and another."

"Yeah, I heard a rumor. I don't know if it's true."

"What's that?"

"That you're conducting an investigation into Bradley's. . . ." His voice trails off.

"Murder. Well, not exactly, or at least I wouldn't call it an investigation. I did ask a few questions and apparently got some people upset, so I've backed off."

"May I ask what you've uncovered so far?"

"As far as the murder? Not much."

He persists. "I mean like motive, suspects."

I shake my head. "Not anything substantial." Not anything at all, I could have told him, but he has me curious now about his own motive.

"You may have heard that Bradley and I had been on the outs just before he died." So is that it? *What are people saying about me?*

"I heard that."

"I thought maybe you'd be around to talk."

"I didn't see the point of it. Jesse told me it was something silly, I forget exactly what." I might as well hear his version of it.

"Well, it had to do with buying vegetables from Byron Holmes."

"Yeah, I remember now, but I figured there must have been something more than that."

"You didn't find that sufficiently convincing?"

"I've never known people to stop speaking over vegetables."

He frowns, starts to say something, then thinks better of it.

"But it doesn't matter what I think. Whatever it was I was doing, and I'm not sure myself, it's over, and if you say you had a falling out over Byron Holmes' produce, that's fine with me."

"You asked me and I told you," he says with a little heat. "Here comes your friend." He waves at Jesse across the parking lot. "I've got to go make a roux." He walks back to the Mercedes, retrieves his burlap bag, and disappears into the Rosewood.

As I watch Jesse walking toward me in white shorts that look familiar, I reflect on one thing Sam Rivers said. *You didn't find that sufficiently convincing?* That's not something people say about factual matters, but about stories, lies.

"You driving this or just resting on it?" Jesse arrives wearing a quizzical expression.

"It's about a two-hour story. What are you doing for lunch?"

"I'm free," she says, "if you promise not to talk about dinner the other night with your friend."

"Fine. I'd just as soon forget it."

"But you are going to tell me everything?"

"Everything. And last night was particularly eventful."

"And you see you were wrong."

"I am Lazarus come from the dead, come back to tell you all."

"That's T. S. Eliot," she says. "Don't forget I was an English major. Is this a rental?"

"Yep. My car's in the shop, but that's part of the story."

"That's one ugly car."

"You got a favorite lunch place?"

"There's a little place in Sevierville that Sam Rivers likes. Vietnamese couple. Bradley used to—" She stops and winces. "Sorry. I was just going to say that Bradley used to eat there a lot. I've got to stop avoiding places I associate with him."

"So Vietnamese it is."

"See if you can cheer me up in two hours."

"I'll try. Get in."

"Are you kidding? I wouldn't be caught dead in that car. I'll drive."

"I've got groceries."

"So why don't I follow you to the lake house, and then I'll drive you to Sevierville."

"Fine. Do you need to change, or do they allow shorts at this place?"

"The Vietnamese are very permissive."

"I believe you were wearing those the other day at the old pond."

"Part of the time," she says.

AFTER lunch, driving back from Sevierville, she's still trying to sort things out. "So you were sure it was Cotton May that shot up your car and now you're not?" She is driving too fast on a narrow blacktop road that runs past small fields and white frame houses.

"I'm less sure, but I think I can find out."

"But you said you gave your word to that man."

"We have to make a distinction here. I gave my word to Deathridge that I wouldn't interfere in a murder investigation . Now we're talking about somebody who shot at me and vandalized my car."

"That's a very fine distinction."

"Maybe so, but I'm going to talk to Byron Holmes this afternoon."

"What could he possibly tell you?"

"The same people who shot at me may have tried to burn down his barn. I don't know for sure who they are, but I think he does."

"Except he's not going to tell you."

"Things have changed. I'm in it now. People are shooting at me, trying to run me out of town. And now I'm not doing this for the McLean family. I'm doing it for myself."

"I want you to stop too," she says. "You could end up like Bradley and it would be my fault."

"From this point on it wouldn't be your fault. I hereby absolve you of any responsibility. From this point it's all me."

"Bobby, don't be silly. I wanted you to look into it, but it's gotten serious. Can't we go back to drinking martinis on the deck and watching the sunset and maybe some innocent flirtation?"

"We can. Right after I do this one last thing," I say. "So could you drop me off, and I'll call Byron Holmes and then it's all martinis and sunsets and God knows what."

"Have you ever noticed how one last thing always leads to another?" she says, and she is right. Or at least this one last thing turns out to be the beginning of something else.

I TRY calling Byron Holmes repeatedly with no success, so in the late afternoon, disregarding his warning, I drive over to the farm. Pulling up the long driveway, I see that his barn is still there, his truck is gone, and his young Mexican field hand is sitting on his front steps watching me intently as I get out of the car. I walk up to the porch, hoping to learn of Byron Holmes' whereabouts, but that proves more difficult than I have anticipated since Jesús has little English and I have only the remnants of high-school Spanish. But through a combination of gestures and a few shared words I learn, first, that Jesús is waiting for his brother to take him home—*hermano*, I recognize—and, secondly, that Byron Holmes has disappeared.

Turning an imaginary steering wheel, I suggest that perhaps he is out making deliveries, but Jesús disputes this by pantomiming a tomato-picking motion with his hands and repeating *No,* which I interpret to mean there's nothing harvested for him to deliver. I try the front door, but it's locked.

I point to the barn and ask about the fire. Jesús gestures for me to follow, and leads me to the charred wall. There's still the smell of gasoline in the grass beside the wall, and it appears to be an amateurish job. Somebody has simply splashed gasoline against the side of the barn and lit it. But I also note that the fire has been set on the side of the barn visible from the house, which does not strike me as especially bright even for an amateur arsonist. But then I reconsider. Whoever set the fire didn't particularly care if it was spotted from the house. It was simply the act of arson that was the message, and I see the parallel with the BMW. Not too much damage, just enough to constitute a warning.

The two of us stand looking at the charred wall in silence." So what do you think happened to Byron Holmes?" I ask after a time, not really expecting an answer.

Jesús looks at me with a blank expression.

I try again. "*Dondé es?*"

"*Muerto,*" he says.

"Dead? Byron Holmes is dead? Did you see something? Are you certain?" I search my Spanish memory. "*Seguro?*"

"*No,*" he says. He spreads his arms and shrugs, as if to say I don't know but it's possible.

"You're guessing he's dead, *muerto,* but you don't know for sure? *Seguro?*"

He shakes his head." *No,*" and repeats the shrug. He points to the charred wall and then makes his right hand into a gun, the index finger extended and the thumb cocked. He places his finger to his temple. "*Asesinato,*" he says.

All of this I translate as, "No, I am not certain but my best guess is that the people who set fire to his barn killed him."

XX

THAT is my first thought too, but the wild card in all this is the man himself. My father once said that Byron Holmes talked like a character in a novel, and when I call Jesse with the news of his disappearance, she says something similar.

"That's just Byron Holmes."

"Meaning?"

"He's acting out one of his stories."

"You don't think it's serious?"

"Did you report it?"

"I'm going to call as soon as I hang up with you."

"They won't think it's serious either."

She's right. I talk to a deputy named Jeremy Carter, the only civil officer I have spoken to in the Sheriff's Department. I tell him what I know, including the half-hearted attempt to burn the barn.

"Let's give it a few days," he says. "I've got a feeling he'll turn up."

"You want to go look around out there? I could meet you."

He pauses. "I know Byron Holmes," he says. "He was my twelfth grade English teacher. You may not know that he's always been a little theatrical."

"That seems to be the consensus."

"If you don't hear something in a few days, call back."

"How can I be sure I deal with you? I don't seem to get along very well with your colleagues. Jim McKinney ran me out of a bar in Parris City a few nights ago."

"Is that so?" Deputy Carter sounds amused. "Just leave me a message and I'll call you back, but I don't think it'll come to that. Byron

Holmes is thought of around here as something of a local character. There's a lot of stories, and his going missing wouldn't be thought of as unusual by people that know him."

I've never thought of Byron Holmes as a local character, but I have to agree with the deputy that the odds are against his being dead, which cheers me up considerably, and I decide to have a drink.

In the kitchen, I hear the cell phone ringing back on the deck, but the full martini glass retards my progress and it has stopped by the time I reach it. I retrieve the number of the caller, a Knoxville number, I see, and dial it.

I am informed that I have reached the voice mail of Agent Lloyd Emerson of the Tennessee Bureau of Investigation. Agent Emerson is out of the office, and I am given the hours when he can be reached and a number to be used in an emergency. I click off and walk back to the living room, find a yellow legal pad and write down the emergency number. I figure getting a call from any police agency constitutes an emergency so I start punching in the number but then look at my watch and see it's just after five. I was apparently the last name on Agent Emerson's list of things to do today, and he is in all likelihood in his car on the way home. I should at least give him time to get comfortable.

I walk back to the deck to ponder the question of why I have received a call from the Tennessee Bureau of Investigation. Is Byron Holmes somehow mixed up in it? No, John Deathridge. He said he would give it some thought, and apparently Agent Lloyd Emerson was what he came up with. He can't help me, but maybe the Tennessee Bureau of Investigation can.

I give Agent Emerson forty-five minutes, then make the call from the deck.

"This is Lloyd Emerson." His tone is not encouraging.

"My name is Robert O'Brian. You called me about an hour ago, or somebody from your office did."

"John Deathridge asked me to get in touch with you." His tone softens a bit, but is still wary.

"That's what I figured. He was my boss until a few weeks ago, and I asked him to help me out on something down here in McLean County. Is this a good time, or should I wait till you're back in the office?"

B. J. Leggett

"Good as any," he says. "Tell me about it."

"You want the long version or the short version?"

"Might as well get it all."

"Let me look at my notes." I pull the legal pad across the table and flip it open.

"You got notes?" Emerson laughs. "Is this going to take a while?"

"Not long. It'll go faster with the notes."

"I've got a glass of Wild Turkey over ice on the coffee table," he says. "I'm going to trust you to get through your notes before I get through the whiskey."

I tell him everything that's happened, or almost everything, between the time of my arrival in McLean County and the disappearance of Byron Holmes. He interrupts twice, once to clarify my relationship with the McLean family and the second time, at the end, to ask if Byron Holmes has offered any evidence of a local drug ring.

"No evidence," I say, "unless you count barn burning."

"You got anything solid?"

"Well, I got a car with the windows shot out, I got a slug taken from my back seat, and I got a photograph of the shooter's boot print."

I hear the clinking of ice. "From what you've told me, there's two things going on here," he says, "and there's no indication they're related. I mean the drugs and the murder. The drug thing, hell, what would be surprising was that there wasn't drug trafficking in McLean County. It's a tradition down there. Seventy-five years ago it would have been selling moonshine. They've just switched drugs. And these mountain boys seem to think it's their right—make a little corn whiskey, sell a little weed or what have you. Their own property, they ought to be able to do what they want to on it." Emerson pauses. "Like the old boy who's charged with having sexual congress with a cow. He can't understand the charge, keeps saying 'but it was *my cow*.'"

I laugh appreciatively. "I'm not naive about these things. I worked in a police department, and I was as cynical as the next man, but I've never seen an outfit as bad as this bunch. All I'm saying is nothing's going to happen with Bradley McLean's murder or anything else as long as they're left in charge. I know you can't come riding in here like the Lone Ranger and clean everything up, but what can you do? What would it take for the TBI to intervene?"

"One of two things," Emerson says, "and don't get me wrong. I've heard some things about McLean County law enforcement like everybody else in the business, but you know as well as I do that rumor's one thing and evidence is another."

"One of two things, you said."

"One, we could be asked by local law enforcement to aid in an investigation, whether it's drugs or murder. You and I both know that ain't likely to happen. The other way would be that we can present solid evidence that there's corruption there or some other malfeasance or incompetency that would require us to step in and take over an investigation."

"That wouldn't be easy."

"It's happened."

"So you're saying I get you evidence against Giles or McKinney and you're in?"

"I'm not the one that makes that decision, but yes, most likely. And just between us, there are people here who would love an excuse to bust Giles or McKinney. You're not the first man that's ever suspected something's going on down there."

"Do you know them?"

"Never met either one of them, but I've heard stories. Did you ever hear the story about McKinney and the prostitute?"

"Is this a joke?"

"True story, supposedly. They were trying this young woman in Adair for prostitution, which she admitted to, and she pointed to the deputy in the courtroom and said he had been one of her customers, and McKinney says, 'Worst piece of ass I ever had.' Anyway, you've got my number. You find something solid, give me a call. In the meantime, try to stay out of trouble. You're just a private citizen now like everybody else."

"Deathridge told me the same thing, in so many words."

"John's a smart man. If he worked down there, we'd probably already know who killed that fellow." He pauses, and I hear the click of ice cubes again and imagine the last of the Wild Turkey being drained away. "I may be talking to you again, but I doubt it." And Agent Emerson is gone.

I doubt it too, given that the bar has just been set pretty high, and that I'm no match for Stanton Giles. The only way I'll be talking to Lloyd Emerson again will be with the help of somebody who knows more about the criminal element of McLean County than I do, and, except for the criminals themselves, that seems to boil down to Byron Holmes, who is unfortunately unavailable for consultation.

XXI

I AM *Lazarus come from the dead, Come back to tell you all*, the letter begins, quoting the Eliot line I had cited in Wilson's parking lot not so long ago. I was apprised of it by a phone call from Miss Edna, who told me that I had my first real mail if the junkers had not resorted to pencil. A package, she said. From Knoxville. She would hold it for me for the next time I was in town, which turned out to be thirty minutes later, so intense was my curiosity. At the post office I noted that the small package was indeed addressed in pencil in large block letters, no return address, a Knoxville postmark.

"Looks like a child's hand," Miss Edna said, hoping for more information. When none was forthcoming she asked if I had children, and as I made my escape, I heard her remarking to another patron how odd that such a handsome young man had never gotten married.

When I open the package back at the lake house, I see that it contains a single folded sheet and, underneath it, something that makes me look back at the address. Has there been a mistake? Under the letter is a small digital camera. A camera? Why would somebody send me a camera? Then I see that attached to the camera is a short cable of the kind used to download images, which provides a possible answer to my question. I unfold the sheet, and look at the bottom for a signature. There is none, but when I read the Eliot line, it's as good as a signature, the literary epigraph being Byron Holmes' signature of a sort, one he employed in almost everything he's ever written.

I read the short text, also in pencil in large block letters. *This will explain things you may have found mysterious. You'll note that the sequence is important. Note especially number three. Do with them as you will.*

B. J. Leggett

That is all. I read it over again. *You'll note that the sequence is important.* I take that as a reference to images stored in the camera. I assume I'm about to view some photographs taken by my correspondent, but why does my correspondent feel it necessary to hide his identity and employ a highly cryptic style? First possibility—it's just Byron Holmes being Byron Holmes, playing his version of Deep Throat to my Bob Woodward. Second possibility—it's a message from a man on the run, not wishing to reveal anything should it fall into the wrong hands. Third possibility—it's a combination of one and two. Fourth possibility—the writer is not Byron Holmes, but someone who genuinely has something to reveal to me and does not wish to betray his identity.

I dismiss that. The Eliot quotation says Byron Holmes. How many other people in McLean County can quote from "The Love Song of J. Alfred Prufrock"? Well, Jesse of course, and, who knows, maybe there are hundreds of poetry lovers in McLean County. Perhaps an Eliot reading group meets monthly to discuss the obscurities of the *Four Quartets.*

I turn on the camera and locate the control to view the stored images. What appears is a shot of two men, possibly of Mexican descent, unloading a truck. In the background are a barn and other farm buildings. In the second shot the men are carrying small bales, which I recognize, into what appears to be a metal storage shed. Third shot—they are shoveling something onto a large sheet of plastic lying in front of the door of the shed. There may be two other men in the background conversing, although on the camera's small screen they are difficult to make out. Fourth shot—one of the workmen carries more bales into the shed; the other carries the folded sheet of plastic. Fifth shot—same scene but one of the men in the background is pointing toward the camera. Sixth shot—the two workmen are looking toward the camera, one of them pointing. Seventh shot—the two workmen are running toward the camera, the two men in the background watching with interest. Eighth shot—the two workmen, now closer, are running toward the camera, but now I notice that one of them appears to have something in his right hand.

I read the letter again. *This will explain things you may have found mysterious.* Yes. Byron Holmes' sudden disappearance is no mystery. Had he stayed he might have ended up like Bradley McLean. *Note especially number three.* I click to the third photograph, the men shoveling something onto the sheet of plastic. They have dropped one of the bales and are being directed to clean it up by the two men in the background. Why should I note this especially? Because there might be traces of it on the ground in front of the storage shed? Or is he directing me to the two men in the background? This is the first shot in which they appear.

I try to picture the scene. A portly man of some years who resembles the French novelist Gustav Flaubert is running across a field pursued by two Mexican laborers. How did he outrun them? He had a good head start, but how far did he have to go? That would depend on where the photographs were taken. That crucial bit of information has been omitted, but I think I know.

I LEAVE the car in Byron Holmes' gravel drive and walk back to the barn. It is a typical East Tennessee barn with a wide hall down the middle, open on both ends, two stalls on the right side, one on the left, and what looks to be a tack room, a hayloft above. I walk through the open hallway to the fields below that extend to the creek marking the back property line. Expecting to spot the storage shed in the photographs from somewhere along the bank of the creek, I walk the property line, but see nothing except empty fields. Making my way down the bank, I find a crossing, and climb up the other side. Now I'm somewhat more vulnerable, trespassing on somebody else's farm, that of Cotton May, as I recall.

I walk through last year's broom sedge, knee-high and yellow now. On a well-managed farm this would have been burned off in the spring or plowed under. Cotton May obviously does not depend on the bounty of the land. I have my eye on a rise covered with locust trees. It seems a likely spot for secreting oneself while photographing criminal activity. From the trees I look down on the farm, surprisingly far away, a house, a barn, and several outbuildings that look familiar, but not the metal shed from the photographs. This is approximately where Byron Holmes stood and where he was spotted. The buildings looked closer in his photographs because he obviously used a long-range lens, which also explains how he made his escape. His pursuers were not as close as they appeared.

I take several photographs from the hilltop with Byron Holmes' camera just to verify the scene—same house and barn and outbuildings, absent storage shed. (*Your honor, I submit these photographs as evidence that the defendants, learning that their clandestine activities had been recorded, have attempted to alter the crime scene.*) What I need as a clincher is a photograph of the foundation where the shed stood and a sample of the soil at the spot of photograph three. (*Your honor, this soil sample will reveal traces of the content of the bales being stored in a shed that has mysteriously disappeared.*) To stroll across a drug trafficker's farm lot with a camera would, however, be pushing my luck and risking the loss of the evidence I already have, which is considerable.

Enough, I think, back at the lake house, to venture another call to Agent Emerson. First, though, I want to look at the photographs on a computer screen. Maybe there are other surprises, like the two shadowy men in the background. Be interesting if they are recognizable. Be even more interesting if at least one of them turns out to be a resident of McLean County, like, say, Cotton May.

I do not find Cotton May in the photographs, but I find something better. On the computer they are crystal clear, and I see that the object in the right hand of Byron Holmes' pursuer is not a weapon, as I had thought, but a glove he has apparently taken off. As for the four men, three of them are unfamiliar to me, but one is enough.

Or maybe not. Time to take stock. Byron Holmes has, against all odds, collected evidence of wrongdoing in McLean County, but is it of any value? It would be foolish of me even to let local law enforcement know that I possess it, and the state police, in Agent Emerson's account, have set an impossibly high bar for intervention. The newspapers? Obviously, Byron Holmes could have taken that option and chose not to. Not my call. He sent the photographs to me, so I assume he meant me to make use of them. I have to give it a shot, high bar or not.

I locate Emerson's cell number and check the time—after six. He should be at home, maybe into his second Wild Turkey.

"I didn't expect to hear from you again," he says.

"I didn't expect to be calling you."

"You must have something."

"I have two sets of photographs I'd like to send you along with some commentary explaining the circumstances."

"You took these?"

"A friend took the first set using a telephoto lens. I took the second set without one from the same place a few days later, just to confirm the location. I believe my commentary will make everything clear."

"Why don't you just tell me what you've got?" Agent Emerson is apparently not intrigued.

"I think you need to see the photographs."

"Well at least tell me what they're photographs of."

"The first set shows what I believe you will agree is criminal activity of a fairly serious nature. The second set shows the crime scene after it has been somewhat altered."

"Are we talking drugs here?"

"Yes."

Agent Emerson pauses, as if to better articulate his response. "I believe I made it clear to you in our previous conversation that the Bureau is not likely to intervene in a McLean County drug investigation unless we're invited, and we're not likely to be invited. If that's all you got, I'm not interested in your photographs."

"I believe you also said that the Bureau could intervene in the case of malfeasance or corruption on the part of local law enforcement."

"That's right."

"And I believe you said you knew of Deputy Jim McKinney of the McLean County Sheriff's Office."

"That's right."

"Would you recognize him if you saw him?"

"I believe we have photographs of the sheriff and chief deputy of McLean County."

"I'm going to send these to your office, and you can do with them as you will."

XXII

APPARENTLY Agent Emerson's will is to do nothing, hardly surprising. I imagine the TBI brass sitting around a table, speaking in turn.

Can of worms.

Wouldn't touch it.

Not our problem

Stanton Giles' problem.

Drugs? Probably couldn't buy a bottle of aspirin down there.

How many residents of McLean County does it take to run a drug operation?

Whatever the reason, nothing happens, and after a week I decide to call Lloyd Emerson for an explanation. What I get instead is a curious conversation with a no-nonsense woman who answers Emerson's number. I identify myself and ask to speak to him. That will not be possible at the moment, she tells me.

"Could I call back later?"

"Agent Emerson is on special assignment," she says.

"Meaning?"

"He will not be available for the immediate future."

"I have his personal cell number and—"

"He'll not be accepting any calls."

"When do you expect him to be available?"

"I don't have that information. Now, if you'll excuse me." And there is a click and a dial tone.

I interpret our exchange to mean simply that Agent Emerson doesn't wish to speak to me about certain matters in McLean County, and I imagine another scene at the TBI office. *What do I say if Mr. O'Brian calls?* the no-nonsense woman is asking. *Tell him I'm on special assignment,* Emerson replies. *What does that mean exactly?* she asks. *I don't know. I just made it up. Sounds good though.* Emerson grins. *Did you hear the one about the old boy who had sexual congress with a goat?*

So that, as they say, is that. I have given it my best shot, but nothing is going to happen. I stand on the deck, cell phone in hand, feeling like a kid who's just gotten his knuckles rapped. I look across Lake Eleanor at the mountains to the east, pondering my own immediate future, which does not appear promising at the moment. A mental checklist seems in order. *One, a dead end at TBI; any chance of criminal justice in McLean County now appears quite remote. Two, successful launch of a second novel appears equally remote. Three, relations with Jesse McLean appear problematic.*

Number three turns out to be an understatement. I call Jesse later in the afternoon and invite her over for a drink. I have decided, after much internal debate, to tell her about the mysterious letter from Byron Holmes, the photographs, the call to the TBI, the whole bit. And I do. In great detail.

"When was that?" she asks when I finish and take a sip of my drink, waiting for a response. "I mean when did you get the letter?" We are in our customary spot on the deck. She is wearing faded jeans and a black silk blouse.

"I've just told you something incredibly interesting and your response is, When did this happen?"

"When did you get the letter?" she repeats, and it is becoming clear the direction the conversation is about to take.

"Early last week."

"Why didn't you tell me?"

"I'm telling you now."

"We've had this conversation before. You said you were going to tell me everything."

"About Bradley. I said I was going to tell you everything about Bradley. As far as I know this has nothing to do with Bradley."

She has acquired a wounded look. "Why do you keep things from me? What possible reason would you have? I thought we were close. Maybe I've got the wrong idea about us."

"I haven't told anybody except the guy at TBI."

"I'm not just anybody," she says. "I thought we were in this together."

"You're right, and I finally came around to that."

"What's happened to us?" She seems genuinely surprised and mystified, as if she were looking at me for the first time. "We got off to such a great start and now it doesn't feel right."

"I'm sorry."

"You're more interested in Byron Holmes' feelings than in mine."

"I know it looks that way." But this isn't about Byron Holmes.

"You keep me at a distance. I thought—never mind what I thought. I've got to go." She stands and retrieves a ring of keys noisily from the glass tabletop.

"You haven't finished your drink."

"This has been a problem from the beginning. You just want to talk and drink martinis. You keep pretending this is just a social relationship." She gives me an incredulous look. "Is this about my family?"

I'm not sure how to answer that but I shake my head.

"This is not working," she says." We need a serious talk."

"I'm up for it." This has been brewing for a long time.

"Not now."

"Any time, Jesse."

She starts to say something else but stops herself, and I see she is crying.

"I don't understand what just happened. How could I make you so unhappy without even knowing it?"

"You were the only good thing in my miserable life, and now even that's turned bad." She walks into the house through the open French doors. "I won't be seeing you for a while," she says over her shoulder.

"What do you mean? Are you going away?"

"I was going to tell you today," she says from the living room, and then I hear the slam of the front door.

Another dead end. Two dead ends, maybe three counting the novel. Which leads me to consider my options. I can stay in Prosperity, forget about the novel, forget about criminal investigations, find something else to do, try to make up with Jesse, eat expensive dinners at the

Rosewood Café, have drinks on the deck and watch the sunset. Or I can return to Knoxville, rent a dreary apartment, see if Deathridge will still take me back. The first is infinitely more appealing, but I know I'm heading inexorably toward the second. I decide to wait a little longer before making the call to Deathridge, dreading the prospect of slinking back to the jeers of my former colleagues and no doubt acquiring yet another nickname in the process.

XXIII

I SEEM to be one of the few readers of fiction who occasionally questions the motives of narrators who are confiding to me their most intimate feelings and experiences. *Why are you telling me this*? I can't help asking. A quite sophisticated reader with whom I once discussed the issue responded, in effect, that this is just the way fiction works. It's not a question we need to raise, she said, because we accept the convention of the unmotivated narrator. Even to raise the question risks confusing a Philip Roth novel, say, with something else. Maybe so, but it still bothers me at times, and I want to confess at this point that my own narrative is not entirely without motivation.

After I reach the conclusion that my Prosperity escapade is over I decide to put it all down on paper, beginning with my retirement from the Knoxville Police Department and ending, I assume, with my packing up and heading back to Knoxville, Bradley McLean's murder unsolved and the novel unwritten.

If I can't write a novel, I reason, I can write something. And so I begin my account of the Bradley McLean affair, thinking, I must also confess, that if I get it right it might, with some creative rewriting, become the basis of a story the present participants will not recognize as their own. Or maybe not, but then what else do I have to do? With Eddie and Jesse now boycotting me and Byron Holmes in hiding, address unknown, I have become the hermit of McLean County.

So I pull out my legal pad and felt-tip pens and set up shop under the umbrella on the deck. I start with the retirement party at Kelly's, which seems the logical beginning, then loop back to Bradley's funeral and my re-introduction to Jesse McLean. And for the first time I put into words my version of the Billy Ratliff incident. The writing does not exactly flow, but unlike my attempts at the novel, it comes steadily, and by the third day of composition, sitting at my station on the deck, I have reached the point of my entry into Prosperity, coming down off the ridge pulling a rental trailer. I'm at the fork, trying to decide which road leads to the lake house, when I look up from the legal pad to see a swirl of dust rounding the bend of the lake. It's late afternoon, and I've already decided this is to be the last page for the day, so I cap the pen, flip the pad shut, and walk over to the railing, glad of a diversion after three days without seeing another human being.

As the dust gets closer, I recognized the car and walk down the wooden steps and around the side of the house. In the driveway Jesse sits behind the wheel of her mother's black Mercedes. She makes no move to get out, leaning forward and working intently with her CD player. I open the passenger-side door.

"Almost martini time," I say over the music.

She punches the music off and pats the seat beside her. "Sit down." She is wearing what looks to be a man's work shirt over jeans and she bears a serious expression.

I sit. "You don't want to come up?"

"I can't, got to get back. I just came over to say good-bye."

Her pronouncement has the desired effect. "You mean temporarily or permanently?"

"I guess that's still to be determined," she says.

"Then a farewell drink is certainly in order."

"I've just got a minute. There's a million things to do, shut up the house, stop the mail. You know, all that."

"So you're going to be away for quite a while. With your mother, I assume."

"We haven't decided how long. We're flying to New York tomorrow and then, after a couple of days there, on to Dublin."

"Ireland? You're going to Ireland? Jesus. I would have thought something like that would have come up in conversation."

"I was going to tell you the other day but I was too upset."

"Was there something in particular that led to it? I mean, Ireland—"

"Several things," she says. "One, that's where Mother's side of the family's from—Cork in the southwest—and she's always talked about going. Two, after Bradley's death she got a letter from one of her relatives inviting us over." She pauses for a moment. "And this is a good time for a change of scenery for her. She's hardly been out of the house since the funeral."

"When somebody gives you three reasons she can't come to your party, none of them is the real reason."

"Did you just make that up?"

"It's not original with me, but I used it in something I was writing a couple of days ago."

"So you think I haven't told you the real reason?"

"I don't know. Have you?"

"Okay, try this. Mother's going to be just as miserable in Ireland as she is here. I'm the one that needs to get away for a while. From McLean County and Bradley's murder and maybe you most of all."

"You've given it a lot of thought?"

"But it's still muddled. And while I'm away you need to give some thought to your particular hang-ups about younger sisters of high school friends or whatever your problem is."

"I promise, but there's a possibility I won't be here when you get back. The novel's not going well, so I got no excuse to stay. Maybe I'll go to Ireland."

"Not funny. But please stay until I get back. Would you at least do that?"

"Of course, if that's what you want, but why at least? I'm not the one taking off tomorrow for Western Europe."

"No, but you're the one—" She stops abruptly and turns to face me, leaning forward with a little smile. "If I knew how to finish that sentence I wouldn't be in such a muddle." She opens her arms to me and we embrace in the front seat of her mother's car like a couple of teenagers.

"A lot's gone on since that afternoon in the church basement," she says over my shoulder.

"Quite a bit."

"I was sure something was going to happen with us." She turns away, staring through the windshield.

"It has."

"Not exactly what I had in mind," she says, turning the key in the ignition.

When I see the second column of dust, my first thought is that it's Jesse coming back to resume our running battle, but as it gets closer I note that the car is white and official-looking. I don't recognize it or the man who is exiting as I come around the side of the house, although his dark suit and sunglasses give him a Secret Service look, or maybe Tommy Lee Jones in *Men in Black*.

We meet in the middle of the driveway and he sticks out a hand. "Lloyd Emerson," he says, "and I'm hoping you're Robert O'Brian."

"I'd about given up on you."

"Well, we're a bureaucracy and it takes us a while to get moving. But we haven't exactly been idle. Just because you don't know about it don't mean it ain't happening."

"So you're in it? I appreciate it very much."

"Don't thank me. I got out-voted. My position was don't touch it—nothing but trouble. Bad press. Local resentment. And probably bad outcome. Official corruption's a hard thing to prove, especially if you're dealing with people been in the business a long time. But your photographs impressed some people."

I don't quite know how to respond, since I don't know why he's here. I gesture over my shoulder toward the house. "I was about to fix myself a drink. Could I fix you one?"

"You got whiskey?"

"I got George Dickel."

"That'll do fine," he says.

I take him in through the front door, pointing out the Catherine Wiley as we walk into the living room. "Have a seat and I'll locate the whiskey."

"Nice place," he says standing at the French doors looking down the lake.

"I believe I've mentioned the McLean family. They're letting me stay here while I do some writing." Not exactly true now. "Well, originally that was the plan."

"And your connection is through the son."

"Bradley. We were friends at one point in high school. His sister got me into it actually. Thought the local people weren't doing anything."

"Unless something changes we're not looking into that," he says. "Just the drugs and possible police involvement."

"I figured that, but then you never know what'll turn up when you start poking around. You take water with your whiskey?"

"No water, but a little ice would fix me up just fine."

When I come back with the drinks, he is seated on the sofa, his jacket removed.

"Thanks," he says, looking at his watch, when I place his glass on the coffee table. "It's after office hours so I can drink this guilt free." He raises his glass. "Cheers," he says wearily.

I take a chair on the other side of the table and raise my glass. "You don't show much enthusiasm for this assignment. I hope that's not a bad omen."

"I'm not looking forward to dealing with Stanton Giles, if that's what you mean."

"*Mean little mother* I believe was my ex-partner's phrase."

"He got that right."

We drink in silence for a time. I want to ask him exactly why he's here, what he wants from me, but I figure he'll get around to it in his own way. And he does.

"That's what I wanted to talk to you about," he says finally. "That's a reckless bunch, especially McKinney, and I'm a little concerned about you out here five miles from anywhere. Be easy to have a little accident—house fire, explosion—you already got shot at, as I recall."

"I think I can handle myself okay. I've got my service revolver in the bedroom."

"It's the isolation that worries me."

"I appreciate your concern about my safety, but I'd like to stick around when—"

He holds up a hand. "This is not exactly altruism on my part." He sips his whiskey. "As of now you're my only potential witness. You're the only one that can testify to the provenance of the photographs that put McKinney at the scene. Unless your man has come out of hiding." This last a kind of question.

"I haven't heard a thing. Just the one letter."

"I'm not sure we can count on him, and if something was to happen to you then I'm screwed, and I'm thinking maybe McKinney, say, would understand that too."

"How would he know I'm involved?"

"He knows you're the one's been poking around, and he probably knows you're a buddy to the one that got run off. Anyway, things are going to start popping pretty quickly, and what I'm asking is that until we see where we stand you pack up and head back to Knoxville. We don't have a big budget but we could put you up in, say, a Holiday Inn."

"I don't want to be completely out of it. I am an ex-policeman, you understand."

"I know that."

"Before I promise anything I'd like to know what it is you're planning to do."

"We have a search warrant for the May farm. We've identified the two workers in the photographs. They work for May, and we have warrants for their arrest, along with May and McKinney. We haven't to this point identified the other person in the photographs. We have a court order to examine the bank records of May and McKinney. We tried to have Giles included, but the judge wouldn't go for it."

"When does this start?"

"Maybe tomorrow, if we can coordinate it. We want to make all the arrests as near to the same time as possible. Then we'll search the farm of Charles "Cotton" May with dogs for drugs or residue of drugs, then try to find the money, or at least some suspicious bank transactions. That's the way it would work ideally, but you know how that goes. Seldom works the way you draw it up."

"The money's likely to be the hard part."

"Right. I don't know how smart these people are. Anyway, that's the plan, and I'm thinking that until we see what the deal is you ought to be somewhere with some people around."

"Might be a long time."

"Could be, or it could be that somebody comes clean right off the bat, and my witness is off the hook."

"What about Adair?"

"Instead of Knoxville?"

"Right. I'm still around but not so vulnerable."

"I'll take that if I have to, but I wouldn't be strolling around the square."

"At least I can visit my car."

He gives me a quizzical look over his whiskey.

"It's in a body shop in Adair. I told you about that little incident."

"Right."

"I'm thinking I may be there a while. The prospect of somebody coming clean doesn't strike me as very probable."

"No, but we got other ways of finding out things. It's like the old boy that had an idiot son." He stirs his ice with a finger. "Took him to town with him one day, selling tomatoes out of the back of his truck. Had to run an errand. Told the kid not to say anything. See, he didn't want people to find out. Guy comes up starts asking about the tomatoes. Are they local? Kid doesn't say anything. Are they Granger County? Nothing. Are they Florida tomatoes? Kid just stares at him. Guy calls him a fucking idiot and stalks off." Emerson pauses to sip again. "Father comes back. Kid says, 'I didn't say anything but he found out anyway.'"

Emerson looks at me for a response, but I'm still pondering my sudden change of plan. "I don't think they've got a Holiday Inn in Adair."

"It was just an example." Emerson tilts the ice from his glass into his mouth and chews on it. "Holiday Inn or comparable." He studies his empty glass. "I might have another one of these," he says. "Or maybe a half. I've got to drive back to Knoxville tonight and God only knows what's coming at me tomorrow."

XXIV

THE plaque in the rhododendrons identifies it as the Kinzer House, built in 1927-28 by Alexander Kinzer, President of Prosperity Logging and Mining. It is, the plaque also informs me, a classic example of the Federalist style, listed in the National Registry. Its three stories remained the residence of the Kinzer family until 1942, when it was sold at auction. In the 1990's it was completely remodeled and became a popular bed and breakfast, as it remains today. The plaque is silent on the years between the forties and the nineties, when, I assume, it fell on hard times.

I'm standing before the Kinzer House, suitcases in hand, as the result of a phone call to Miss Helen. "If you were obliged to be in Adair for, say, a couple of weeks, where would you stay?" I asked her after Agent Emerson's departure.

"Well, I always recommend the Kinzer House," she said. "It's very comfortable and they have this wonderful breakfast, I'm told. Is this for you?"

"Somebody I know." I lied only because Agent Emerson's departing advice had been not to divulge my destination.

"I'm sure your friend will find it pleasant. I've never stayed there myself. I don't have much occasion to be in Adair, but it's gotten quite a reputation, and I know the owners slightly."

"Thanks for the information—I'll pass it on. By the way, the Ireland trip caught me off guard. Had you known about it?"

"It was unexpected," she said, "but I've long since stopped being surprised by anything Jesse does. She's a very impulsive young woman." There was a meaningful pause. "As you no doubt have learned in recent weeks."

B. J. Leggett

There was something knowing in her voice, which led me to conclude that Jesse had confided in her aunt. "She's a little disappointed in me at the moment."

"She has no reason to be, as far as I can tell. You've acted honorably, if I may say so."

Somebody has obviously been talking about our non-affair, either Jesse or her mother, but I decided not to pursue this line of discussion, which could end only in some sort of lame excuse on my part. "Thank you, and thanks again for the recommendation. I'll pass it on to my friend."

It was hard to lie to her, especially after being characterized as honorable, but it would have been difficult to explain why I was leaving the lake house, and so it is I stand reading the plaque in the rhododendrons. It's not Holiday Inn or comparable, but I was unable to face the prospect of two weeks or more in a strip mall off Highway 411. Better to supplement the TBI's witness protection fund.

The Kinzer House turns out to be a good though somewhat quirky choice. I'm led up a flight of stairs to my room by an elderly lady named Martha Crossnoe, who unlocks the door and hands me the key. The room looks nice enough in an over-stuffed sort of way, and Ms. Crossnoe points out its features—working fireplace, window air conditioner, flat-screen TV. She also recites the rules of the house. Coffee and soft drinks available in the sun room. Wine and cocktails at 5:00. Breakfast at 9:30. And the owners are quite insistent that guests arrive on time. There is only one seating, and this is the opportunity to get to know the other guests, who will be seated together around a large dining table.

Ms. Crossnoe obviously doesn't like my expression when I hear that I will be getting to know the other guests. She informs me tersely that the Kinzer House is known for its breakfasts.

Indeed, breakfast turns out to be something of a bone of contention between me and one of the owners, Chuck of the team of Chuck and Walter. Retrieving one of the suitcases from the parlor, I run into Chuck, who introduces himself and we engage in small talk about the inn. They bought it ten years earlier, he tells me, upgraded the amenities and the room rates, and inaugurated the three-course breakfast.

I have never heard of a three-course breakfast, am not particularly interested in one, and suggest to Chuck that I would be perfectly content with coffee, dry toast, and the Knoxville paper. It's at this point I learn that Chuck, a bit overweight, with short curly hair of an unnatural blond tint, is the chef (Walter, more reserved, serving as business manager), and Chuck is visibly stung by my aversion to what has become the Kinzer House's signature.

"Well," he says with a dismissive wave, "I guess you're not a breakfast *person*. Fine. We'll send your coffee and toast to your room. You'll find the newspaper outside your door sometime after 7:00." He turns to go.

"Nothing against your breakfast, you understand. I'm sure it's wonderful. In fact, Helen Gates, who recommended you, mentioned the breakfast in particular."

My acquaintance with Miss Helen helps to ease his expression, which has formed itself into a pout. "You know Helen Gates?"

"Yes, and her niece Jesse McLean." I'm now becoming something of a name-dropper, and so I drop one more. "As a chef you may be interested to know that the other night Jesse introduced me to one of your colleagues, Sam Rivers of the famed Rosewood Café."

My credentials have now put me back in his good graces. "You've eaten at the Rosewood?"

"Yes."

He touches my arm. "Walter and I get over there whenever we can. Isn't it wonderful?"

"We liked it a good deal."

"So enjoy your stay, Mr. O'Brian. Maybe one morning you'll even deign to have breakfast with us." He gives me a little wave and walks back toward the kitchen. Now that the three-course breakfast has been settled I feel somewhat better about my prospects at the Kinzer House and take the suitcase up to my room to unpack.

I decide also to skip the five o'clock cocktail hour, opting instead to drink alone, having had the forethought to pack the ingredients for my late afternoon martini along with the latest P.D. James novel for entertainment. The room is quite large and comfortable and I'm content for the moment, but suspect that will last maybe a couple of days. If the TBI investigation of drug trafficking in McLean County drags on, I'll have to make other plans. But one day at a time. At the moment I require dinner, and so I venture out into downtown Adair, locate a small not-so-bad restaurant and manage my first day in hiding without incident.

The days that follow, or at least the afternoons and evenings, are a blur of indifferent restaurants, chance encounters with Chuck or Walter, TV cooking shows, and P. D. James' Adam Dalgliesh solving a double homicide. The mornings, however, are a different matter.

When I was very young I watched a local TV show called *Sheriff Sandy's Western Theater*, in which, after singing a few cowboy songs, Sheriff Sandy showed old black and white westerns. One of the conventions of these movies was the whirling newspaper. Whenever it was necessary to condense a series of events, it was done through newspaper headlines, which spiraled toward the viewer then froze. *JACKSON GANG ROBS CARSON CITY BANK.* Then in rapid order, *POSSE FORMED TO TRACK JACKSON GANG. ROBBER GANG TRAPPED IN CANYON HIDEOUT.* Something like that. At the Kinzer House I am reminded of those old movie headlines.

When I hear a soft knock on the door the first morning, I open it to a tray containing a pot of coffee, a plate of toast, a vase with a single yellow rose, and a newspaper. Inside, I place the tray on the table in front of the couch and turn my attention to the newspaper. Probably too soon for any news on the TBI front, I'm thinking as I unfold it. The headline is uncustomarily large and satisfying—*MCLEAN COUNTY DEPUTY ARRESTED IN DRUG INVESTIGATION*—but the details are sketchy. Lloyd Emerson of the Tennessee Bureau of Investigation announced the arrest of James McKinney, longtime chief deputy for McLean County. Readers are informed that Deputy McKinney, married, the father of two teenage boys, has served in the McLean County Sheriff's Office for more than a decade. Prior to his service he worked as a salesman for Giles Chevrolet. Sheriff Stanton Giles, also his previous employer, announced he would release a statement as soon as the facts were in. At the moment, he assumed that Deputy McKinney was the victim of a vicious political smear campaign in advance of the November elections.

The initial charge against McKinney is interstate transportation of drugs for resale, although Agent Emerson said other charges could follow. Deputy McKinney is currently in custody in Knoxville, the TBI having determined the Adair facilities would be inappropriate for the former chief deputy. A bail hearing has been set for Tuesday.

There is no mention of Cotton May or the two Mexican field hands, and my first thought is that Agent Emerson's carefully-laid plans have somehow gone awry. I reread the story as I sip Chuck's coffee and pose to myself a number of obvious questions. The most obvious—has the TBI found actual evidence of drug trafficking, or is McKinney's arrest based solely on Byron Holmes' photographs? There are many others, but—and this, is what I find most astounding—they will be answered as the week unfolds. A morning ritual develops. I lie awake awaiting the sound of the steps on the stairs and the knock on the door, quickly retrieve my breakfast tray and newspaper, head for the sofa, pour the coffee, and search for the McLean county drug story.

On the second morning I learn that a large cache of drugs has been unearthed on the farm of a McLean County businessman. It is difficult for me to think of Charles "Cotton" May as a businessman, but the story identifies him as an executive at May Transport in Adair, owned by Ellison May, his father. According to Agent Emerson, drug-sniffing dogs detected a tarpaulin containing cocaine, marijuana, and prescription drugs buried in an overgrown field on the farm owned by the younger Mr. May.

A warrant for the arrest of Mr. May and two employees has been issued, but it appears that the three fugitives have fled McLean County. The third morning produces nothing new, but on the fourth I learn that Charles "Cotton" May and two employees have been arrested in south Texas and are being transported back to Tennessee. On a more alarming note, I learn that James McKinney is now free, the bail money having been supplied by a brother in Atlanta.

By the fifth morning the story has lost its front-page appeal and is relegated to section two. What now appears is mostly background material. Charles May was once arrested for robbing a convenience story, but the charges were eventually dropped. The two field workers are in the country illegally. Both have criminal records in Mexico. Two

B. J. Leggett

years ago Deputy McKinney successfully defended himself against the charge of police brutality and violation of a defendant's civil rights. Sheriff Stanton Giles expressed shock that drugs had made their way into tiny McLean County.

I wonder just how much the TBI has passed on to Giles. Does he know of the existence of the photographs? Does he know of Byron Holmes' involvement in the investigation? Or my own? I figure it's about time to talk to Agent Emerson.

During my fifth afternoon at the Kinzer House absolute boredom impels me to call Emerson on his cell phone, and he answers after the first ring.

"I assumed you were going to keep me informed," I say without preamble.

"I assumed you were reading the newspapers," he says.

"I hope that's not everything you know."

"It hasn't gone all that well," he says.

"You've got four people in custody, including the second meanest man in McLean County."

"That's about all we've got. And by the way, only the two Mexicans are still in jail. McKinney and May are out on bail, so you shouldn't make yourself conspicuous for the time being. You may be all we got."

"Nobody's talking?"

"Nope."

"Nobody's implicated Giles?"

"Nope, and we got no money and no money trail. Given the size of the operation there's a lot of money around somewhere, but McKinney and May don't seem to have it. What we need to do is find the money."

"What about the Mexicans? Can't you give them a deal?"

"They're professionals, and I'm not sure how much they know about that end of the operation. Probably nothing."

"I would think May might be the soft spot there. He's not talking?"

"Nope."

"But you found the stuff on his property. How does he get around that?"

"Says it was in a remote field that he's never farmed. Anybody could've planted it there. He suspects his neighbor Byron Holmes."

"Well, he hasn't lost his sense of humor."

"Smartass. The thing is May's afraid of McKinney and McKinney's a tough son of a bitch. So, bottom line, we don't know much more than we did the last time I talked to you, and we've played our hand. Without your photographs we still don't have a case against McKinney."

"But you do have the photographs. And the drugs."

Agent Emerson is, however, undeterred in his gloom. "I think I was right from the beginning," he says. "This is one we should never have taken on. I think the possibility of getting Giles made some people use bad judgment."

"You're not going to get him?"

"I don't see it happening. He's too well insulated in that bureaucracy he's got set up. I feel a little bit like the old lady that was up against the insurance company. She told somebody that it had been so hard collecting her husband's insurance that sometimes she wished he hadn't died."

"So I shouldn't have sent you the photographs."

"Sometimes I wish you hadn't," he says.

XXV

I RECOGNIZE the voice on the phone but her words do not immediately register. "Your little friend has written you again," she says.

"My little friend."

"You have another letter with the big printing," Miss Edna says. "Are you still out at the lake?"

"At the moment I'm in Adair, and I was wondering how you found me, but then of course that's the magic of the cell phone."

"You probably don't want to drive all this way for one letter."

Actually, I do. It would be fascinating to get Byron Holmes' take on recent events, and after a week and a half at the Kinzer House any excuse for diversion is welcome. I check my watch. "I'm not sure I can make it by closing time, but I would like to get it as soon as I can."

"If you're not here when I close up, I'll take it home with me. You remember where I live?"

"I do remember."

"I'll see you in an hour or so," she says.

It's still light when I reach Prosperity, and I locate Miss Edna's white frame house on Sevierville Pike, not far from the location of the house I grew up in. After my father left, Mother took a place in town and the house was sold and eventually demolished to make room for a Gulf station, now abandoned in its turn. It's a sad sight, sitting in its overgrown lot, but it brings back no memories.

Miss Edna meets me at the door and hands me the envelope. "If you'd like to come in, I could offer you a glass of sherry." Miss Edna's sherry bill was the source of much speculation when I was young.

"I'd love to but I've got to get back. I was sort of in the middle of something when you called. Thanks again." I give her a wave and head down the front steps before she can protest. Miss Edna's company is not entirely unwelcome. I could have caught up on twenty years of gossip, but I'm curious about what my little friend has to say.

Back at the Kinzer House, I sit back on the sofa and tear open the letter. One typed page, single-spaced, unsigned, but with Byron Holmes' signature epigraphs, two of them this time. These, however, are not the usual literary quotations, bordering, as they do, on the pedantic. Both appear to have been taken from criminology texts.

> *Properly defined, money laundering is a three-stage process. It requires, first, moving the funds from direct association with the crime; second, disguising the trail to foil pursuit; and, third, making the funds again available to the instigator, with their occupational origins hidden from view.*
> —R. T. Naylor, *Wages of Crime*

The second quotation answers the question that the first one raised—why is he telling me all this?

> *A cash-based service business provides an ideal milieu for money laundering. By running illicit cash through the business, the launderer disguises its source. By reporting it as income of that business, he hides its trail. By paying it out (to fictitious accounts) as business expenses, he makes it available again as legitimate funds. . . . Restaurants and bars—especially high-end ones—are excellent money-laundering businesses because of the ease with which they are able to fabricate receipts and the difficulties of fixing legitimate expenses. A creative chef can work as much magic in his books as in his sauté pan.*
> —Gordon Jeffers, *The Money Trail*

The body of the letter is somewhat more direct in its argument.

180   *B. J. Leggett*

1. A Currency Transaction Report (CTR), which identifies the depositor and explains the origin of the cash, is required for bank deposits of $10,000 and over, but it is possible for businesses that normally generate large amounts of cash to be exempted from filing CTRs. Such is the case with a local high-end restaurant.

2. In so far as can be determined through anecdotal evidence, said restaurant also appears to pay in cash for most of its supplies, produce, labor, rentals, etc.

3. If there exist duplicate accounts to which said restaurant pays fabricated business expenses, then it could be said to meet Professor Jeffers' criteria for a money-laundering enterprise. Whether these accounts exist could only be determined by an authorized body such as the TBI, which, according to recent newspaper articles, is conducting an investigation in the neighborhood.

I read it through again and phone Agent Emerson. "I've got something here that might cheer you up."

"I could use it. Shoot."

"It's a letter from the same source that furnished the photographs."

"I was hoping we might hear from him."

"It's unsigned, but it's got to be him. The first two parts are from some textbooks on money laundering. The third part is Byron Holmes playing detective."

"Just read it and I'll draw my own conclusions."

My reading, as undramatic as possible, produces a long silence. "You get all that?"

"I got it. Some time tomorrow I'll drop by there. I've heard of the place but I forget the name."

"It's called the Rosewood Café. The guy that runs it is an Atlanta chef named Sam Rivers."

"You've met him?"

"I have, yes, and I've eaten in his restaurant. High-end, like the man says. You think we've got something here?"

"Probably not, but it's more than anything else we've got. A little talk with Chef Rivers couldn't hurt."

"I hope you'll keep me in the loop."

"I'll be in touch. In the meantime don't make yourself conspicuous. McKinney's mentioned your name, and he's extremely pissed."

"He's not back on duty?"

"Administrative leave, but that only means he can't officially shoot you." He pauses. "This fellow Rivers strike you as the criminal type?"

"I'd have to say no, or maybe just in the prices on the menu. By the way, Bradley McLean was also involved with the restaurant. McLean money supposedly banked it."

"Now there's an interesting connection," Emerson says. "I'll let you know something after I talk to the chef."

He does let me know with a phone call the following afternoon. "I just left the Rosewood Café."

"So?"

"First off, your friend was right. The restaurant is exempted from filing currency transaction reports because of its large cash business. Nothing wrong with that."

"Anything else?"

"The chef was cooperative, but stopped short of showing me the books."

"Did he have a reason?"

"Said he was not the principal owner. Didn't have the authority."

"And the owner is?"

"That would be your McLean family."

"Puts a little different slant on it," I say. "I mean the money laundering possibility."

"Right," he says. "I did ask him what the restaurant's largest monthly disbursements were, and he gave me a figure for wine and liquor that I thought was exorbitant until I saw the wine list. Hell, a man could buy a case of the kind of stuff I drink for the price of one of his bottles."

"Knoxville distributor?"

"Atlanta, I think. Just a minute." Agent Emerson is apparently consulting his notes. "Krieger Imports, Atlanta."

"Now there's an interesting connection," I say.

"How do you mean?"

"I don't know if I told you, but Rivers once had a cooking show on the Food Network."

"Okay."

"The name on this account where he's sending a great deal of money is the same as that of one of his former colleagues, a woman who has a show on that network."

"You know that for a fact?"

"I watched it yesterday afternoon. It's called *Healthy Appetite*. Her name is Ellie Krieger. Probably a coincidence."

"Probably."

"Not a common name though. Could be that it's a fake account, a name he had in his head."

"I wouldn't want to bet on it, but it bears looking into."

"A dinner at the Rosewood Café says it's a dummy account."

"Well, if you're right, there won't be a Rosewood Café much longer. Have to shut it down for money laundering. And if it's as popular as they say, I guess I'd be one of the most hated men in East Tennessee. Kind of like the old boy over in Parris County that got himself elected sheriff. He was going along pretty good until he decided to shut down cock fighting in the county. Never won another election."

"You're lucky you're not elected."

"Right," Emerson says. "And that my boss's lunch of choice is a Diet Pepsi and a Slim Jim."

He finds that a satisfactory exit line and breaks the connection before I can reconsider my ill-conceived bet. Of course it's a coincidence. Nobody would be brazen enough to use a former colleague's name for a fraudulent bank account.

XXVI

I DON'T hear anything from Agent Emerson for the next couple of days, and the McLean County drug bust has by this time disappeared from the Knoxville newspaper. To combat absolute boredom I devote most of my time now to bringing my account of the Bradley McLean affair up to date. I decide that present tense works better than past tense with the narrative, go back to the beginning and change every verb. By the end of the second week at the Kinzer House I've reached the moment of my last conversation with Agent Emerson. He's discussing his superior's dining habits. "His lunch of choice is a Diet Pepsi and a stick of beef jerky," I write, then cross out *stick of beef jerky* and substitute *Slim Jim* as snappier and more concise. I add another paragraph to get Emerson off-stage, then close the tablet and toss it on the coffee table, awaiting further developments.

Deprived now of my chief diversion, I try to fill the afternoons with small tasks. I do my laundry. I replenish my supply of gin and olives. I phone the body shop to discover that the BMW is ready, and have it delivered to the Kinzer House. I take it out for a test drive. (Okay, but is there a faint tinkle of glass when I shut the passenger-side door?) I phone Miss Helen to see if she has heard anything from Jesse. (No.) I phone Eddie in Knoxville for no particular reason. (He's out of the office but will return my call.) I return the rental car. Running out of tasks, I watch *Healthy Appetite* with Ellie Krieger on the Food Network and wonder how Agent Emerson is progressing with the Atlanta bank account.

While Ellie Krieger is chopping an onion, the cell phone beside me rings and I expect to hear Agent Emerson's laconic voice. It's Eddie.

B. J. Leggett

"I hear you're having a little excitement down there," he says.

"Some people are. I'm mostly reading about it in the newspapers."

"That's not what I've been told. My source says you're right in the middle of it."

"Your source must know more than I do."

"Well, he was involved with the interrogation of Deputy McKinney. McKinney says you're mostly responsible for the trumped-up charges against him. Claims there's a long-running conspiracy that involves you, your old schoolteacher, and the whole McLean family."

"News to me."

"What about some photographs he claims were taken by the schoolteacher during the unloading of fertilizer, turned over to the TBI?"

"That's true, except it wasn't fertilizer."

"Course you'd have to prove that," he says.

"I think it actually has been proven with analysis of a soil sample where one of the bags was dropped."

"That's what the TBI man said, but I thought he might have been bluffing."

"You seem to know quite a bit about this interrogation. Like somebody that was in the room. I believe I may actually be talking to the source."

"I wasn't in the room."

"On the other side of the glass?"

"Right. You knew that they kept McKinney up here, and the TBI wanted somebody from the department to observe, just to cover all the bases. Deathridge asked me to do it—I figured because of my connection with you."

"So you could fill me in?"

"He didn't tell me not to."

"And you heard it all."

"Not that there was that much to hear," he says. "Except for his conspiracy theory, McKinney didn't have a lot to say. I pretty much concluded that there wasn't going to be a confession. If they get him it's going to have to be some other way."

"I think that's what the TBI's concluded also."

"You've talked to this guy Emerson?"

"Several times. He's a little discouraged but there's a new development." I tell him about Byron Holmes's letter and the money-laundering angle.

"I wouldn't count on that," Eddie says, "but the main reason I called is to tell you to watch your back. You probably know that McKinney's out. It would be to his advantage if you disappeared. Emerson says you're not at the lake house anymore."

"I'm staying at a place called the Kinzer House in Adair. Bored out of my mind."

"What is it with you and houses with names?"

"Eddie, I've missed your sarcasm. There's nobody down here I can have a decent conversation with."

"What about your lady friend?"

"She's out of the country, and that's all over, I think."

"Too bad, but I don't know that she was quite right for you."

"You didn't give her a chance, but never mind that. Did you get any results on that slug we found in the car."

".357 Magnum, like I thought."

"That would be consistent with McKinney's Colt Python."

"And a lot of other guns," he says. "You have to have the gun to get a match."

"That might be somewhat easier than it was a couple of weeks ago."

"The man's got more serious problems at the moment than shooting out a windshield."

"Still, it would be good to know."

"We don't have the gun. Probably it's at the McLean County Sheriff's Office. Your friend Emerson would know."

"Right. But this is not the time."

"First things first," Eddie says. "Let me know what you hear on the money laundering. In the meantime, you need to take care of yourself. Do you have your little .38 with you?"

"I can almost see it from here."

"You wouldn't want to meet up with McKinney unarmed on a dark country road," he says.

"I believe we've already done that once. Of course he didn't know we were unarmed. We may have been luckier than I thought at the time. I thought he was just trying to scare us. He may have been trying to kill us."

"That was certainly a possibility," Eddie says, "and that's the reason I wanted to get you out of that place."

"I appreciate your concern."

"Now that you and your lady are over it maybe you'll think about coming back up here."

"Maybe. Eventually."

"Deathridge's saving your job for you."

"I've got to write the novel."

"You back on that?"

"I've had a breakthrough. Filled up a substantial number of legal pads." I don't tell him that the story they contain is more or less factual. Or that its conclusion is contingent on events over which I have no control. Not the ideal situation for a writer.

As IT turns out, that's not strictly true—that I have no control over subsequent events. Emerson phones later that afternoon. "We need to talk," he says. "Is there somewhere inconspicuous we can meet?"

"What about the Atlanta bank account?"

"I'll tell you all about it, but we need a place to meet. Where did you end up?"

"This place called the Kinzer House. It's a block off the square. Are you in town?"

"What if I come over there?"

I give him the directions and the room number. "If you run into Chuck or Walter, just tell them you're an old friend from Knoxville."

Twenty minutes later he's at the door. "I said Holiday Inn or comparable. You're not expecting us to keep you up in a place like this?"

"No problem. I'm paying the difference. Sit down and tell me about it."

He decides on the sofa, and I take the over-stuffed chair across the coffee table where the yellow legal pad still lies. "So tell me about the

Atlanta bank account. What's the verdict?"

"I guess the bottom line is inconclusive. I'm still trying to decide whether or not you lost the bet," Emerson says. "There is a Krieger Imports, so I guess technically you lost the bet, but if it turned out to be a dummy company I'd be willing to give it to you. But finding that out is a different problem. Krieger Imports is a private company that's owned by a firm called Russell and Lewiston, which has extensive real estate holdings in Atlanta and no doubt a room full of lawyers on retainer. So right now you'd have to say Krieger Imports is a legitimate company. But if your theory's right, the money from the drugs on Cotton May's farm is ending up in Atlanta hotels and shopping malls."

"But at the moment it's just a theory."

"Right."

"So the Atlanta account could be a dead end."

"Could be."

"Even if it gives every appearance of a money-laundering scheme."

"You got to have something solid," he says. "Like somebody involved talking."

"What about Sam Rivers?"

"He talks and we're shutting down criminal operations in two states."

"You haven't had any contact with him since the first conversation?"

"As far as I know, he's ignorant of our little Georgia adventure. The last thing I said to him was 'sorry to inconvenience you.'"

"Any reason that you're waiting?"

"I wanted to get something definite, which I don't have, and I wanted to talk to you. You might be able to help us."

"Whatever I can do."

"Would you object to indulging in a slight deception?"

"As long as it's not against the law."

"This would not be illegal, and it wouldn't even be exactly a lie, just a little misleading."

"You want to let me in on it?"

"I'm close but I haven't quite got it worked out. In the morning, I think. I thought I might drive over to your little town and visit Chef Rivers. You game to meet me?"

B. J. Leggett

"Sure."

"Is there any place over there to eat breakfast?"

"I understand that the old guys have breakfast at the BP station. That's the only other place to eat in town other than the Rosewood, and it doesn't serve breakfast."

"Okay, I'll meet you at the BP station at, say, eight-thirty or so?"

"Fine."

"So if you want to get something to eat in Prosperity, you got a restaurant that serves hundred dollar bottles of wine, and you got a gas station."

"That's pretty much it," I say as we walk to the door.

"There's got to be a story there somewhere," Agent Emerson says. "Maybe you could find a place for it in the book you're working on."

"Maybe so."

"And what about a crack TBI man that breaks up a ring of drug runners and money launderers?"

I'm thinking it probably would be a bad idea to tell him that a character named Agent Emerson, although arriving late in the narrative, has become increasingly dominant in the book I'm currently working on.

"Of course you'd have to change the name," he says smiling at the prospect of becoming a character in a novel.

"Yeah, and the names of everybody else involved and the names of the towns and the county and maybe even the state."

"Of course that wouldn't fool anybody in McLean County," he says.

"William Faulkner created an entire county in Mississippi, along with its past, but people just assumed he was recounting local history."

"So maybe it works both ways," Agent Emerson says. "If you make it up they think it really happened, and if it really happened they think you made it up."

XXVII

"Interrogation can be an art like anything else," Agent Emerson says. We are in a booth at the BP Food Mart, facing each other over empty breakfast plates. There are three other booths around the perimeter of the room, one occupied by a couple of teenagers, a second by the town elders, including Mr. Wilson, and the last by what I take to be Latino farm workers, engaged in voluble discourse.

"In what way exactly is it an art?" I figure I'm supposed to ask.

"Indirection," he says. "I read somewhere that your great writer works by implication and innuendo. He never just comes out and says here's what I mean. And in a good interrogation you never say did you do it? You always come at it from an angle."

"I was never good at it. Eddie Carpenter, my partner, was pretty good."

"There, you see. There's another way it's an art. Some people are born with the gift and some people aren't."

"I'm inclined to agree with you." I attempt to move us away from the topic of interrogation as art, but Agent Emerson is not to be moved.

"I'm not suggesting that there aren't things that can be taught," he says. "Like the difference between interrogating your hardened criminal and somebody like our chef. Your professional criminal just wants to know what kind of deal you're prepared to give him. What you got? What's in it for me? He doesn't especially care that you know he's guilty. Your ordinary citizen like Chef Rivers is a different matter. He may be hiding something that's become enormous in his mind. He'd like to tell you, but only if you can find a way to make it easy for him."

"Okay." I'm pretty sure I'm about to learn techniques for making it

B. J. Leggett

easy for criminals to confess.

"Like some more coffee?" I shake my head, but he's looking back toward the food counter. "I'm going to warm this up."

He gets up and strides back to the serving line, and across the room I see Mr. Wilson making his way toward the booth.

"Haven't seen you in the store for a while," he says, standing beside the potato chip rack. "You been out of town?"

"I have been, actually." I'm pondering how much I should say when Emerson returns with his coffee.

"Lloyd Emerson," he says, sticking out his hand. "Enjoying your local cuisine."

Mr. Wilson introduces himself as the proprietor of the local grocery store. "I believe I've seen your name in the newspaper. You're the TBI man."

"You got me," Emerson says.

"I just want you to know that people here are generally on your side," Mr. Wilson says. "I think we all knew that something was going on."

"I appreciate it. We'll do what we can." Emerson slides into his seat. "Good to meet you."

Mr. Wilson takes the cue. "Come by the store sometime, Robert," he says. "We'll talk." He walks back to join his cohorts, who stare at us with the guilelessness of children.

"I didn't know whether you wanted to be identified."

"I'm not a secret agent," he says.

"Did you get my little deception worked out?"

"All in good time," he says. "I need to give you a preamble. As I was saying, we need to find a way to make it easy for Chef Rivers to tell us what he knows." He pauses. "Assuming he knows something, and you got to assume he does—first rule of interrogation. I'm the author, by the way, of an interoffice memo on interrogation."

"So you wrote the book."

"Three of the techniques I listed seem pertinent to this particular situation. The most important, and this is where you come in, is what I called The Lesser of Two Evils." He shifts in the booth, reaches down into the side pocket of his jacket and pulls out a folded sheet of paper.

"Look this over. We don't have to follow it exactly but it's more or less the way I'll be heading."

It's like a half page of movie dialog.

"You see where the deception comes in."

"Yes."

"It's not a lie."

"Right."

"More like an implication."

"Right."

"And you see how suddenly the admission of money laundering seems less significant."

"I can see that."

"Anyway we'll try it, along with what I called Mitigating Circumstances, which depends on allowing the suspect to see that it wasn't really his fault. The other I called The Crack in the Dam, and it relies on the principle that if you can get your man to admit something small, apparently not criminal, just a little trickle, then the dam breaks and everything pours out."

"Does any of this actually work?"

Emerson grins. "Not ever in the way that you expect," he says. "The problem is that your average law-breaker is not intelligent enough to play his part correctly. But this chef seems like a real smart guy, so we'll hope for the best." He gets halfway up then sits back down. "There's one other thing," he says, extracting two twenties from a roll of bills and placing them on the table in front of me. "You're now a paid consultant," he says—then, when I start to protest—"All in good time."

When we get to the door I see one of the Latinos gesture toward us and say something to his companions, the only part of which I recognize is *la policíno.*

Outside in the parking lot, Emerson retrieves his cell phone and a small notebook from inside his jacket. He finds what he's looking for and punches in the number. "I wonder if Chef Rivers is available," he says. "This is Lloyd Emerson." And then, after a long pause, "Mr. Rivers, Lloyd Emerson. I'm in town and I wonder if I might stop by. Something's come up and I wanted to get your take on it." Another pause. "I know, but this won't take more than ten minutes." He looks

B. J. Leggett

at me and winks as he listens to the response. "Okay, good. And, by the way, I'll have Robert O'Brian with me. I believe you know him. See you in about fifteen minutes."

The Rosewood Café is within sight of the BP parking lot. "Fifteen minutes?"

"Let him think about it. Why don't you leave your car here and ride with me. We'll take a fifteen minute tour of your town."

"I don't think that'll take fifteen minutes."

"Well, we can drive out toward the lake," Emerson says. "You can show me the spot where you and your partner got bushwhacked."

We drive past the Rosewood and turn left onto the lake road. "Our chef was a little more reluctant this time," Emerson says. "Claimed he was especially busy this morning, which I took as a good sign. You don't want your suspects to be too cooperative. Might make you think you were wrong."

"He's a very unlikely suspect. The criminal population among chefs must be very small."

"Probably right under English teachers," Emerson says. "And if he's been engaged in money laundering I've got a strong suspicion it wasn't his idea. But, hell, people fool me all the time."

I tell him about Bernie Dukes' idea that a good detective can pick out the guilty man in a crowd.

"I hope you set him straight," Emerson says. "I knew this old boy—"

"That's the woods down that hill where Eddie and I took cover."

He pulls off the road onto the turnaround and we take in the scene, a grove of large trees with the lake behind. "You ever figure out who the shooter was?"

"At the time I thought it was Cotton May. We'd had a small confrontation earlier in the evening. Now I'm thinking it was McKinney. Easy enough to establish if you've got his gun. Probably twenty slugs in the tree trunks."

"Well, maybe if he beats the drug charge we can get him on assault on a police officer." He looks at his watch. "You got your part down?" He makes a u-turn from the wide shoulder.

"It's a small part. I'm not expecting him to break down and confess."

"No, you wouldn't expect that," Emerson says. "But just for the hell of it, would you look in the glove compartment and retrieve that little digital recorder?"

I find the recorder and we ride back to the Rosewood Café in silence.

Rivers meets us at the door, relocks it, and motions us into the bar. "I can give you ten minutes," he says, walking behind the bar. "Can I offer you some water or a soft drink?"

"Thanks, but we just had breakfast at your competition down the street." Emerson pulls out a bar stool and sits down, motioning for me to join him. "I hope you don't mind Mr. O'Brian's presence here. He's serving as a paid consultant in the drug investigation."

"How's it going—the drug investigation?" If he's nervous he doesn't show it. He's searching among bottles of water in the cooler behind the bar and finally chooses one. He makes a point of inspecting his glass carefully, then pours the water. "It was a little warm in the kitchen," he says. "Worse part about being a cook. You got a confession yet?"

"They're sticking to their stories." Emerson frowns. "McKinney says frame-up, May says somebody buried the drugs on his back forty without his knowledge. They're not fooling anybody, but they're not as bad as the fellow that was accused of starting a hotel fire by smoking in bed. He claimed the bed was already on fire when he got into it."

If this is another interrogation technique—Lightening the Mood—it doesn't have the desired effect. I laugh on cue but Rivers doesn't appear to get it. He stares at Emerson and takes a sip of his water. "What is it you wanted to talk about?"

"Are you aware that Mr. O'Brian was conducting a sort of unofficial inquiry into Bradley McLean's death?" Emerson asks. "You want to sit down?"

"I'll just stand here if it's okay with you," Rivers says.

"You were aware of Mr. O'Brian's little inquiry?"

"I think everybody in town was aware of it."

"Well, that's the reason we're here," Emerson says. "He's talked to some people close to McLean, and. . . ." He pauses. "Why don't I let him tell you?"

Rivers' gaze shifts to me.

"I talked to several people who knew Bradley," I begin.

B. J. Leggett

"You didn't talk to me."

"Except for that day in front of Wilson's."

"We just happened to run into each other."

"Right. Among the people I talked to was Jill Haynes. We had a very interesting conversation." This is the deception. Not a lie, just a deception. I did in fact have an interesting conversation with her, but her name is now out there because she's someone Bradley McLean might well have confided in. "I had conversations with several local people actually, and my conclusion was that shortly before his death Bradley McLean had come to suspect that the Rosewood was being used to launder drug money." This is also not a lie. That is the conclusion I reached, although not quite in the way that I implied.

Rivers finishes his water, then sets the glass on the bar. "Then you came to the wrong conclusion," he says. "What are you saying?"

"That there may be a connection between the drug trafficking and Bradley's death." I say it almost exactly as Emerson wrote it. "I think I'll have a glass of water after all."

He selects a glass, pours the water, and slides the glass across the bar. "Since I'm the one that keeps the books here, I should take this as an accusation?"

"Not necessarily."

"He found out the Rosewood was being used to launder drug money and I killed him? Jesus Christ." He turns away, shaking his head. "Jesus Christ. I can't believe this."

So The Lesser of Two Evils is on the table, and my part is done.

"No, Mr. O'Brian is not suggesting you killed Bradley McLean, and neither am I," Emerson says. "It's possible, however, that you may suspect or know who did kill him."

"And why would that be? Jesus Christ, you come in here—"

"Let me make this clear," Emerson says. "I do not believe that you killed Bradley McLean. That's not what we're talking about here. I do however have reason to believe that you were, perhaps against your will, perhaps due to coercion or threat, forced to participate in a money-laundering scheme which may be related to McLean's death."

Rivers, clearly shaken now, starts to speak but then decides against it.

"And I can also tell you that if coercion could be established, your responsibility would be significantly downgraded—perhaps even down to a suspended sentence in the best of circumstances."

Rivers has apparently determined that silence is the proper strategy. He has turned and is looking back into the empty dining room, eyes narrowed, as if something interesting is going on there.

"You have every right not to make any statement on possible money laundering at your restaurant," Emerson says. "On the other hand, if I'm right that you were forced into it, then it might be best for you to establish that. Let me ask you again—and you don't have to answer—was there coercion?"

Rivers stares at him for a moment, then turns away. "If you call setting fire to my restaurant coercion."

To his credit, Emerson does not betray what he must be thinking, *Got him*. In a matter-of-fact voice he says instead, "Of course you'd need some proof of that."

"I could show you the wall out behind the kitchen," Rivers says.

"I take it we're talking about Jim McKinney."

Rivers nods and closes his eyes.

"He came to you?" Emerson sees his opening, and the dam, if it does not burst, at the least loses its containment.

Rivers nods.

"And said what?"

"He had a way of routing money through one of my restaurant accounts to a bank in Atlanta. No risk, he said. Relatively small amounts. Just for a few months."

"He didn't say where the money came from?"

Rivers shakes his head.

"And you said okay?"

"No. I said I can't do it."

"And he said?"

"He said this conversation never took place, and I agreed to that. I was afraid of the man."

"With good reason," Emerson says. "He came back?"

"No, there was a note in my mailbox that said something like restaurants are highly susceptible to fire and it mentioned a recent

B. J. Leggett

restaurant fire in Chattanooga that had been in the newspaper."

"Do you have the note?"

Rivers shakes his head.

"And he came back to see you?"

"The next day. And I told him again I just couldn't do it."

"So you turned him down twice. What changed your mind?"

"A couple of days later I came in early and smelled smoke. The back outside wall of the kitchen was on fire. I got it out with a fire extinguisher we keep in the kitchen. There was a strong smell of gasoline, and I didn't have any question about what had happened."

"So then you agreed?"

"I told him I would do it for three or four months. Of course that was a joke. I was a little naive."

"And so it began."

"Right."

"Did you ever consider just closing the restaurant down, moving someplace else?"

"I thought about it. I thought about a lot of things."

"So why not?"

"I don't want to be immodest, but the Rosewood is famous. It's been compared to the French Laundry in Napa Valley. People come here from all over the country. I didn't want to close it down."

"I understand," Emerson says. "Back to the money. How was it delivered to you?"

"I rent this farm house off 411, about halfway to Adair, fairly remote. On the back porch there's a trunk I bought at an antique store. I got a note in the mailbox that said for me to check the trunk. Maybe once a week, sometimes twice, there would be a paper bag of money in it. I guess it was delivered while I was here at the restaurant. I never saw anybody actually put it in there."

"The same amount every time?"

"Oh, no, different amounts. There would be a sheet giving the amount to be sent to the account, and another amount. . . ." He pauses. "For me."

"So you took a percentage of the cash?" Emerson says, frowning. "That may complicate the coercion argument."

"I never took it for myself." Rivers keeps looking out over the empty dining room. "I plowed it back into the restaurant. I never took a dime for myself."

"That's good. That's a fine line but I think we can still make the argument."

"After a while I realized this was not a temporary arrangement, and the amounts of cash in the trunk kept getting bigger—too much for one account. I was given the names of other accounts to send payments to."

"These were in Atlanta also?"

"Yes."

"Same bank?"

"No, different banks."

"After we've finished here I'll ask you to write down for me the names of the accounts and the banks. But right now go on with your story."

"I told McKinney he had broken our agreement, but nothing ever changed except bigger sacks of money. But by this point I knew I was in too deep. I was engaged in a criminal act with no way to extricate myself. It went on right up to McKinney's arrest."

"Even after Bradley McLean found out?" Emerson's question silences him momentarily, and he simply nods.

"We're going to have to talk about this. How did he find out?"

"I told you everything I know about the money laundering," he says finally. "I had nothing to do with Bradley's death."

"How did he find out?"

Rivers' recital of the money-laundering operation has been impersonal, almost as if it has been rehearsed, but now he wears a pained expression. "I'd like for him to leave," he says.

"Of course." Emerson tilts his head toward the door. "Robert, I'll probably see you later this afternoon or tonight. At your place."

I let myself out, walk to my car at the BP and drive back to Adair. On the way I conclude that, whatever Agent Emerson's skills in the art of interrogation, Sam Rivers' revelations came much too easily.

B. J. Leggett

XXVIII

It's nearly seven and I've given up on Emerson, figuring something has gone wrong, when I hear the tap on the door.

"It's not locked."

"Running late." He comes in pulling a fifth of bourbon from a paper bag. "I stopped at Toddy's there on the corner. You got ice?"

I direct him to the ice and glasses on the bathroom cadenza and sit down on the sofa.

"We got a lot done today," he says from the bathroom. "Deserve a drink. Can I fix you one?"

"Sure."

"You take water?"

"Just ice."

He comes back with the drinks, my glass extended. "A toast," he says. "Here's to Chef Rivers. Man just broke the case for us."

"I'll drink to that. What did you do with him?"

"Well, at the moment he's in protective custody in Knoxville, but I swear I don't know exactly what to do with him." He takes a swallow of whiskey. "I'll figure it out." He sits across from me in one of the over-stuffed chairs.

"You want to tell me about it?"

He gets up from his chair. "I hated for you to miss it, but this is almost as good." He reaches into a coat pocket, takes out the recorder, and sets it on the coffee table. "It's all there, so you can get it almost first hand. This is just between us, you understand. I figure since you pretty much set it up, and your having been a policeman. . . . Anyway, I wouldn't want it to get around."

"I understand."

Leaning over the coffee table, he punches the play button, then immediately stops it. "I guess I should fill in the gap between the time you left and when I started recording." He sits down. "He was reluctant to talk about Bradley McLean, and I asked him if he had incriminating evidence against someone involved. He nodded, and I told him I was pretty sure we could work out a deal of some kind in exchange for his cooperation. He asked if I could protect him. He said he was pretty sure he would be shot like Bradley if he told me what he knew. I told him I thought I could protect him." He turns to me, still trying to think it through. "I've got to get him out of East Tennessee. And I think we can cut a deal. He testifies, he doesn't serve time."

Emerson swirls his drink and takes another swallow. "I asked him if anything he might tell me incriminated himself in Bradley McLean's murder. He said he wasn't sure but he didn't think so. So then I suggested we record the interview for his own protection. I couldn't claim he told me something that wasn't on there. He thought about it and said okay, so here we are."

He gets up again, punches the play button and then fast forwards. "I'm going to skip over the preliminary stuff—identifying myself, Rivers, the time, where we are, the fact he's given permission, etcetera."

He locates the true beginning, punches the play button and returns to his chair. And this is what we hear.

Emerson: "Let's start with the question I asked you before. How did Bradley McLean find out that the Rosewood was being used to launder money?"

Rivers: "I'm not exactly sure—he never told me—but I think that when I was away he took a look at the books. He had the run of the place because he was the principal owner and—"

Emerson: "And he came to you?"

Rivers: "Yes."

Emerson: "At the restaurant?"

Rivers: "At the restaurant. He said he knew what was going on and it had to stop."

Emerson: "He wasn't more specific than that?"

Rivers: "We weren't on very good terms at that point, hardly speaking. No, he just said something like 'I know what's going on and it's got to stop.' It had to do with his sister. I—"

Emerson: "I'm sorry?"

Rivers: "His sister—I had been having this relationship with his sister and he wasn't happy about it."

Emerson: "Back to the money, how did you respond to what he said about the money?"

Rivers: "I told him that I was forced into it, that it was not my idea. He said he didn't care how I got into it, I had to get myself out. I didn't get myself out, he's reporting it to the district prosecutor. And then he walks out."

Emerson: "And not the sheriff?"

Rivers: "What do you mean?"

Emerson: "The logical thing for him to say is that he's going to report it to the police, which in your case would be the sheriff's office."

Rivers: "He knew that office was corrupt. He hated Stanton Giles, and I think the feeling was mutual."

Emerson: "So the next time you talked to him?"

Rivers: "Bradley? That was the only conversation I had with him about it."

Emerson: "And when was that?"

Rivers: "About two days before his death."

Emerson: "So two days after McLean learns of the money laundering he's shot."

Rivers: "Well, I don't know when he learned about it. Two days after our conversation about it. Actually about a day and a half."

Emerson: "He told you it had to stop. What did you do?"

Rivers: "What he told me. I tried to stop it. I called McKinney, told him I couldn't do it any more. And then—"

Emerson: "Before you leave that, what was McKinney's response?"

Rivers: "He just laughed. He said you don't seem to realize what's going on here. No way you can get out. You're in this for the duration. He went on like that. I couldn't see any solution. He won't let me quit and Bradley's going to turn me in. I'm screwed either way."

Emerson: "So what did you do? I mean, you're—"

Rivers: "I did something I'll regret for the rest of my life. I didn't think it through, I didn't consider the consequences. If I had thought—"

Emerson: "And what was that?"

Rivers: "I told McKinney that Bradley knew. He was going to report it if I didn't get out. I thought maybe—I don't know what I thought."

Emerson: "What was McKinney's response?"

Rivers: "He said he would take care of it."

Emerson: "And those were his exact words?"

Rivers: "Pretty much."

Emerson: "Take care of it? Not take care of him?"

Rivers: "It, I think."

Emerson: "And then what happened? And by the way, did you consider informing Bradley McLean that he might be in some danger?"

Rivers: "I did think about it—what to do—but I never thought it would. . . ."

Emerson: "Lead to murder, you mean."

Rivers: "Yes—I never thought—I mean, Jesus."

Emerson: "So you never mentioned your conversation with McKinney to Bradley McLean?"

Rivers: "I didn't see him again. He was dead less than two days later. I mean, if I had had time, maybe I would have—I don't know—"

Emerson: "And the next time you talked to McKinney?"

Rivers: "He called me at the restaurant and said for me to check the trunk tonight and if I ever pulled another trick like that they'd find me in somebody's tobacco field with a bullet in my head."

Emerson: "He didn't refer to Bradley McLean?"

Rivers: "No."

Emerson: "He didn't say something like 'It's taken care of'?"

Rivers: "No."

Emerson: "And this phone call was after McLean's body was discovered."

Rivers: "Actually, no."

Emerson: "No? What do you mean?"

Rivers: "He called me on the morning of the day the body was found, but the body wasn't found until about noon, according to the newspapers."

Emerson: "Let me make sure I'm understanding you. McKinney is talking about a body in a field shot through the head several hours before

B. J. Leggett

such a body is discovered."

Rivers: "Three, I think."

Emerson: "Three?"

Rivers: "Three hours before the body was discovered. He called me about nine. The sheriff's office was notified about twelve, according to the article."

Emerson: "And you're sure about the language? He used the words tobacco field."

Rivers: "I'm sure."

Emerson: "Would you be willing to testify to this under oath?"

Rivers: [Silence.]

Emerson: "I can understand your problem. He's done it once, he could do it again."

Rivers: "I don't think I would live very long if McKinney knew I was going to be a witness."

Emerson: "We can protect you. For starters, I think we can make a strong argument for denying McKinney bail when we make the murder charge. For precisely this reason. Is there anybody else involved who would be a threat? What about Cotton May?"

Rivers: "He's just a kid with an attitude. I actually know him—he doesn't scare me. If you can keep McKinney away from me, I'll testify."

Emerson: "Good. I'll do whatever I need to do, you have my word on that. Is there anything else relating to the murder or the money laundering you can tell me?"

Rivers: "I never spoke to McKinney again. The money was always there in the trunk. I transferred it to the Atlanta accounts—up to the point where McKinney was arrested."

Emerson: "And then the money stopped?"

Rivers: "Right."

Emerson: "Going back to something you said earlier—your relationship with Bradley McLean's sister. Did she have any knowledge of the money-laundering scheme?"

Rivers: [Silence.]

Emerson: "You do understand the question."

Rivers: "I understand—why would you ask me something like that?"

Emerson: "Confirmation of what you've just told me."

Rivers: "I think you'd have to ask her that question."

Emerson: "I plan to. I'm going to turn this off now. I think we've got—"

He stops the recorder. "I believe that's worth another drink," he says.

I hand him my glass. "An interesting question about Jesse McLean."

"I made some inquiries," he says from the bathroom. "Apparently she's out of the country at the moment."

"She's in Ireland with her mother. Your question seemed to catch him by surprise."

"It sure put him off story." He returns with the drinks." I have to tell you one other thing because it affects our dinner bet."

"He's closing the restaurant."

"No, actually he's got an assistant who's going to run it until he can figure things out. This has to do with the Atlanta account."

"Krieger Imports."

"Right. After the interview I asked him about the name of the company. He gave me a blank look. 'This lady named Ellie Krieger,' I said. 'She has a cooking show on the Food Network.' He says, 'I know who you're talking about, but I didn't set up that account. Somebody in Atlanta probably set it up.'"

"So it was just a coincidence," I say.

"Pure coincidence," he says. "But I can't claim a win either since that's what got us to this point. Here I was prepared to buy your dinner at the Rosewood Café, hundred-dollar bottle of wine, but the bet's off. Pure coincidence."

Emerson is in such a fine mood that I don't have the heart to bring up my reservations about Sam Rivers' story.

B. J. Leggett

XXIX

With McKinney's bail revoked I return to the lake house and write the conclusion to the Bradley McLean murder investigation. But even as I'm putting it down I keep thinking it's too neat an ending—the two of us staring at a digital recorder telling us exactly what we want to hear. Well, almost exactly. Jesse's role is becoming a little blurred, but almost exactly.

It doesn't feel right. Things fell too readily into place, and I know if I ever manage to turn it into a novel I'll have to change the ending. After a few days of stewing about it I call Emerson to compare notes. "Didn't it seem to you that Rivers' story was a little too well-rehearsed? Like he'd had it all ready for you?"

"Think about it," Emerson says. "If you were laundering money through your restaurant, no matter what the circumstances, you'd have a story ready."

"Maybe so, but still—"

"That's not my problem with Rivers' story," Emerson says.

"You got a problem?"

"A small problem," he says. "I think we can take care of it. Cotton May wants to give us McKinney in exchange for a deal."

"Why is that a problem?"

"He's got a different story."

"Different from Rivers'."

"Right. He doesn't know Rivers' version—we haven't put it out," Emerson says. "But his version contradicts it at almost every turn."

"So what's his version?"

"According to May, Bradley McLean and Sam Rivers were willing participants in the money-laundering scheme."

"No coercion?"

"McKinney went to Rivers with the scheme, Rivers talked to McLean, they made a counteroffer on the percentage and they had a deal."

"What about the fire at the restaurant?"

"I'll get to that, but you can see my problem here. We've got a good witness—well-known local celebrity chef—and May undermines his story."

"But if Bradley McLean was a willing participant why is he dead?"

"That's maybe the most interesting part of his story. He got killed, May said, because he kept demanding a bigger piece of the action. He kept raising the ante, and his trump card was threatening to expose the whole operation, drugs and all."

"He was willing to incriminate himself?"

"According to May, he and Rivers had concocted a story of coercion and they had a charred kitchen wall to back it up."

"They set the fire?"

"That's what he says."

"If he's telling the truth, that explains why Rivers had his story all set for you."

"If he's telling the truth," Emerson says.

"You don't believe him."

"We've got two stories here," Emerson says. "And one of them is a lie."

"Or both."

"Well, could be, but the odds are that one of them is true, and it would be to my advantage if the chef's story is true. Or close to it. We're trying to make the case that the second highest ranking law enforcement officer of McLean County is guilty of drug-dealing, money-laundering and murder." He pauses. "On the one hand, I've got a well-respected local man willing to testify to the money laundering and the murder of a prominent citizen who sought to expose McKinney's criminal activities. In this account, Mr. McLean is a hero, and I would be willing to put that case to a jury. You no doubt would agree that it's a pretty tight case with Byron Holmes' photographs and Sam Rivers' testimony."

"Almost perfect. I was thinking maybe too perfect."

"On the other hand," Emerson says, "we've got a two-bit criminal who's giving testimony in exchange for a plea. And in his testimony the local hero is now one of the bad guys who gets whacked because of pure greed. Which one do you like?"

"You might not have a choice. What's to prevent Cotton May from telling his story anyway? Or McKinney, for that matter."

"Well, if McKinney tells it, it's a confession of murder. That's fine with me, but it's not going to happen. In May's case I don't think he'll be doing much talking when he's informed that if his story is true, we're adding the charge of accessory to homicide."

"So you've already made up your mind."

"Well, finally, it's somebody else's decision, but we need Rivers' testimony, and we got nothing that says it's not what happened except Cotton May. So, yeah, we're going with it."

"I hate to sound naive, but what about truth and justice? If May is telling the truth, then—"

"Justice?" Emerson's voice betrays his impatience. "Whether he's telling the truth or not, McLean ended up with a bullet just above the right ear. There's your justice and maybe a little more."

BYRON Holmes has also deemed it safe to return, but not, as I would have thought, in triumph. He's skeptical of the more or less official version of events, parts of which have now been leaked to the newspapers.

"A start," he says. "But they didn't get it quite right." We are back on the deck with a bottle of the good wine. The summer is winding down, and there are spots of orange and red in the trees along the river.

"You mean the money laundering."

"Once again the McLean family emerges untouched by the law," he says. "Does this take you back?"

"Not exactly untouched. Bradley's dead. You don't buy the coercion."

"Jim McKinney is certainly capable of that but, no, Bradley McLean was up to his neck in that scheme. Saved the McLean empire actually. The rumor was he was facing financial collapse. Overextended himself and then this economic downturn came along. Saved by drug money and comes out looking like a hero."

"You don't actually have any evidence of this, I'm guessing."

"I've talked to some people in the financial community. That's all I'm saying. He was in trouble and then, mysteriously, he's solvent again. I don't think it was such a big mystery."

"Still, they got McKinney."

"They didn't get Stanton Giles."

"You still working on your investigative piece?"

"Still at it," he says, draining his glass.

"That was the last bottle of Miss Helen's wine, but I've got some ordinary stuff I picked up in Adair."

"I'm game," he says.

"I'm still interested in what you know about the McLean family's involvement in all of this."

"Another bottle might just loosen me up," he says. "Pleasant out here."

"I'm going to miss it."

"You leaving?"

"I'm pretty much done with what I came to do."

"So you finished the book."

"Except for the ending. You might be able to help me out with that."

B. J. Leggett

XXX

I'M in bed, thinking about making arrangements for a U-Haul trailer, when I hear the sound in the living room, somebody walking across the hardwood floor. The bedroom door is open and I can see that a light has been switched on somewhere in the house. I hear the steps approaching, see the silhouette at the door, and then the overhead light comes on.

Jesse stands in the doorway, her finger still on the light switch. She's wearing jeans and a white tee-shirt. "I'm back," she says.

"Welcome home. I appreciated all the postcards." I pull myself up into a sitting position, my back against the headboard.

"I figured we needed a break."

"A lot's happened."

"Aunt Helen filled me in. We'll talk about it later. How's your writing?"

"I've got a draft. It may be a little too close to recent events."

"Am I in there?"

"Everybody's in there."

"Maybe that's the only way you can work."

"Looks like it."

"What's it about?"

"I've decided it's about money and class, mostly money."

"Sounds interesting. You got a title?"

"I thought I might name it after our little town."

"Prosperity," she says. "It doesn't have the ring of Brief Nudity but okay. Are you wearing anything under that sheet?"

"Pajama bottoms. I've missed you. Nobody's asked me anything like that in weeks. How was the trip?"

"Okay. Some good times. A lot of relatives. A few revelations."

"From the relatives?"

"From Mother actually. We discovered Irish whiskey and consumed a bit of it together. There were a good number of heart-to-hearts and a few confessions, a few mysteries solved."

"I don't know that I'm following you."

"Oh, deep into her Irish cups one night Mother told me about a certain promise you made to her and then a second promise not to reveal the first promise. Very foolish."

"I know. I'm afraid I was no match for her."

"Neither am I, but you're released from both promises with your honor intact."

"She said that?"

"Well, not the part about the honor, but yes."

"Speaking of revelations, there's something I need to tell you."

"You haven't been fooling around in my absence?"

"No, you were asking about the novel and I said it stayed pretty close to recent events, but that's not true of the ending."

"The ending of the novel."

"Right. In the novel the murdered man and the chef are more heavily involved with the money-laundering operation."

"You mean they weren't forced into it."

"That's right. Willing participants. Even though the TBI agent goes for the coercion angle, the narrator sees through it."

"Does he have any evidence for his version?"

"You mean in the novel?"

"Yes."

"Only circumstantial—financial rumors, the word of one of the drug dealers that may or may not be true, the views of a local writer who's looked into the victim's financial situation, things like that."

"Is that the extent of your revelation?"

"Well, maybe one other small one. The sister of the murdered man also knows about the money-laundering scheme but keeps it from the narrator. Trying to preserve the family honor, I guess."

"You mean in the novel."

"Yes."

"She knows her brother is engaged in money laundering."

"Yes."

"How would he know that, your narrator?"

"Mainly intuition on his part, but also because it feels right—the relationship between the brother and sister and the chef—very protective of each other. And at one point the chef character almost lets something slip—about the sister."

"But doesn't she get the narrator involved in the first place?"

"That's right. In the novel she has a real conflict. She wants to bring her brother's killer to justice, and she thinks the narrator might be of some help there. But family honor trumps everything else so she withholds the key piece of evidence. Just a small betrayal in a family practiced at it."

"Is your narrator drawn to this character, the sister?"

"Absolutely smitten."

"How could that be if she's deceived him?"

"Happens all the time. You're familiar with the institution of marriage."

"And you're going to publish all this?"

"My agent has a draft, and he thinks he can place it."

"Is this your revenge against my family?"

"It's just a novel. There'll be a disclaimer up front."

"You didn't answer my question," she says.

"Revenge for what?"

"Billy Ratliff."

"I wondered if you knew. I managed to work him into the novel also."

"So that's what it's about," she says. "You've finally got your revenge."

"I was thinking more along the lines of setting things straight."

"But what if it isn't true?"

"It's a novel. It's fiction."

"Maybe we could negotiate the ending."

"I don't think so."

"I came over here with a proposal in mind," she says, "I mean, before you told me all this."

"Okay."

"What I propose to do is turn off the light, take my clothes off, and join you in there."

"You think that's a good idea? It could complicate things."

"While I was on the trip I read something that seems to apply here," she says. "It was a quotation. 'You can never hope to untangle all the circumstances that led you to this moment. Embrace your fate.'"

"Some kind of Eastern wisdom?"

"It was that Canadian singer Leonard Cohen," she says.

"Figures. He's a Buddhist and he wears a fedora."

"I don't know what the fedora has to do with anything."

"It's been my experience that people who wear fedoras occasionally say things like that."

She thinks about this for a moment. "Are you going to put this scene in there too?"

"It hadn't occurred to me. But now that you bring it up."

"It could go on forever," she says. "The novel."

"No, I think it's about done."

"So what happens now?"

"When you came in I was just thinking about where to rent a U-Haul. My old job's still open."

"More negotiations." She holds my gaze while her hand searches the wall for the light switch. "I can see I've got my work cut out for me," she says and turns off the light.

B. J. Leggett is Professor Emeritus of The University of Tennessee, Knoxville, where he held the title of Distinguished Professor of Humanities. He has authored numerous studies of modern poetry and criticism, including books on A. E. Housman, Philip Larkin, and Wallace Stevens. *Prosperity* is his second novel. *Playing Out the String* was published in 2004.